FOREVER RESCUED BY LOVE

FOREVER RESCUED BY LOVE

Flynn's Crossing Romantic Suspense Series
Book 12

Yvonne Kohano

Nanokas Press

A Division of Kochanowski Enterprises LLC

FOREVER RESCUED BY LOVE
FLYNN'S CROSSING ROMANTIC SUSPENSE SERIES BOOK 12

Copyright © 2018 by Yvonne Kohano

Nanokas Press/KE Press books may be ordered through booksellers or by contacting:

Kochanowski Enterprises LLC
PO Box 1274
Clackamas, OR 97015-9594
www.yvonnekohano.com
yvonne@yvonnekohano.com

Forever Rescued by Love is a work of fiction. People, places, events, and situations are the product of the author's imagination. Any resemblance to actual persons, living or dead, or historical events, is purely coincidental.

Any people depicted in stock imagery provided by DepositPhotos are models, and such images are being used for illustrative purposes only.

Certain stock imagery ©DepositPhotos
Cover design: John Kochanowski

ISBN: 978-1-940738-42-0 (sc)
        978-1-940738-61-1 (e)

Nanokas Press First Edition: 08-17-2018

Also by Yvonne Kohano

FLYNN'S CROSSING ROMANTIC SUSPENSE SERIES

Pictures of Redemption, Book 1
(Serena & Dane)

Flashes of Fire, Book 2
(DK & Vince)

Naked Intolerances, Book 3
(Gabby & Rick)

Gratefully Ever Yours, A Flynn's Crossing Seasonal
Novella

Tastes and Consequences, Book 4
(Mac & Roxy)

Blooms on the Bones, Book 5
(Tess & Powers)

Wine Into Water, Book 6
(Marguerite & Deke)

Love and the Christmas Tree Nymph, A Flynn's Crossing
Seasonal Novella

Love's Touch of Justice, Book 7
(Jake & Marlee)

This Proposal Between Us, A Flynn's Crossing Seasonal
Novella

Measure Twice, Love Once, Book 8
(Geno and Agnes)

State Fair Date Dare, A Flynn's Crossing Seasonal Novella

Love's Fiery Prescription, Book 9
(Noah and Nicolle)

Love's Fiery Resolution, Book 10
(Gideon and Danielle)

Riffing with the Muse, Book 11
(Kaane and Angel)

Forever Rescued by Love, Book 12
(Rock and Jenn)!

Subscribe to Yvonne Kohano's enewsletter to be among the first to learn about new releases and special offers.

GET YOUR FREE NOVELLA PREQUEL at
www.YvonneKohano.com.

FOREVER RESCUED BY LOVE

Prologue – Twenty Years Ago

"Sit."

He didn't want to sit.

"I said, sit."

She treated him like a baby. "But Aunt Debby – "

"Don't but me. You sit and do as I say. I know you don't want to, Rock, but this is for the best."

He sat, mainly because he wouldn't win the argument. Like with Ma, what Aunt Debby said, you did.

Stupid songs crackled through Uncle Rowan's old speakers, saying stupid things like Santa was going to come or something. Everyone knew there isn't a Santa. His brothers had known, which is why they snickered when he got excited a couple of years ago about going to the Main Street parade. He thought he was going to see the big man in person. They didn't tell him until later it was really the guy from the barber shop dressed up in a costume.

"Dumb as a bag of rocks, that's what you are." They made fun of him for a month over that. Big brothers could be mean.

He kicked mud into the fire. It sounded like a hissing snake. He could do that when girls were around. Girls hated snakes. They'd probably scream. The idea made him feel a little better.

A van pulled up, blaring carols loud enough to drown out the Santa songs once the doors slid open. His gaze darted that way in a surge of hope one of the occupants would be a boy his age. The family tumbled out with a mixture of groans and laughter. He blew out a disappointed sigh. Girls. All girls. He went back to examining the dirty toes of his boots.

Aunt Debby bustled out of the cottage, the one no one used except during this season. "Welcome to Cedar Ridge Tree Farm. Have you visited us before?"

"Yes, we've bought our trees here for the past sixteen years. It's part of our holiday tradition."

"Oh, it's good to see you again, and you know the drill. Here's a saw. Please remember to leave a few branches below your cut so the roots grow a new tree. My husband and nephews are up on the hill, if you need help carrying your selection."

The girls made noises like a flock of angry chickens. Why did they all sound like squeaky little birds? He hated girls. They were stupid.

He swung his boots in the mud and kicked again, missing the fire this time. Maybe if he closed his eyes, he could beam himself back to his room, where he could read the Star Trek comic book he swiped from his brother. Jake wouldn't miss it, not since he discovered those magazines with the pictures of girls on the inside. Beaming was cool, and he thought he should give it a try.

"Hello, how are you? My name is Jenn, short for Jennifer. I live in San Francisco. This is a beautiful place. I love the forest. Do you live here?"

He squeezed his eyes shut harder, wishing himself back on the ranch with everything in him.

"I love Christmas, don't you? I love the tree, and twinkling lights, and Santa."

That voice, chirpy and cheery like his teacher's, rivaled the music. He had to admit, his teacher was cool. This girl invading his private space, not so much.

"Can't you talk?"

Where was a good lightning bolt when you needed it? It could hit the girl, and she'd vaporize, and then he wouldn't have to say anything.

"I feel sorry for anyone who can't communicate. I like the way that word sounds, don't you? Communicate. Anyway, I'm sorry you can't talk."

She sounded sad. Sad, and sorry for him. He wasn't sure why words picked this minute to burst out of him.

"I can talk fine."

Why did he open his mouth? He hated this stupid job. Stupid, stupid, stupid. His brothers got to go up the mountain and help people saw trees and carry them down and use that cool new bagger Uncle Rowan got this year. Most of all, he hated girls. But Aunt Debby would be on his case if he didn't do his job.

He lifted the basket tied with red and green ribbons, extending it in her direction without looking at her and willing his mouth to stay shut.

"Why thank you, I'd love a candy cane. Do you know how they're made?"

He had never given it a thought. Staring at the candy in its crinkly wrappers, he couldn't picture how someone would make them. He didn't want to ask her about it though.

"They're made by pulling sugar by hand, at least the original ones were, and that was over three hundred years ago. Some people say they were hung on the first Christmas trees people set up in their houses, and that was over a hundred and fifty years ago."

That was kind of interesting. But he wasn't going to ask her how she knew so much stuff. It would make him look dumb, and the last he thing he wanted was to look dumb in front of a stupid girl, particularly one who might be a fun person, if she wasn't a girl.

"What happened to your arm?"

Okay, she was kind of neat when she talked about the candy, but couldn't she tell what was wrong?

"Broke it."

"How?" She sucked on the candy cane. The sound reminded him about snakes, so he kicked slushy dirt into the fire. She didn't shriek like he'd hoped.

"I love fires, real wood fires. They smell so smoky, and they remind me of Christmas."

Maybe it didn't sound like snakes hissing. She never stopped talking.

"You don't talk much. I talk a lot, because people are so interesting, don't you think? I am talkative, my dad says, because I am precocious."

He had no clue what she was talking about. She was like that weird bug he found in the barn last summer, the one he kept in a jar. Did she look like a weird bug? He lifted his eyes for a peek. Damn, as Deke would say. Busted.

She smiled at him, wider than the tractor's tires. She looked stupid, all dressed up in red and green like she was Santa's elf. She even had fake ears, like Spock's, and she kept pushing brown hair behind them. Her brown eyes looked too big, like a bug's, and that idea made him smile.

If anything, her grin grew wider as she stuck out her hand in his direction. "Like I said, I'm Jenn." She kept the hand in the air, wagging it up and down.

He glanced over his shoulder to see if his aunt watched them. If he wasn't polite, she'd be out here doing something to make him look dumber in front of this stupid girl. He lifted his arm as slowly as he could manage, ready to slap palms and pull back fast.

Her hand grabbed his. Despite the cold winter day, her skin felt warm and soft, and her fingers gripped hard. She didn't let go, shaking their joined hands up and down like a pump. His hand felt warm and funny.

"And you are?" She wiggled her other fingers in the air, pumping all the while.

His eyes stayed stuck on her face. "Rock."

She cocked her head with a sudden solemn expression.

"You mumble a lot. I think people who mumble are shy. Are you shy?"

"I'm not shy." He yanked his hand away, cradling it against his stomach. He might have eaten too many candy canes, because when he looked at the girl, his belly rolled like it did when the truck rode over a hill too fast.

"Oh, that's good, because I like to talk to people and get to know all about them and I like to learn how things work. Do you like to learn things? How does this work? Like, do you plant the trees and have to water them and stuff or do they grow wild or what?"

He had to shut her up, because she made his head spin and his stomach felt even stranger and he couldn't stop staring at her like he had at that bug. It hadn't been an ugly bug. Neither was she. Words tumbled out of him once more.

"Do you want some cider? It's hot."

She jumped up, extending her hand to him again. "I would adore some cider. Don't you love that word, adore? It's so sophisticated."

He wasn't sure that was a good thing, whatever it meant. But she still held her hand out to him. Stupid girl, but he'd be a polite gentleman like his aunt wanted. He took her hand, and her fingers gripped tight with more strength than he would have given any girl credit for.

Then he looked back at her face. When she grinned at him like he was the best thing to happen to her ever, he forgot about beaming to anywhere but here.

Chapter 1

Dust blanketed his brain. Something about fire. He was supposed to build a fire. They needed the fire for warmth and for safety. They relied on him to keep them safe.

"Rock? You up yet?"

He blinked into the darkness, attempting to comprehend why the familiar tones were speaking in the Middle East, thousands of miles from where they should be.

"Why didn't he unchain the road? Why isn't the fire started?"

Twisted sheets cold with soaked sweat held Rock in tangled ropes. He struggled against them, trying to break free, and blinked eyes gritty with sand.

"He probably overslept, Rowan. The poor boy's tired."

He'd only awakened to the echoes of his own screams half a dozen times last night. Hard work helped keep the nightmares at bay. If it stopped them altogether, he'd work himself into physical collapse.

"Rock? We need to get things set up. People will start arriving in half an hour, and you know it always looks better to have things ready than to be rushing around like you don't know what you're doing."

The lighter tones snapped in his mind with rubber band reflexes. His Ma, bless her heart. She was the only girl he'd ever told he loved. The women he'd known in the biblical sense, not so much.

"Are you decent?"

He glanced down at his rumpled clothes. He was dressed. Did that count? Last night, after fighting off the sleep for as long as he could to keep the demons away, he'd dropped his boots to the floor and pulled the blanket up, praying once again for release from these worldly bonds.

"Do you think we should go in?" Uncle Rowan sounded uncertain. It was a tone Rock had become used to. Everyone walked around him like he was a bomb about to blow.

"Of course we should go in. It will be fine. He's probably sleeping hard. He always was a hard sleeper, my Rock was."

Not any more, Ma. Not any more.

As he pushed into a standing position, the door opened on hinges creaking from lack of attention. This cabin was little more than a shack, with unheated running water and a woodstove but little else in terms of amenities. He'd slept in worse places. Cold wind blew in with the arrivals, both of whom squinted with concern until they found him in the darkness.

"There's my boy. Good morning, honey. Did you sleep well?"

The civilized question accompanied a worried glance at the bed, with its mess of sheets and knotted blanket. Ma lifted on her toes and he reached down to kiss her cheek. She sniffed twice, and her frown deepened.

"Why don't you go to the ranch and take a shower, honey? Rowan and I can run things for a time. Don't want to scare the customers, now do we?"

"Ma, I'll, ah, clean up here. Can you and Uncle Rowan start the fire outside? I'll be along." God, he needed some coffee.

"Come on, Emie. The boy needs to wake up. We'll get things going. Not like we haven't been doing this for decades." His uncle didn't sound pleased by the prospect of readying the tree farm for its holiday business, but his determination hadn't faded with age, despite what his body said differently. If he didn't like the way Rock ran things, he shouldn't have given it to him in the first place.

And that was it. Uncle Rowan had run the Christmas tree farm as one of his many ranching and farming enterprises. Few people would look at Rock's uncle and assume he was wealthy in both land and businesses. Unfortunately, none of his direct offspring were interested in his holdings, and one by one, he divested himself of property, either selling out to Deke, Rock's oldest brother, to grow the ancestral ranch, or gifting things, like he'd done with Rock.

Rock scrubbed a hand over his face. His gratitude wasn't in question. When he returned to Flynn's Crossing, he had no clue what he was going to do, other than escape the godforsaken corners of the planet where he'd landed in the last few years. The pain of everything weighed on him more than a truckload of his nickname. It would be better to crawl off like a scorpion and sting anyone who drew close, except the stings only hurt others and didn't kill him. In the end, home was the only place he had left to hide.

Even if he could never hide from himself. His counselor reminded him of this on a regular basis. That was the same counselor his number two brother, Jake, insisted he see. Nothing like having a sheriff's deputy pull up, lights flashing, to drag your ass to a session. Jake stood outside the center like a sentry for the hour Rock spent saying nothing to the counselor. He didn't want to talk. He was afraid of what might come out of him if he did.

Not that Deke was any less insistent, but he executed his attempts at normalcy with more subtlety. "Hey Rock, do you think you could give me a hand moving the cattle down for the winter? I could sure use the help. Besides, it will feel good to be on a horse for a few days, don't you think?"

Yes, being on a horse and in nature was indeed wonderful, as long as he didn't need to talk to anyone. Unfortunately, Deke also wanted him to talk, about what had happened and about why he was a shell of the man he'd once been. Empty of words, empty of emotions, he felt drained of everything by his nightly trips to hell.

Rock poked at the snapping logs. They would burn long after darkness filled the forest surrounding the fire pit with the sounds of night creatures. This was usually his favorite time of day, losing himself in the dancing embers and letting his mind drift to the only semblance of peace in his aloneness.

Except he wasn't alone. Deke leaned back against a stump, his boots crossed at the ankles as if he sat in a fine leather chair. The cabin door banged open, and Jake emerged with three beers in his hands. Rock hadn't invited them. No, they showed up. His peace and quiet shattered with their intrusion, like the clink of the bottles his brothers insisted on using in salute.

"To Friday night, hanging out with the bros."

Jake and Deke drank. Rock stared at the fire, wishing them gone.

Both men looked at Rock. He caught their hasty glances at each other. He didn't dwell on the worry in their faces.

Deke settled back as Jake rolled a chunk of log over to Rock's other side. He sat on it and shifted a few times with an audible grunt of discomfort. Rock winced in momentary guilt. He'd offer his brother his own seat on a blanket in the dirt, but it wasn't any better.

"Hey, remember the old plastic chairs they used to have out here? You know, the white ones? They must be around. Have you looked for them, Rock?"

Taking a long slug out of his bottle seemed like a good way to avoid a long explanation. When he lowered the bottle, he said, "Broke."

His brothers regarded him in silence, as if they expected him to elaborate further. Deke rolled his eyes.

"Have you considered buying new ones? People like to sit by the fire after they select their tree. You know, have hot cider and linger for fine conversation."

Rock raised his eyes enough to connect with Deke, then Jake. He took another sip of his beer and returned to his examination of the fire.

"Aahhh," Jake said.

A pocket of pitch caught and sparked high, making that snapping log burn much brighter than before. In the added glow, Jake glanced around as if assessing their perimeter.

"Things seem to be getting a little shabby around here. Or is it the light?"

"No, it's not the light. In fact, the lack of light may make it look better."

The echo of disapproval in his brothers' tones settled at the base of Rock's neck, making the hairs stand up along with his temper. He couldn't limit the first reaction, but he sure as hell could switch off the second. He'd mastered the fine art of controlling his reactions to almost everything.

"Do you need some help? Because I could come by tomorrow and – "

"I'm fine."

Jake frowned, though whether it was at his brusque reply or turning down the help, he wasn't sure. It didn't matter. His family would show up and do whatever they wanted, no matter what he said.

"How's counseling going?" Deke's question carried too casual a tone for it to be unplanned.

Rock said nothing, lifting his beer only to find it empty. He chucked the bottle into the darkness toward the trees. Let them think what they wanted about that little move.

Deke leaned forward, a sure sign he was about to deliver a lecture. "Now listen, Rock, we know you've been through a lot."

They had no clue what he'd been through, and the reason behind that was simple. Rock hadn't told them. Not Deke. Not Jake. Not Ma. And certainly not that counselor. The fact the mission had been classified and buried so deep under shitloads of red tape and black ops guaranteed they'd never know.

"We can't imagine what it must be like, to live with those kinds of memories of death and destruction."

Damn right they couldn't. He, on the other hand, relived it every night, often multiple times on instant replay.

"Nothing will bring back the years you lost but talking about it will help you cope," Jake said.

Talk? Talk achieved nothing. It didn't bring back the dead, didn't restore his faith, and didn't make life worth living.

"So, how about we come over tomorrow and help you out here? You know, like old times, the three of us trying to get away with all the holiday cookies Aunt Debby and Ma baked for the customers, and seeing who could throw a tree the furthest, and generally acting like idiots."

Deke broke off his walk down memory lane with a grin and a sip from his beer. Jake lifted his in a salute. They both watched him expectantly. He hated the hope he saw in their eyes.

But there was no hope for him. In time, they'd come to realize that, and he wished that reality would come to them without pain. He knew it would be hard, particularly on Ma, but they would all be better off in the long run.

And he'd have some peace at last.

Chapter 2

"Shush. If you make noise, we'll be kicked out of here."

Jenn sneaked a look into the tote bag. Dark eyes shown at her, the cocked ears and red and green bow between them all that was visible. With luck, Princess Sweet Pea would hold off barking in fierce protective mode until the line in front of them disappeared. Jenn really needed that scone, the one thick with blueberries and the promise of lemon, according to the tag. And maybe a large espresso. She wanted today to be a joyous day, and nothing sang out joy like sugar and caffeine.

"We're going to the mountains for the weekend, Princess, to Flynn's Crossing, and maybe visit that Christmas tree farm, the one Mom and Dad loved so much."

The dog hadn't shared an opinion about the destination. She hadn't told her sister about her need to escape the city, much less to a place none of them had visited in a very long while. Memories swarmed over her of that last time, the dividing line between innocent happiness and intense sorrow.

"Oh, excuse me." A man brushed against her and stopped, giving her an assessing glance. She considered returning his broad grin until her purse rustled, and the tiniest of warning growls sounded from its depths.

She shook the bag. "Quiet, Princess."

The woman behind her said, "What did you say, dear?"

Jenn smiled with an inward sigh and gave the bag a stronger shake, hoping Princess would take the hint. She made small talk with the older woman until a cell phone sounded. The woman gave an apologetic smile and dove for the call. By the sound of it, it was a husband. By the look of the woman's beaming face, it was a good marriage.

Jenn sighed, nostalgia gripping her. Why did she detonate the good things in her life? Like her last boyfriend, who was a great guy. He had a good job in sales, liked the same things she did, didn't blanch when she launched into animated conversations with complete strangers, and had that cute thing going with glasses that made him look like Clark Kent. It had all been great, until – well, until she tried to fix him.

She couldn't help it. He could have been so much more at work. He was bright, but didn't apply himself, not like he could. She'd only had a few suggestions. In the end, he said she 'shoulded' him to death. That should have been a clue for her, but no. Fixing things, people and companies, was the only thing she knew.

"What can I get for you?"

The round man behind the counter held tongs and an open paper bag. His high wattage smile radiated friendliness and joy. This is what she remembered about Flynn's Crossing. People were nice. The thought of a warm hand in hers flashed through her mind. She craved some nice in her life.

The tote bag's strap jumped on her shoulder, and Princess's brown and black head popped out, tongue panting, with an opinion of her own. "Ruff. Ruff-ruff-grrr."

Crap. Jenn finally stood in front of the promised land, and now she'd be thrown out. No lemon-blueberry scone. No savory quiche to heat up in the hotel microwave for dinner, either. And no cookies. Her eyes flashed to those chocolate chips as her rambunctious dog continued her tirade.

"Oh, isn't that cute? Is it a boy or a girl? Look at those ribbons."

The woman behind her keened over Sweet Pea, who took it upon herself to act stately and allow herself to be petted. She wasn't one of those sweet trembly pocket dogs. No, her

Princess Sweet Pea was a finger-grabbing, skin-puncturing monster, and Jenn needed to order food and go, before the dog revealed her true nature.

"Here. Your doggie might like this."

The man behind the counter extended the tongs, and Jenn lifted her eyes to tell him she didn't feed her human food. It was bad for her teeth, not to mention creating a gaseous situation that rivaled a frat boy fart fest.

"It's a dog biscuit. A new thing we're trying. See if your doggie likes it. What's her name?"

Jenn blinked. In the city, aka San Francisco, she'd been forced to slink out of more places than she cared to think about because Sweet Pea decided to make a scene. But this nice baker offered her dog treats instead of the door.

"Thank you," she stammered, taking the little biscuit. "Here, Sweet Pea. What do you say to the nice man?"

The dog sniffed the biscuit with open distain. A suspicious lick followed. Then she grabbed it, and Jenn pulled back just in time to avoid getting a new set of holes to match the plentiful scars marking her fingertips.

Why did she think she could fix a company or manage a relationship? She couldn't even train her dog.

"And what would you like, miss?"

Jenn pointed and mumbled her selections, her eyes fixed on the path of the tongs. Her confusion rose as she followed the man's movements. "No, I only need one scone."

The baker smiled and continued to add a second one to the bag. "These are loaded with sparkles of sunshine. Baked them myself. You look like you could use a little joy in your day today, miss. The second one's on the house."

Yes, nice people lived in Flynn's Crossing, and why that made tears prick her eyes, she wasn't sure she knew.

>>>>>

The baker was right. His scone embodied tastes of sunshine and happiness as she munched her way up Main Street. Eye-catching window displays encouraged her to linger in front of the shops, marveling at the goods displayed inside. From food to art, kitchenware to flowers, she had no trouble imagining she could happily find everything she needed in life within these few blocks.

Jenn's cell phone rang as she reached the small park at the end of the street. She flicked screen, seeing her older sister's picture, and considered letting it go to voicemail. It would accomplish nothing, though. With a heaving sigh, she sank on to a bench and connected the call.

"Jenn, where are you?"

No greeting. No shooting the breeze. No pleasantries whatsoever.

"Hi Kate. How's your morning going?"

Silence met her cheeriness head on. Jenn lifted Princess out of her bag and placed her on the ground. The dog promptly moved to the end of her leash and pulled hard. When Jenn didn't come along for the desired sniff, the fur ball growled.

"Jenn, I thought we were going to work on your resume and networking profiles today. You know, to update things with a new look, one that would be more appealing to potential employers."

Yes, that was what her sister had said they would do today. Jenn didn't need another walk down memory lane, analyzing how things had gone sideways. She couldn't stand to listen to her sister's lectures, nor did she want to spend the day revising her deeply revised resume and reviewing job posting sites she'd already been over daily for months. Her sister wouldn't understand why she needed this adventure so badly.

This is what her life had been reduced to, struggling to find a new job in a market turning every cold shoulder in her direction. She thought it would be easier, but she was wired in a way that produced challenges and drama and dead ends. If she could curb her need to poke her nose into things, she might have a more peaceful life.

"I decided I needed time off, Kate. You know, weekend, relaxation, a little bit of fun."

The sound of a pen tapping came through the line, the impatient gesture one Jenn had seen aimed in her direction far too often recently.

"It seems you've had plenty of that over the last few months, don't you think? It's time to get back to work. Do you want to live in my guest bedroom forever?"

There it was, the friction between them. When Kate offered her a soft place to land, Jenn jumped at it. Her condo was the only big asset she had left, other than her retirement account. Selling it hadn't been a problem in the hot Bay Area real estate market. Committing to someplace else would have to wait until she had a new job.

Princess yipped her frantic bark, the one meaning she didn't like being held back from something she wanted. Jenn's gaze followed the line of the leash to its end and found Princess nose to nose with a dog twice her size. At the other end of that leash, an older woman smiled indulgently at the canine interchange.

Jenn dropped the phone and jumped to her feet, reeling Princess in as fast as she could. She knew what was coming, and it wouldn't be good. Despite her quick moves, Princess was faster. The little dog leaped up with an open mouth and sank her tiny teeth into the other dog's inquisitive nose.

"Yelp!"

The other dog jumped back with a crescendo of pitiful whines. The woman scooped up her dog and gaped at Jenn in shocked disbelief.

"Your dog just bit my dog."

"I'm sorry, I'm so sorry. Princess, say you're sorry." Jenn lifted the Yorkie and waved an admonishing hand in front of her nose. Princess lunged, this time for her index finger.

"You should learn to control your dog. I certainly hope it has had its shots. I will have to report this to the authorities."

"No, please, I'm sorry. Princess has had all her shots. See? This is her rabies tag and her license." Jenn flashed the metal to the other woman, who peered at it while stroking her whimpering pet's head. That animal cowered and looked at anything other than the fur bundle in Jenn's arms. Princess, on the other hand, gazed back as if supremely satisfied with herself.

"Your dog is dangerous. If you can't control the animal, you shouldn't have it out in public."

Jenn could only continue to apologize and squeeze her little dog tighter as Sweet Pea tried to wiggle out of her arms. When the woman marched away with an aggravated backward glance, Jenn gave her a weak smile.

She sank back on the bench and shoved the dog in the tote. When Princess protested with a series of barks, she zipped the top closed and set her on the ground under the bench. By the time she picked up her phone once more, her sister was in full tirade.

"I heard all that, Jenn. I keep telling you, that dog is a menace. She has impulse control problems, not unlike someone else we know."

"Hey, listen, I need to go. I don't want to monopolize this park for too long, you know?"

Kate continued to lecture, but Jenn signed off. It made her so tired. Her sisters and her father didn't understand why she left what was, in their minds, a perfectly good job. When she told them the job came with problems, they huffed and shook their heads in response. Every position had shortcomings, they had warned her, and her expectations were set too high. When they thought she'd behaved carelessly and acted on a whim, she heard all about her lifelong issues with leaping before she looked and never shutting the hell up.

"How did we get into this, Princess?"

The dog rumbled in deep disgust in the bag. Jenn retrieved the remainder of the first scone and popped it into her mouth, but the flavor didn't seem quite so sunny now. Depression over everything that had occurred over the past year reared up with unexpected intensity.

She was stuck in a rut. Her world grew smaller with each passing week. Money would become the deciding factor in taking anything, any job at all, if only to find her freedom again. That only accented her blues.

Main Street, Flynn's Crossing, wavered as tears filled her eyes. She was usually the most upbeat, optimistic person around. She could conquer any mountain, smile wide enough to fill any ocean, and make anyone her friend. People were basically good, she believed, until that belief was crushed under moral lapses so huge, she still couldn't process them completely.

"What am I going to do?"

No one responded to her question, not even Princess.

Window shopping had lost its appeal. If she didn't have a job, she certainly couldn't fantasize about what her life could look like with her own home and furnishings, clothes that were current fashion, and a new pair of boots. She'd dearly love a new pair of boots. She loved boots, and the ones she stared at now on her feet, her favorites, showed their wear.

She dropped her head back, mostly to keep the tears from finding a low spot and trailing down her face. It was embarrassing enough that she owned a four-pound attack beast she couldn't control. It was even worse to be sitting in a public place on a beautiful day, crying her eyes out. Blinking a few times, she focused on the building across the street to clear her vision.

The old structure's brick façade stretching up three stories with tall windows set at close intervals. A cheese shop occupied the street level. Its display included bottles and cutting boards, a large picnic basket, and signs advertising artisanal cheeses and meats inside. A 'Help Wanted' notice hung next to the door.

That would be a fun place to work. No one came into a shop like that unless they were looking for something happy. No moral dilemmas, no ethical issues, just good food and fun. It wouldn't pay much, but like the bakery, the smile quotient would be high.

She sniffed again, scrubbing at the one tear she hadn't been able to control. She glanced down the street, busy on this Saturday morning, but with none of the loud blare of traffic and rancid smell of exhaust and trash of the big city. Birds tittered in the park's bushes and trees over the other town sounds. People passed by and smiled at her, unaware she had a monster hiding in her tote bag and a pain as large as this county in her heart.

Where would she go? What would she do? There was no place like home, and she had no idea where that place was anymore.

A mental kick was in order. She sounded like a melodramatic heroine in an old movie, or better yet, like she was looking for a wizard. No one was going to take care of her and her little dog too if she didn't do it herself. New resolve to fix her life had her biting into the second scone.

Jenn eyed the cheese store again. She knew next to nothing about cheese other than she liked to eat it. That had never stopped her in the past. She could learn about any subject, given a little time.

Her drying eyes wandered. A nice place like this was bound to have other jobs she could do. She could cobble together little bits of work until she found something bigger. Getting out from under the combined thumbs of her well-meaning but overbearing sisters and her worried but equally nosey father suddenly sounded like the best Christmas present she could give herself.

She lifted her tote off the ground and peered inside. "Princess, what do you think? Could you learn to like Flynn's Crossing?"

Bright eyes stared back at her without comment, which she took to be another positive sign. She smiled, knowing it was a risky step to take, but that's what most of her life had been about. Standing and slinging the tote over her shoulder, she glanced up above the cheese shop.

And there it was, two stories higher, the third sign she needed. 'For Rent.'

Chapter 3

Dawn came obscenely early, and for that, he was grateful. The sun didn't officially rise until almost oh-eight-thirty, but light grew beforehand in the mountains. He'd left the old curtains open last night. The yawning abyss of emptiness gave him an odd comfort when the nightmares woke him on the hour. His endurance wore thinner with each rotation of the planet. A few more weeks of this and he would be gone.

Because of that, he berated himself multiple times each day for making a promise to Uncle Rowan.

"I'm deeding this to you because frankly, I'm getting too old to cope with it. Hauling trees down that hill and tying them on tops of cars is more than I want to do, not to mention clearing the trails and making sure they aren't too slippery and all the other stuff that goes into making this place safe for customers."

Rock had kicked at the dirt, hard as clay back then with the summer lack of rain, not meeting his uncle's eyes.

"I don't have to tell you about the history of this place. You know it. Been in the family for generations and all that. Too bad none of my girls are interested in the family legacy. I figured you'd like it as something to do for a couple of months out of the year, while you figure out what comes next."

If his uncle had realized he'd provided the perfect place to hide out and lay low, he probably would have rethought his transfer of property title. When Rock shoved his meager possessions into his two duffels and marched them to the old truck he'd picked up used, his mother nipped at his heels in no time.

"Rock, honey, are you sure this is a good idea? I mean, you've been gone for years, and it's so nice having you around the ranch. I know the boys love having you nearby too. You always were between a rock and a hard place, being the middle child, but that doesn't mean you have to disappear on us again."

He'd had a pang of guilt strong enough to make him pause in the act of climbing behind the wheel. Emileen Kermarrec still favored those tie-dyed hippy clothes, like a bright butterfly flitting between all their lives. Deep creases marred Ma's face now, and he had contributed to those too. Worry made her frown at him, and he wrapped her in a hard hug and lifted her off her feet.

"I love you, Ma. I just need some space. Things to process, you know?"

Since that had amounted to a long speech in his recent conversation pattern, Ma fell quiet. She bit her lip but smiled as she waved him off. It was another of life's guarantees that she'd show up at the tree farm at least a couple of times a week with food and whatever else she took into her head he needed to live at the tiny cabin. He had to time things right, or she'd be the first to know.

A glance at his watch spurred him forward. Light the woodstove. Light the fire outside. Unchain the driveway. Get ready for customers. He had to leave something of value behind, though who would take this on, he wasn't sure.

The first three families to arrive were friends, making a day of their outing to the area. Their happy chatter dimmed a bit when their eyes scrutinized the trail up the hill to the taller trees. Yes, it was steep and not exactly wide, because Rock hadn't cleared it. Blackberry bramble caught on jeans and coats and sometimes gloves. Dead brown branches circled the bases of some trees because he hadn't clipped those off either. As his brothers so aptly pointed out last night, the farm was going to pot right along with him. These families didn't linger once their trees were tied on board.

The rest of the day wasn't much different. One more hour and he could chain himself in once more. One more hour of trying to be as civil as he could. He didn't make small talk, and soon, most folks wandered off to find their tree, pay him, and head on their way with minimal fuss. At one time, people stayed for an hour or more, visiting, listening to Uncle Rowan's stories and sharing their own. They ate cookies and drank cider and left with candy canes sticking out of their mouths.

Shit, he'd forgotten to make the cider today. He hadn't handed out candy canes either. His Ma would take a stick to him if she knew. The memories that recalled gave him a ghost of a grin.

With twenty minutes to go, he thought about closing early. The sky darkened as the wind picked up. He doubted people would be cutting their trees this late.

As he hitched up his jacket collar and set his boots in the direction of the entrance, headlights pinned him in their overly bright glow. Lifting an arm to shield his eyes, he stepped to the side in resignation. The car made a weirdly silent passage by him, like a ghost ship, and continued up to the parking area. He trudged after it, hoping this party would hurry and get the hell out.

A woman emerged from the driver side, boots and rear end first, talking faster than a freeway mile to someone else in the car.

"I think it's better if you stay in the car, don't you? After all, it's getting dark. I promise I'll make this quick. Then we can get home and set up our tree."

Thank hell for that. She might like one of the trees right next to her car. They were little, like the car. He didn't think it would carry much more weight than that. It looked foreign and expensive and this woman would probably cry about the tree sap leaking on her pristine roof. Too bad. You cut a tree, you live with sap. He headed for the saws, hoping he wouldn't have to provide too much of the usual spiel.

"Hi. I'm so excited to be here again. My family's been cutting our trees here for ages and now after a long break, I'm back to cut my own. The couple who used to run this place, are they still around? Do you have any cider? I'd like to have mine before I hike the hillside."

The woman followed him, chattering loudly enough to cause crows to squawk and head for other treetops. He wished he could do the same. At least she'd know the drill. He turned with a saw in his hand and lost his train of thought when his gaze settled on her.

"Oh," she said, staring at him with wide eyes mimicking the round circle of red lips.

He might have said the same, if he was the talkative type. As it was, he had a momentary flash of uncertainty. The woman had long brown hair swept to one side, a felt hat that belonged anywhere other than the woods, and nice leather gloves on hands she now held to her cheeks. He cursed his observation skills, because a quick pass told him she wasn't dressed for this, nor would she be able to carry any tree, little or not, in boots with heels that would undoubtedly cause a twisted knee or worse on the trails.

The woman's hands dropped and a smile he swore was forced came to her lips. She took a tentative step forward, then another, and raised a hand to him.

"I'm sorry, I tend to babble when I get excited. Tell me, does the same family still own this place?"

He nodded once, ignoring the outstretched hand. Restlessness made him want to step back from her, a feeling he didn't understand.

"Oh, so you're what, a son? Or do you just work here?" She glanced around as if looking for others to come bounding out of the forest. When her eyes settled back on him, the intensity in the sharp gaze amped up his ill-ease.

If she'd been coming here for years, there would be a reason for that. He remembered good times, when he and Deke and Jake, and later, the twins, came leaping out of the trees. Aunt Debby and Ma used to read them the riot act for scaring the customers that way.

He reached out and put the long stick with the saw bolted on its end in her hand, and she jumped when the wood hit her palm. Her fingers closed on it as she stared at him once more. Big questions loomed in brown eyes that regarded him closely enough to freeze his movements as if a sniper's bead was on him.

She said, "Do we know each other?"

He glanced away, unwilling to engage and yet having that sinking feeling he'd be given no choice. He'd have to help her find a tree and carry it to her car. Whoever was still in the car should come out and help her.

"Your car's open."

Her expression turned puzzled and she glanced back. When she swiveled again, her smile had returned. "Oh, that's okay. She likes the fresh air."

Two women then, so no help for it. He'd be cutting and carrying and bagging and tying. In resignation, he closed his glove over the saw and pulled.

She pulled back.

"I've got this. I may look small, but I'm strong. This isn't my first rodeo. I wonder where that saying comes from? Something else to look up, after I get done with cheese, of course. Did you know that cheese-making dates to before recorded history? The number of methods and kinds and qualities would make your head spin. For example, take cheddar. Did you know it's not naturally orange?"

Why the hell should he care? And did this woman ever shut up? He turned to the nearest trail toward the cedars, hoping she'd fall in love with the first tree she saw.

"Oh, no, I want a white fir. This way, right?"

Off she went, much to his dismay. That trail was the steepest, the rockiest, and the narrowest. He gave himself a mental kick for not clearing it better as he glanced at her high-heeled boots.

His gaze traveled north, hard to avoid as her hips swayed with each step she took. His view of her climb was a damned sight better than any he'd seen in a long time.

"I don't remember there being so many vines around. Was there a problem this year?"

She paused long enough to consider him over her shoulder. The look was more friendly than flirtatious, but that didn't stop his body from having a profound urge to reach out and capture her before she climbed further. For her own safety, of course.

"The trees look worse this year too. Was it because of the drought? Because we had a lot of rain this fall. In fact, I heard that the totals since the middle of October rivaled – "

He saw it coming the second her foot hit the muddy hillside. The boot slipped in her distraction. The heel caught in the exposed root of an old fir too tall for a holiday tree. She reached out her hands to catch herself, closing on a blackberry vine with long, nasty spines.

Her breath left her body in a whoosh loud enough to echo in the forest. His long strides covered the slope fast, but that didn't keep her from landing, cute butt first, in the mud. For the first time since she arrived, she was silent.

Rock reached her side as she examined the palms of her no longer nice gloves, flexing and straightening her fingers.

"Are you hurt?" What a moronic thing to say.

After a moment, she sniffed as if trying to hold back tears. "No, thank you. I hurt my dignity more than my body. But that's the way my life's been going recently. Pretty much in the mud."

A deep inhale marked the end of her statement. She looked up at him, fierce determination on her face. She gave a single nod as if they'd just agreed to something and glanced around at the forest.

"I like that one." She pointed to a ten-footer with dense branches and a nice cone shape. "It will fit beautifully in my new apartment. Did I tell you it has twelve-foot ceilings? And tall windows, and I plan to put the tree in front of one of those, so everyone can see it when they're shopping. It's hard to feel stressed or unhappy when you're looking at a decorated Christmas tree, don't you think? But then of course you do. You run a Christmas tree farm."

A slight waver in her voice accompanied this latest addition to her long storytelling. She winced as she flexed her gloved fingers and shifted to put her feet under her, grimacing with a quick inhale. The distress she tried to hide sparked the rescuer side of him he never could control. He reached out a hand to help her up, and after a moment's hesitation, she grabbed it.

When he pulled her upright, he didn't let go right away, fearing she might fall again. Her hand felt elfin in his, a fitting description for her with her red and green hat and matching scarf. She stared up at him in dazed confusion, and he wondered if he should ask if she hit her head.

Was it bad of him to hate letting her go? There was something about her that gave him a sense of comfort and peace. Those things had been sorely lacking in his life over the last couple of years.

Her hand slipped free as she spun away, trying to look over her shoulder. He noted the contorted frown, and he could understand why. She wore a thick coating of mud from her ill-fated landing. The weight of it alone would tell her all she needed to know.

And still, she asked, like she couldn't help hearing herself talk. "How bad is it?"

He closed his eyes for a moment, because he didn't need to examine her further to know. It would be forever imprinted on his brain. A perfect inverted mud heart marked her read end, accenting the curves filling her fancy jeans.

"Guess you'll have to hose me off," she said, a suggestion of mirth in her voice.

Oh yeah, that was exactly what he wanted to do, because there was no doubt wet denim would unmask what little bit had been left to his imagination.

"So, let's do this, shall we? I want that tree. Can you cut him about so high off the ground, please? Oh, I did it. I called the tree him. Is that correct? I'd read trees that flower should be considered female, but firs, because they don't technically flower, would be considered male. Do you agree? How do they pollinate, anyway? To plant new trees, do you collect the cones and seeds and plant those in the forest, or do you start seedlings? How long does it take to grow as tall as this one?"

He put the saw to the trunk and heaved with pent-up frustration. Unfortunately, the cut of the blade through green wood wasn't loud enough to drown out her voice, and he wondered if he'd be pushed to act on his next thought. Cut his own head off at the neck, all the better to avoid her continuous flood of words.

Chapter 4

Why couldn't she stop talking? Yes, her nickname growing up was Precocious, but she thought she had more control by now. Around this beast of a man, she might have to staple her lips together to keep the torrent of sound from coming out.

It was easy to understand why. When he'd stepped out of the forest, Jenn thought first of Big Foot or Sasquatch. He wasn't particularly tall, but he made up for that by being wide in the shoulders, and she bet it wasn't only the heavy camouflage jacket he wore. His beard extended almost half a foot from his lips, matching shaggy long hair, all the color of old linen. When he followed her to the clearing, she wondered if she should stay in the car.

"What do you think, Princess? Get the tree, or hightail it out of here?"

The dog gave a bored yawn and rounded her cushioned seat once before settling. Princess Sweet Pea wasn't fond of the great outdoors or exercise. City life suited her perfectly.

In the end, memories of good times outweighed any of her worries. Carols played and smoke from the fire rose lazily. While the place looked more run down than she remembered, she chalked it up to the magic of childhood compared to adult reality.

When she straightened with her customary smile on her face, the shock of piercing pale blue mixed with hints of gray in his eyes drooped her grin. Their color changed, deepened to remnants of the sky.

But while the color changed, the lack of emotion did not. Empty, devoid of happiness, but without sadness too. She felt sorry for him immediately, which was always a dangerous place for her to be.

Those eyes were like beamed magnets for her attention every time she glanced at him. She caught him staring a couple of times, like he couldn't figure her out, and that seemed to darken their color. Then he'd frown, or at least she thought that's what it was under all that hair, and they'd lighten. She pegged his age as ten years her senior, but all that fuzz made it hard to tell. Despite his appearance, something about him made her feel safe and secure.

So here she was, prattling on because what she felt around him was nerves. Not the nervous kind of nerves, but the kind with a pitch of excitement, on the cusp of something. That, and her ankle hurt like the dickens.

Dickens. How appropriate. 'A Christmas Carol' and all that. When the big man hefted the tree on his shoulder as if it weighed no more than a toothpick, she bit back a purely feminine sigh.

That feeling didn't last long, though, because she had to concentrate hard to keep from groaning as she followed him down the hill. Each step was like knives jabbing in her foot, caught in a vise of pain. His long strides covered the slope easily. She minced along, hoping he didn't turn around to watch her slow progress.

Each small step for womankind reminded her of the mud caking her backside. It didn't take long for the wet to penetrate her jeans, reminding her is was the beginning of December. Forget hosing off. She'd take the car someplace to be detailed, no matter what the cost. Flynn's Crossing must have a shop for that. She didn't want to look at her boots. Why hadn't she thought about how hard it was to walk in the forest in heels before she decided to come cut a tree?

Ahead of her, the big man stopped dead in his tracks, sliding the tree off his shoulder to stand it next to him. He stared at something on the ground without moving so much as a hair on his overgrown head.

"Ggrrr."

Oh heaven and hell, she knew that sound.

"Princess? No. Get back in the car, Princess. Back to bed."

"Ggrrr. Arh-ruff."

In the fading light, she saw the small body trailing the red leash dart toward the big man. She started moving too, but only a step further, the pain was too much.

"Ow!"

The man turned to check on her, and Princess kept coming. She latched on to his pants leg with a ferocious bark, or as ferocious as a dog weighing four pounds would. He didn't seem to notice. He released the tree and lumbered over to where Jenn stood on one leg, looked her up and down, and lifted her up in his arms like she weighed no more than a bag of groceries.

She knew her mouth hung open. She knew she should do something about her dog hanging off the man's leg. She knew she should tell him to put her down. But something in her brain short-circuited when she stared into his darkening eyes.

He set her on the largest log by the fire with such care, she wondered if she'd imagined the act at all. He stripped off his leather gloves, exposing hands thick with sinew but without the harsh wear and tear she'd expect from someone making his living off farming. Gentle fingers probed through muddy leather on her ankle. Taking advantage of the situation, Princess let go of his leg and snapped at his hands.

"Princess, please, be a good dog and go back to the car. I promise I'll be right there and we'll go home."

Yvonne Kohano

The man glanced up at her and down at the dog. She thought she heard a huff which might have been humor. He snapped his fingers in front of Princess's nose twice. "No."

The dog blinked fast in apparent surprise. Her head tilted to one side, sagging her red and green bow over one pointy furred ear. Jenn swore her eyes narrowed as the little monster lunged once more for the fingers in front of her nose.

"No. Bad dog."

Princess froze in midflight. She dropped back on her haunches and tilted her head again. Her lips peeled back, and her tongue lolled out panting. Jenn swore the dog smiled.

"Wow. Look at that. You must be a magician with animals." Never had Jenn been able to convince the dog to do anything she didn't darned well want to do.

The man went back to examining her ankle. His testing touch remained gentle but firm. "Does this hurt?"

Oh yowzah, hot-diggedity, yes indeedy. She must have sucked serious air, because his gaze shot up to meet hers. His next move, sliding the zipper down on the inside of the boot, surprised her almost as much as the stormy seas of his eyes when they pinned her in his view.

The boot slid off with a protesting creak, exposing her spirited Christmas socks. He paused and shook his head, a small jerk. His fingers wrapped around the ankle, manipulating it with slow movements. The warmth of his skin bled through the socks and felt good, too good. This was so embarrassing. She was getting turned on by a man checking her twisted ankle. And he wasn't just any man, but a mysterious mountain of a man who stirred a welcoming place inside her.

"I don't think it's broken, but you should go to the hospital and have it x-rayed."

That had her gasping again, bringing his attention back to her face with narrowed eyes. She wished he didn't narrow them. They were mesmerizing opened wide, and basking in their glow heated her from the inside out.

"Should I get you an ambulance?"

This time she kept her lips sealed but gulped hard. She shook her head.

Shaking her head brought a deeper frown from her rescuer. She couldn't tell him the sad truth. She had no health insurance and no extra cash to pay for care out of pocket. She had a new job, granted, not a fancy one, but it meant she had to stand on her feet. And she had a perfectly beautiful tree she would be completely incapable of hauling up to the third floor.

"I should be going."

The man frowned at her.

"Home, I mean. Well, my new apartment. I really love that tree. I hate cutting down a tree that doesn't get used. I hope someone else will want it. That's why I don't go to commercial lots, because I don't want to see all the trees that don't get selected. Plus, this is such an interesting and fun experience."

The man's face twitched, and she thought she saw the hint of a smile lift one side of his lips. Hard to tell, carpet of beard and all.

"Fun?"

The single word captured her attention, along with the dancing light in his eyes. He should always look this way. He wasn't anywhere nearly as imposing in good humor.

"Is there someone at home to help you with the tree?"

She shot a quick glance at the tree lying on the ground, now being sniffed with great interest by her little dog. "No. I just moved here, you see. To Main Street in town. I, ah, don't know many people yet."

A sigh of gargantuan proportions blew out of the man as he stood. He scratched his ear, his gaze on the dog sitting with unusual patience at his feet. Hands landed on his hips as he shook his head.

"I can bring it for you." He continued to examine Sweet Pea, and the dog returned the attention with an uncharacteristic wiggle of wagging tail.

"Really? You'd do that? I'd really appreciate it. I bought a stand and everything already, though I don't have any decorations, at least not here. I have to pick up some things from my sister's house and from storage. I was going to do that tomorrow, but now, maybe I'll wait a day or two until my ankle feels better. I can't have her worrying about me, you know. She's nosey but well-meaning, and she wants me to take any job, but I don't want to. Plus, I hate feeling beholding to her for giving me a roof right now."

The man's eyes shifted to her in slow motion, as if he didn't know what to make of her. She couldn't blame him. The way she was acting, even she didn't know what to make of herself.

"I'll drive."

She glanced at the only other vehicle in the clearing, an old pick-up, then at her car. "I can drive myself." At least she thought she could. Her left foot wasn't used for much in her automatic.

He nodded once in a decisive fashion, walking over to the tree. He stared at the dog for a moment, and Princess stared up at him.

"Car," he said, snapped his fingers and pointed at the open door of the hybrid. Princess didn't even hesitate. She trotted over to the car and took that mighty leap inside. Jenn could only stare dumbfounded.

The man lifted the tree and tossed it easily in the back of the truck. He returned to her, and with his arms extended, she had no problem envisioning him lifting her in his arms again. Part of her wanted to be a girlie-girl and allow it. Pride had a different opinion.

"I can walk," she said, pushing her palms on the log for leverage. His hand appeared under her nose, palm up. She drifted into the grip with as much of her scattered dignity she had remaining and allowed him to pull her up.

A glint of humor mixed with puzzlement shown in his eyes. Up close, they seemed dark blue now, though it could be a trick of the faded light and reflections of the fire. He didn't respond to her thanks and didn't move to his vehicle until she had safely hobbled over to hers and landed in the seat, mud and all.

"Well, that was an interesting adventure, wasn't it, Princess?"

In response, the dog gave what could be a grin.

Jenn glanced in the rearview mirror as the truck lights appeared on her back bumper. When they drove the distance into town, he was never more than a length behind her. His presence brought her a feeling of comfort and security in what had been a crazy, wild afternoon.

Chapter 5

She drove like a city girl, tentative on the turns along the twisty road. Just as well, since she didn't seem to realize the edge of the road turned to soft-crusted dirt and she narrowly missed ending up with a set of tires buried in the silt more than once. She waved at him a couple of times. Rock didn't wave back.

Why the hell was he doing this? It was her own damned fault for wearing such ridiculous boots. And leaving the door open was an invitation for the dog to get into trouble. He had no problem picturing the rat-thing heading into the woods where he would be expected to spend half the night searching for it.

She angled into a curb spot, which was probably just as well. He bet she wouldn't be able to parallel park. He continued a few spaces further and backed the truck up to align it with ease. He'd learned to steer on a tractor, along with parking it in a slot designed for something much smaller, his dad's idea of teaching the boys how to drive.

He saw her struggle briefly with a large shoulder bag, with no sign of the rat-dog. She straightened as he closed his gloved hands around the tree trunk in the back. His task would be simple. Carry the tree to her apartment, refuse any offer of money, if she was going to offer, that is, and head home without conversation.

Except nothing ever turned out like he planned, and he should sure as hell know that by now. The woman unlocked a door between two shops, pushing it wide. She hung on to the doorframe as he approached, her smile genuinely grateful. He didn't want to dwell on how he wanted that smile to stay in place, without the horrified sorrow she'd worn as he examined her ankle before.

What was her story, anyway? He shouldn't care. He shouldn't, but that sense of the familiar kept eating at him like sand fleas in the desert.

He stopped at the doorway, putting a hand on it to hold it open. He gestured with the tree for her to precede him. She glanced up the stairs, then back at him.

"Why don't you go first? I'm at the very top, on the right. It may take me a while to navigate it."

Her chuckle held no humor, and as he examined her closer, he noticed fine lines of tightness in a face paler than before. Those eyes were an interesting mix of browns and golds. Her mouth carried a pretty bow shape when it wasn't flapping. As if he needed any confirmation of her pain, she cringed when toes on her injured foot tapped the floor. He stepped back to the sidewalk, lifted his chin and tracked up the building's façade, gauging the distance.

Why the hell did he do any of it? He couldn't let her suffer like that. It went against everything he believed in, allowing anyone else to suffer. He himself was a different story. The dog growled from her bag as if it agreed.

He leaned the tree against the wall inside the door and turned back to her. He used to tote men his own size in the field, gear and all, and a slip of a woman like her wasn't an issue. When he swung her up with an arm under her legs and the other at her back, her gasp of surprise would have been a nice compliment, if he was wired into that any longer. Her splutter of dismay and requests to be put down were kind of cute as she reeled the big bag in close. The continuous yips of the rat-thing, not so much.

"No."

Both woman and dog fell silent as they reached the first landing, which was a good thing. He expected the dog to obey but doubted his single word would have deterred the woman in the least. His boots made a hollow sound on the wood steps, hollow like his emotions, hollow like his heart. By the time they reached the top floor, she had a key clutched in her hand.

He set her down, leaning her against the doorframe, and turned before she would have a chance to say anything. Trudging back down, he wondered how she'd manage all these stairs now. But that wasn't his concern. He would deliver the tree, apologize for her inconvenience, and be on his way.

When he reached the top floor again, the door stood open and lights shown from inside. He knocked once, receiving no answer from the woman, but the dog growled. He took that as permission and stepped inside.

Her description didn't do the place justice. The ceilings were tall, with a trio of equally tall windows bringing in the quiet lights of Main Street. Exposed brick warmed the interior walls. Painted wood strung between the windows. Doors opened to other rooms in the back, but this front area was open all the way across. She stood with a hand resting on the back of a sofa, balancing on her uninjured foot.

He needed to get out of here. Even though this place lacked decorations and personal touches, it smacked of too much hominess to make him feel comfortable. An empty tree stand stood in front of the center window. As she had promised, it would show its cheery form to anyone walking by below. She struck him as a woman who would put up too many strings of lights and a multitude of shiny ornaments.

"Thank you for everything. You've been my hero today. I guess I didn't think this through when I headed out today. I was so excited to have a place of my own again, you see. My sister has very nice decorations on her tree, all silver and blue, but to me, it looks sterile. I wanted a bright, kaleidoscope Christmas. Does that make sense? But I'm happy to make do with what I have."

He didn't like the sad sound in her voice, like her dismay was bigger than her holiday joy. Instead of responding, he walked the tree over to the stand, put the fir in place, and knelt to tighten the screws. He was almost done when the dog came up and pinned him with its beady eyes.

"Sit," he muttered, mostly because he wanted it to stay out of his way, so he could get done and get gone.

The dog hesitated only a heartbeat before it sat. A minute later, it was giving him that goofy drool-laden grin, its head at a tilt. He didn't trust the little thug for a minute.

"Can you adjust it? A little to the left," Jennifer said. "No, it's tilting, more left."

He fixed it, keeping one eye on the rat-thing.

"That's perfect. Here, water."

He was about to decline the offer of a drink when he realized why she had a pitcher in her hand. He poured it into the stand and stood, trying to avoid looking at the woman who still hadn't shed the elf hat. Her voice rose and fell, and he lost track of her busy words, trying his best not to sneak another look at her. It was exhausting.

Yeah, that was why he was so tired last night that he slept deeper than usual. Her chattering. That must be why he dreamed about her too. She was like an infection, complete with a red and green hat.

"You must have gathered enough wool to weave a blanket by now."

His head snapped back to allow him to focus on neon pink standing four feet away. Gray hair in a braid wound around the crown of her head, bare otherwise despite the winter chill. Jeans and sensible vinyl barn boots darkened her from the waist down, making her jacket glow even brighter.

"Don't give me that glassy-eyed stare like a mean old bear, young man."

No, a bear would take one look at the determined scrunch of Ma's face and he'd run for the nearest tree. Despite knowing he'd never make it, he glanced back at the cabin.

"Rock, Rock, my hard place. Why is there a lock on the chain? Have you been having trouble with trespassers?"

Not unless you counted his brothers, or his uncle, or the woman standing in front of him. Ma put her hands on her hips.

"I didn't hear you drive up, Ma."

"Well that's putting a nose in the middle of obvious. Of course you didn't, because I had to park on the road. It's just as well. I got to see you in your natural state."

He closed his eyes. This was not going to go well, no matter what he did.

"I wish you'd move back home, son. I worry about you out here alone."

Her softened tone, the one he found it impossible to say no to, made him open his eyes and sigh in resignation.

"I'm fine, Ma." That was a total lie, but better than blurting out the truth.

"Good. If you're fine, you won't mind going to your counseling appointment today. Jake had an accident to cover and Deke's negotiating a sale on those crazy cattle of his, and your uncle says you're pigheaded and refuses to deal with you. That left me to make sure you go."

He'd begun shaking his head when she hit Jake's name and kept right on going through the rest. It didn't seem to matter to her.

"You are going, if I have to kick your behind from here to town. I have no problem doing that, because it's for your own good. You think you don't need anyone's help and you don't want to help anyone either. It's time, son, to stop feeling sorry for yourself and pay attention to others around you."

As he had yesterday? His thoughts strayed to the woman and the rat-thing. There was no good reason on the planet why he should have helped her, other than he felt bad about her fall. A squeaky unoiled wheel in his brain warned him differently.

"Come on, come on. Hit the latrine and wash your hands and for heaven's sake, Rock, try to pull a comb through all that shag. You look like a heathen, and I didn't raise any of those."

If he didn't comply, Ma would have no problem taking matters into her own hands. She might be small, but she raised five rough and tumble boys, managed a gruff husband, and mothered a bunkhouse full of ranch hands for more decades than most would have patience for. Plus, he couldn't say no to her.

He was coming out of the cabin when Ma reached down and picked up something from the ground. The color tickled a memory, and when it took full hold, he stopped in his tracks.

"I wonder who lost this. Looks expensive, real leather, and look at those rhinestones." She turned over a narrow red dog leash in her hands.

Oh crap.

On the drive back to town, he tried to think about anything other than the thing now burning a hole in his jacket pocket. As Ma drove in her usual madwoman style, he could think of nothing else. The picture of the rat-dog trailing the red leash burned in his mind. By the time he dropped into a chair in the interior room reminding him of a small box with no escape, thinking about anything else would be a distraction he welcomed.

"How was your weekend?" The dark-skinned counselor sitting across from him wore his interested professional look. Rock didn't hate the guy, but he didn't love this process either. He'd learned Ed was a vet with Afghanistan nightmares and had traveled his own bumpy road back to humanity. Rock didn't feel anything about that other than it wouldn't be his road. Hoo-ah for Ed, though.

Because they'd sit there in silence until he answered, he shrugged.

"How are you doing on expanding your social circle, your interactions with others?"

If Ed meant involuntary interactions, he was golden. He took care of the customers with no chit-chat. That had to count. He nodded to respond.

"Tell me about a conversation this weekend that you consider a step forward."

Did toting a woman, a dog, and a Christmas tree up to a third-floor apartment and listening to her gab count?

Silence stretched again. Ed watched him with empathy, which made Rock squirm. The leash and the need to return it danced around at the edge of his conscious thoughts. Maybe that was why he couldn't help the words from bursting out of him.

"A woman came to the tree farm with a dog."

Ed nodded with so much enthusiasm, he looked like one of those bobble-head dolls. "Good, that's very good. Tell me more. What did you talk about?"

There was the problem. He hadn't talked. He'd listened, against his wishes, and she'd talked, and talked, and talked. That wouldn't satisfy the counselor, he suspected. "Christmas trees."

"Tell me about the dog. What kind was it?"

What kind would it be? He had little experience with small dogs. Growing up, they had big ones at the ranch. Describing it as a rat would probably be considered insensitive.

"Little dog. Lots of hair. Sharp teeth. Ferocious thing." Which, in retrospect, was kind of amusing, given its size.

"You're not a fan, I take it."

Rock shook his head, his hand slipping into his pocket to finger the leash. Ferocious and pampered. The second part probably explained the first.

Ed nodded his head and made a note on a pad. He spent the rest of their hour quizzing Rock on dogs. He didn't mind talking about the dogs he'd had as a kid. That was then and bore no connection to now.

By the time they exited the room, Ed slapped him on the back and congratulated him on a good session. He slipped out of the building, keeping his gaze down to avoid contact with anyone else, and walked up to his mother. She didn't move at first when he approached. Then she smiled.

"You must have had a good session. You look a little more relaxed."

Funny, he didn't feel relaxed. He felt like he had that time they moved the last convoy without a map. That lack of direction tightened his nerves.

Ma jumped into the driver's seat, gunned the engine, and looked over at him. He had a fleeting thought about walking the short distance to deliver the leash, wondering if Ma would allow him out of her sight.

"Hop aboard. Where to now?"

That was his answer. With a resigned sigh, he got into the passenger seat that was almost as old as he was. When he responded with his destination, her eyebrows raised in surprise. Her grin got wider and she might have left some rubber in the parking lot in her happy haste to get moving.

It didn't take them long to cover the distance, and she traveled Main Street from end to end before he said anything.

"Drop me here."

"Please. Drop me here, please. Lordy, anyone would think I raised you in a barn."

"Please." He growled the word, but it made him feel better inside.

"I think I'm going to head into the cheese shop. They have some of the creamiest brie, and I have a craving for it. Will you be long?"

He shook his head, opening his door as she zoomed into a parallel parking spot with an ease the woman last night would never have managed. He rounded the hood and opened his Ma's door, because he didn't want her to start another lecture. Besides, it gave him a delay he found he wanted before he again encountered the petite woman who rattled off data with a speed that rivaled a military intelligence officer.

He waited by the truck until his mother went into the shop, to avoid satisfying her obvious curiosity about his destination. He stepped up to the doorbells alongside the entrance they'd used last night and rang the bell for 3A.

His foot twitched, something it hadn't done in a long time. It was that moment before an operation commenced, that pause before the concentration and the focus and the noise. He tapped impatiently, trying to calm himself. It would take her time to ring open the door, he figured, because she probably had her leg up on a couch.

Minutes passed, and he rang again. No sound came from inside, and he stepped back to examine the windows. The tree stood in the center, still bare of decorations. The room looked dark. No face peered over the sill to find out who was at the door.

He heaved a frustrated sigh, wondering how to handle this. The leash had to belong to the rat-thing. The rat's mistress would need it to control the monster. It did look expensive, and not something she should be without if she wanted any hope of controlling her beast. If he tied it to the doorknob, though, it might end up in the wrong hands. He wasn't sure why he felt it was so important that she have it back. It was like a mission he felt duty-bound to complete.

Resigned, he stepped away and moved over to lean against a lamppost in front of the cheese shop window, hoping the view of him waiting would spur Ma along. When she got to visiting, there was no stopwatch on the planet that would move her. He pulled his coat collar up, not against the cold, but so fewer people would stare as they came by.

A flash of pink flickered inside the shop, catching the bright sunshine of the day. Deeper shadows made it impossible to see further inside. He had no idea how long he'd have to wait. He could go in and prod her along, but he still hated anyplace where a door closed behind him.

Pink flickered again, and this time, Ma appeared in the window and wiggled her fingers at him. She said something over her shoulder, and another face appeared. That one snapped him to attention.

>>>>>

"Yes, that's my son, all broody and gruff. He's a nice young man, but his last few years have been hard. Military duty, you know. I worry about him, I really do."

Jenn opened her mouth, thought the better of it and shut it with a snap.

"So, are you married?"

Jenn wrapped the cheese selections, shaking her head as her hands moved faster.

"Ah, well, there's something about Flynn's Crossing. I know you're new in town, but it doesn't take long. Seems young people come here with no expectations and boom, they fall in love. I'm sure you'll be very happy here, Jennifer."

Love wasn't on her horizon, except she couldn't help darting a glance at the man standing straighter than the lamppost outside.

"Here you go, Mrs. Kermarrec. You'll have to tell me what your son thinks of that brie." Darn. She intended to say family, not son, but the sight of her rescuer undid the connection between her brain and her mouth.

"It's Emie, dear, or if you feel the need to stand on formalities, Miss Emie. Been that to countless generations over the years."

Jenn willed her lips to stay sealed, but there they went, popping open before she could find a stapler.

"What's your son's name?"

Emie looked delighted she'd asked. "Why, that's Rock, my middle boy. Born between a rock and a hard place is what I always teased him. Little did I know. Come on, I'll introduce you."

She linked an unrelenting arm through Jenn's and started pulling, and there was no way to fight it without making a scene. When they approached the door, Rock leaped forward and held it open. His nod acknowledged his mother's words of thanks, but his eyes stayed on Jenn.

That strange sense she knew him hung in the air. She wished she could figure out why he seemed familiar, because until she did, she might have these butterflies in her stomach every time she saw him.

Which wouldn't be again, she assured herself. Matchmaking mother aside, she had no reason to visit the tree farm again any time soon. Except, she had spent a couple of hours looking up ways to clear brush and hit on ruminating goats and lost another hour researching them, because he seemed to need some help with the vines and shrubs.

"Jennifer, this is my son, Rock Kermarrec. Son, this is Jennifer Stanton. Jennifer is new in town, so I thought we could take her under our wing."

If he had any reaction to the idea, he gave no sign. Jenn, on the other hand, found a sudden stream of nonsense coming out of her mouth.

"Pleased to see you again, I mean, to officially meet you. Thank you again for your help yesterday. I still haven't gotten the decorations. Shelley, she owns the shop, and she called and asked me to come in today for training, so here I am. It seems I know more about cheese than I thought. Maybe it's because I like to eat it so much. You know, cheese."

Rock didn't respond, though his eyes seemed to brighten, and his mouth twitched in that expanse of fur. In the sunlight, it had more shades of color than she noticed yesterday, glowing like a rich animal pelt. Highlights ran from top to bottom of the beard and side to side on the moustache. It reminded her of the streaks in Princess's coat after a good brushing. Applying that to the man in front of her brought on a giggle she struggled to stifle.

"Do you two know each other already?" Miss Emie's tone rose in surprise.

"No," came from the man, at the same time Jenn said, "Yes."

Rock's mother swiveled her gaze between them and Jenn rushed to explain.

"I came to the farm where he works to cut a Christmas tree yesterday. I wanted to decorate my apartment, you see, but I wasn't thinking, and I wore these heeled boots, and well, I fell, and he brought my tree home for me. Delivered it. And set it up. He's been very nice to me."

Miss Emie's eyes widened and focused on her son, but Rock wasn't returning her questioning stare. Jenn felt his focused sweep like a physical thing, starting at the top of her head, where she'd piled her hair in a complicated knot to keep it out of the food, to the apron emblazoned with the cheese shop logo covering her from shoulder to knee, to the jeans with their fancy stitching. When they settled on her feet, she blushed in embarrassment.

There was no other solution today. She'd wrapped her ankle in an elastic bandage she picked up at the drugstore down the street, but it was still swollen and none of her boots fit over it. Plus, standing around in heels all day wasn't going to cut it, so she put on the only pair of flats she had with her.

This time, she was sure his mouth twitched. The ghost of a grin formed as he regarded the fuzzy purple slippers. The color was as noisy as his mother's jacket. Technically, they'd be known as mules, since they had no backs. The sound she made as she walked around the shop was a distinct scuffle, no matter how much she tried to pick up her feet as she moved.

Jenn wanted to explain, but she figured she'd jabbered enough already. Trying to change the subject, she moved into territory where she felt safer.

"I spent a little time last night researching brush clearing at the tree farm. I was thinking maybe I could get together with you and the owner to go over what I learned. I'm a consultant, and I'd like to help you develop a strategy to clean things up."

Rock blinked rapidly as if he didn't quite take in what she'd said. A gaze that twinkled at her moments ago faded once more, which was a shame. She suspected if he ever laughed, the ever-changing colors in his crinkled eyes would make a pleasant picture.

"They're one and the same, dear."

She turned to Miss Emie in confusion. "What?"

"Rock owns the tree farm. It used to belong to his Uncle Rowan, but now it's his. That, and a lot of other land."

She didn't miss Rock's brief eye roll at his mother's recitation. Whatever reason he had for being ashamed of being a property owner was probably due to her remarks about the condition of said property yesterday. But she could help him with that. It would be a nice gesture of thanks for his effort with the tree.

"Jennifer?"

The single word drew her attention to the cheese shop owner standing in the gaping doorway. Jenn wasn't a consultant, at least not today. Her new identity was that of clerk in a cheese shop, and she'd better get back to it before she lost the first job in months that paid.

She said goodbye to Miss Emie, surprised by the warm hug she received. Rock gave no indication he cared about her leaving one way or the other, but when she turned at the door to push it closed, she caught him still staring in her direction, even as his mother disappeared up the street.

Chapter 6

"How do you feel about your progress?"

Ed stared at him expectantly, encouragement written as clear as the winter day on his face. Rock paused, saying the only thing that came to mind.

"I drove here today."

Nodding hard enough to cause a breeze, Ed laughed. "Excellent. That willingness to participate in your recovery is a sure sign of progress. How are you doing on expanding your social circle?"

Rock gripped his fingers into fists in his pockets, toying with the red leash he hadn't returned to its rightful owner. Would his thoughts of Jennifer Stanton and the certainty he had about her familiarity be labeled as progress? He doubted the counselor would split hairs over it.

What would the woman say when he returned the leash to her? She'd probably bought a replacement already, but that didn't mean he should keep it. He'd thought about throwing it away and came close to tossing it in the fire last night. He wasn't sure what stopped him.

"Do you have time for a little field trip? I have something in mind that I hope you'll be open to."

Rock had nothing on the calendar, other than the leash thing. He'd even driven himself to his appointment, much to Jake's delight. He told himself that was the only reason he drove himself today, so he could return the leash without an audience.

At his hesitant nod, the counselor grabbed a jacket off the back of his office door and waved Rock through first. "Why don't you drive?"

Ed didn't say anything for the sake of conversation as they drove. The town's congestion, such as it was, changed quickly to small farms and ranches. Rock kept one hand on the wheel and one resting at his hip out of habit, and he noted the counselor's glances at that.

"Left turn coming up, the cinder block building."

Rock slowed, noting the sign. The county's animal shelter was the last place he would have expected this field trip to go.

He pulled into a parking slot but left the truck running. Ed turned toward him, unbuckling his seatbelt. "I bet you're wondering why we're here."

Rock nodded, examining the stack of gray concrete. He could easily imagine the thickness of the walls, the hollowed out noise reflection inside, and the swelter of heat in the summer. The place already depressed him.

Throwing open the door, Ed didn't look back as he said, "Come on."

The counselor turned at the door marked 'office' and stood, one hand on the handle and the other resting where a weapon would. Respect for their shared military journey was the only reason Rock gave a resigned sigh and turned off the engine. When he joined Ed at the door, the man smiled.

"After you," Rock said. He heard the uncertainty in his voice. Along with mysteries, he didn't like surprises. It worried him that he had no primary plan, no back-up escape route, and no way of setting either since he had no idea why he was here.

"Hey Ed," said a blonde behind the counter. She shined a big smile Rock's way too, as she waved them toward an inner doorway.

Rock walked on the balls of his feet, ready to backtrack if the need arose. Brilliant light and earthy animal smells hit him as the door swung shut behind him. The noise in the place stunned his senses as he surveyed the room quickly, and his eyes locked on the cages around them.

Dogs. Big dogs. Little dogs. Hopeful bright eyes and wagging tails, and a few that cowered and didn't meet his gaze. It sickened him to see them. Animals in cages had it no better than humans in cages. The need to run was almost overwhelming. He wanted to release the latches on every gate and let the dogs go, free to run after him or stay in their corners. They would then have a choice.

"Why are we here?"

The words tore out of him without warning, guttural with hurt.

Ed met him eye to eye. "You're a smart man, Rock. I don't think I need to explain it." He cocked his head to one side and raised an eyebrow.

Yeah. Yeah, he got it, and he didn't like it, didn't want to think about it. He refused to see the parallels to his human condition in the fates of these animals. The world designed all sorts of cages. And yet, he had to ask.

"What happens to them?"

Ed shrugged, walking down one aisle. With pronounced hesitation, Rock followed.

"Most get adopted eventually. Some are sent to foster homes because they require socialization or other confidence building. Then they get adopted. Some go to other no-kill shelters with better adoption potential. Some, unfortunately, live here for too darned long."

The man crouched down in front of a cage Rock assumed was empty. The tan and black mound in the back didn't appear to be an animal, but the skin shivered as if in a fever. A quick cowering glance, and its face turned to the corner once more. That look was long enough for mournful timid eyes with what appeared to be tears to register and knock him in the gut hard enough to make him choke.

"Still here, huh, buddy? Don't worry, someone will come for you soon and then you'll find your forever home." The patient soft croon of Ed's voice perked up the animal's ears a little, and the shivering abated, but the dog didn't approach.

"What's this one's story?"

Why was he asking? He needed to get out of here. The need to run and take the dogs with him approached overpowering.

"Not sure. He was a stray, and it took some time for the officers to catch him. Not because he ran, but because he hid under a porch so low, even the dog had to crawl on his belly. The staff named him Ranger, because they found him at a ranger's station. He's been in here a long time already, about four months I think."

No wonder the dog looked so forlorn. Four months in a cage, and who knows what kind of life beforehand. Hiding didn't make him appealing, another feeling Rock was sure the counselor would use as an example.

The dog glanced up once more, meeting Rock's eyes for a fleeting moment. Yeah, I got you, buddy. I understand. He understood all too well.

He executed an abrupt about-face and double-timed out the door, past the startled blonde and out into the sunshine. Inhaling fast, he held his breath as he had been taught to do. The feeling of suffocation came in waves, growing stronger with each passing second. When his oxygen carried him as long as it could, he blew out a gasp and inhaled deeply again.

Walls closed in despite the sunshine. His brain knew he was in the open, but his fear was another story. These panic attacks were something he tried to avoid, and usually he could block the triggers. That dog struck something inside him like a big brass bell, though, and he was powerless to hold it back.

"Keep breathing. In and hold. Out. Again. You're safe, Rock. You and me, we're just going to sit here and breathe."

He wasn't certain how long he hyperventilated. Ed's voice rose and fell in a comforting murmur, not unlike the tone he used with the frightened dog. Rock supposed that was what he was too, an animal trapped in a cage of circumstances' making.

As the episode subsided, he came back to conscious reality slowly. The bite of gravel under his knees. The arm he gripped like a lifeline. The heat of sun on his bowed head. Wet tracks on his face. An ache in his chest from labored breathing.

"Think you can stand?"

Rock nodded, though he was unsure. Muscles under his tightened hand flexed as the man next to him rose, pulling him along. He could see his feet beneath him, but he'd lost his rooting, disconnected from his links to the planet spinning with him as its unwilling passenger.

The next deep breath was easier, and it was harder. The price was his newfound understanding. The counselor didn't need to point out the obvious.

Rock met Ed's concerned gaze, the one filled with sympathy for what he was going through. "I'll drive," Ed said. No words were spoken on their ride back to the center.

In the lot, Ed paused after Rock slipped behind the wheel. "You okay to get home?"

It wasn't home. Rock had a place he stayed until he wouldn't anymore. He'd lost all sense of home, a location of safety and support, because of what he carried inside him. But he nodded, intent on getting on the road.

"Friday, then?"

He nodded again, drumming his fingers on the steering wheel until he noticed what he was doing. He stopped and turned face forward, hoping the counselor got that message too. Dismissing what had happened was easier than acknowledging it in any way.

Barely registering his surroundings, he drove the road out of town in a daze. He hoped the dog found an understanding owner, someone who could make the remainder of its life easier. The alternative was also attractive, that the shelter would take pity on the miserable creature and put it out of its misery. It would be a blessing.

He came to the shelter road and kept on going. At the next turnout, he pulled over, cursing under his breath. This was a crazy venture, showing a complete and total lack of planning on his part. It had come to him in the panic attack, and once embedded in his brain, he couldn't shake it. He had seen the pain and he understood it, and because he understood it, he couldn't ignore it. He hung a u-turn.

When he walked up to the counter, the pretty blonde gave him a delighted grin. Her voice seemed intended to gentle his misgivings too.

"Many veterans find the companionship of a dog gives them peace and solace," she said.

His gaze must have sharpened on her, because her grin faded to a serious expression. "I did two tours," she continued, "so I know."

Rock inhaled and nodded.

"I'd like to adopt a dog."

She waited, her gaze unwavering.

"I want to take Ranger home."

Her smile grew wide as she reached for some forms. "Well, all right then."

An hour later, he and Ranger had been formally introduced. The dog still didn't meet his eyes, nor did he looked particularly excited to be leaving the cage. He walked with his head down and his tail between his legs, paying no attention to the dogs barking in congratulations at his release. He turned his face to the wall as Rock completed the necessary paperwork and the clerk handed a license across the desk. It wasn't until he gave the leash a short tug that Ranger rose and waited, lifting his sorrowful eyes.

There it was again, that kick in the chest. This guy had suffered more than any creature should, and Rock felt the pain like it was his own. He could make him comfortable and give him a warm place to sleep and the outdoors to enjoy once more. Someday, maybe the dog would give a doggie grin again, and Rock sure hoped he'd be around to see it.

It wasn't until Ranger settled in his new dog bed and Rock prepared to hang his coat on the hook by the cabin that he realized the red leash with its shiny stones hung out of his pocket, reminding him that once again, he'd failed in today's mission.

Chapter 7

"Be a good girl, Sweet Pea. I can't afford to buy a new pillow each day."

The little dog gave a huff of probable disbelief accompanied by an innocent expression, but Jenn didn't have time to challenge it. Her boss had a doctor's appointment, and while she had been a tad bit reluctant to allow her newbie clerk to take care of business, it was only for a couple of hours. Today Jenn opened the shop, and she had a plan.

"Princess, this will be awesome, and Shelley will be so pleased, she'll take me off probation early."

Jenn unlocked the shop's door and deactivated the alarm. Her fingers itched to try her idea. It didn't take long to make a space, dust the table, and set out the chalkboard serving platter. A script description of the cheeses seemed appropriate, and she wrote those out in a delicate hand. Her last step would be arranging samples along with knives to cut them.

Her phone dinged, and she dug it out of her pocket while she straightened the bottled goods.

"Hi Shelley. I'm set up for the day. It will be terrific. Take as much time as you need."

A distinct pause met her torrent of words. "Good morning, Jenn. I just wanted to make sure you made it in without any problems."

"Oh yes. I cleaned the back board, checked the orders, and verified the cash drawer. I'm all set."

"Good. I should be in by eleven at the latest. If anything happens that you don't know how to handle, please ask people to come back this afternoon. I'll take care of it."

No, Jenn swore she'd take care of it. Customers trying new cheeses would buy them and she'd be able to show Shelley the register totals supporting her concept.

Jenn glanced at the clock. Ten minutes to opening. She'd been doing this job for ten days now in the countdown to Christmas, and she was certain she had it nailed. She unlocked the front door and hurried back to complete her array of choices.

Moving to the second cold case, she knelt in front of the door and pulled the latch, her thoughts intent on the tangy soft variety she needed inside. Since it was best served slightly warmer, she wanted to give it time to breathe. The plainest crackers would highlight the flavors of the delicate cheese, and Shelley wouldn't mind a box out of her inventory.

Pulling on the door handle, she heard the click. It wasn't a big sound, more like a ping and a clatter. A metallic ring against concrete came next, and Jenn looked down at the handle in her hand.

Her mind didn't process it immediately. The door, still closed, shown in its burnished stainless steel glory in front of her. Behind the door, the cheese she wanted plus all of today's completed orders waited for pick-up or delivery. The chilly handle sat in her hand.

Street noise mixed with the entrance's musical ring. "I'll be right with you," she called out. How hard would it be to jimmy open the fridge door? Prying with the knife told her it would be next to impossible.

Her cell phone sounded an incoming call a second later.

"Jenn, hi. I wanted to make sure you'd be okay for another couple of hours. The doctor, he wants me to head over to the hospital for a couple of tests."

"Shelley, of course. No problem." None at all, except she had a handle in her hand and no idea how she could reattach it to the door. "Everything is absolutely under control." Her boss's stuttered words delivered in a tense tone bit through her distraction. "The hospital. That sounds serious. What can I do?"

Assurances that the best would be taking good care of the shop did little to ease the riot building in Jenn's gut. She had a handle in her hand, and a fridge with a door that didn't budge. Forget Project Cheese-Tasting. People would be arriving for their orders soon.

A rustle of noise reminded her someone had entered. She put her feet under her and prepared to stand up with a welcoming grin on her face. Her knees froze halfway up, about the time her smile reached maximum full velocity.

The man squinted at the chalk board platter, his eyebrows pulled together in a frown. The sight of him jerked her heart. His distinctive blue-gray eyes shifted to examine her from head to toe and settled on her ankle. "It's better?"

She nodded, bustling over to the counter like she had something to do.

"It's barking."

Jenn's attention snapped up to Rock. She didn't want to think about his name, because he lived up to it. Immovable. Solid. A mountain of a man.

And he had some great eyes. Intense and focused, like you were the only one on the planet and nothing else mattered. That focus intensified as his frown deepened.

"Your dog. It's barking its head off. You can hear it out in the street."

Which, crap, just added more greatness into her day. If Princess made too much noise, they'd be thrown out of their new digs, and another layer of complication would join what already came before.

She'd made multi-million dollar recommendations to clients for years. She thought she was a good judge of character, and snap decisions were nothing new. Digging in her jeans pocket, Jenn produced the small keychain and waved it at Rock. "Would you mind?"

He regarded her first, then the keys. She'd say by his expression, he thought the keys might explode on contact.

"Please? If she keeps barking, I'll have to move. This is so convenient, and besides, she's a sweetheart." She could only hope Princess would live up to that pledge.

Rock's eyes shifted between the keys and her face, his expression dipping into an unknown territory. On the last shift, they landed on her hand, and Jenn realized she clutched the fridge door handle along with her keys.

"Please."

His eyes closed briefly, and when he reopened them, she swore they changed in both intensity and color. Warmth flooded her. Synapses blasted in her brain as his beard lifted in what could have been smile.

"What's its name?"

She blinked.

"Your dog," he said, as if he understood her confusion.

"Princess Sweet Pea. She's very friendly." Sending a prayer upstairs, she begged Princess to behave for once in her doggie years.

"And that?" He nodded to her hand.

Desperation. That was all it was, all it could be. She couldn't afford the heat running through her to screw this up. No way, or she'd be back on her way to San Jose.

Hoping the pounding of her heart wasn't showing in her face, she said, "Do you know how to fix a refrigerator handle?"

>>>>>

This was the biggest fucking mess he could figure. He tried to do the right thing, and it backfired. Not only backfired but exposed a cluster fuck of bombs ready to blow up in his face. And all because a pair of smoky brown eyes stirring him in ways he'd sooner forget pleaded with him.

The women behind him continued their animated discussion, the cheese lady in high sales gear and the customer irritated and gruff. It seemed the cheese tray she was scheduled to pick up lay trapped inside the refrigerator he knelt in front of, running his fingers over the handle in his hand. It was better than the alternative, though, the one involving him going into the woman's apartment upstairs to calm the yappy beast.

"I am on a very tight schedule today." An aggravated tone matched the pinched off words.

"Rock will have the door open in a jiffy, Mrs. Ferris, and you'll be on your way."

"Rock Kermarrec? I heard you were back in town. It's nice to see you again."

Yeah, right. He mumbled something he hoped was appropriate without looking up.

How Jenn broke off the metal was a mystery. The locking mechanism jammed inside the door didn't want to budge. As his parents always said, though, when he wanted something, he'd always find a way.

A hiss came over his shoulder. "You can open it, right?"

He stood and met the worry in Jenn's frantic expression. Deep lines formed in her forehead and between her eyebrows, and he shoved his fists in his pockets to fight the urge to smooth the marks away. His fingers closed on her keys as where they tangled with the dog leash. For the life of him, he couldn't figure out why he didn't just shove both items into the woman's hands and walk out the door. He owed her nothing, and the sooner he remembered that, the sooner he could return to his solitude and his plan.

"Mrs. Ferris, how about if I deliver the cheese tray to your office? You said the event isn't until this evening, correct? I can have it to you in plenty of time, for no charge, of course."

Jenn stared up at him with those pleading wide eyes a moment longer before she spun away. If her smile looked forced, it wasn't his business. Nope, she was not his business. She could call a locksmith or a fridge repair man to take care of her problem. It was not his problem.

The customer left in a flurry of bad attitude and Rock tried to follow. He closed his eyes, willing the picture of frantic worry on the face of the petite damsel in distress to disappear from his mind. This was simple. Hand over the items, wish her good luck, and be on his way. Trouble was, he was never very good at doing the things he should do.

"Do you have a toolbox?"

As soon as the words came out of his mouth, he wished he could kick himself.

"I don't know. I can check in the back. I don't want to call Shelley because, um, I don't want to disturb her." She ran a hand over her hair, not that anything was out of place. Her hands landed together, and she lifted them toward him like a prayer. "That's not completely true. I really need this job, Rock. If I call her because there's a little problem, she'll think I can't take care of things. I need to fix this and then explain the funny story of what happened later."

Damn, she blinked fast, and were those tears forming in her eyes? He didn't want to wait around to find out. He'd do the gentlemanly thing and fix her locked door and then he'd hand over her things and never wander in this direction again.

"Tools," he muttered, taking a wide path around her to the door. She said nothing, and he didn't elaborate. The hardware store at the other end of Main would have what he needed.

It wasn't until he pulled his hand out of his pocket that he realized he still clutched pieces in his hand. The fridge handle. The red leash. And the set of keys that weren't his. He examined the foreign emblem on the car lock device, shaking his head. Yeah, those bombs were turning into a minefield under his feet.

He was still shaking his head at his stupidity when he walked into the hardware store and found the things he needed. The cashier tried to make conversation until he pinned her with a glare that told her to hurry things along. He kept his eyes on the pavement as he trudged back up Main Street. He'd fix the damn door and return the leash, but he drew the line at taking care of her dog.

He glanced through the cheese shop's window and paused. The place held a crowd discussing something with great animation. The group parted, and at its center, Jenn handed out something on a tray. She looked every bit the polished salesperson, listening and laughing and pushing another small white cup toward the person across from her.

Then she caught sight of him, and relief flooded her face. She lifted a finger, though if it was to the group or to him, he wasn't sure. It didn't matter. The sooner he got the job done, the sooner he could be on his way. He pushed open the front door and whatever talk had been going on ceased. He knew all eyes were on him, but he stayed focused on Jenn and lifted the plastic bag.

"This shouldn't take long," he assured her. Or maybe he was assuring himself. Those soft brown eyes reminded him of a trusting fawn. He never could hunt, because he couldn't bring himself to hurt anything innocent.

"Thank you, thank you so much, Rock. Here, would you like a sample? It's goat cheese from a local farm."

He shook his head, dropping his gaze to his dusty boots. Do the job, get out the door, and race as far from this one as he could.

A rustle arrived at the same time as the scent of vanilla, and the next thing he knew, Jenn was on the floor next to him, beaming at him with a look he hoped wasn't adoration.

"Can I help? I warn you, I'm not good with mechanical things, but I can hold your tool for you."

Vanilla. The scent turned a key, one he'd forgotten he'd locked long ago. He snuck a look at her, narrowing his eyes to take off the years.

It couldn't be. It shouldn't be. Jenn from then. Jenn from now.

"Where does this path go?"

She trudged along behind him, still clutching the cup of apple cider. When he stopped, she pulled even and gasped in surprise. As she grabbed his arm and squealed in apparent delight, the scent of vanilla washed over him. Even now, that aroma alone was enough to remind him of simpler, innocent times.

"I'm sorry, I didn't mean that to sound like it did. I mean, I barely know you and you don't know me, but I guess it's because you're the first person I really met when I came here, and you've helped me out so much, and I – shit, I should stop babbling."

The briny scents of cheeses and chatter of conversation whipped him back to the present, to the woman from his past invading his present. A blush darkened her cheeks and she patted at that perfect hair again, making Rock want to grab her nervous hands and grip them to keep her from being so unsure. He liked the sure, upbeat, optimistic Jenn better.

What the hell was he thinking? He didn't need this distraction. It didn't fit into his plans, and he'd already deviated from them enough in the past couple of days. He had to stick to the plan. The refrigerator door taunted him to get moving.

Without warning, the room shrank, and he huddled closer to the floor as his vision blurred. He felt a hand on his shoulder, and he flashed back to another hand, pushing him down into the dirt as chunks of concrete flew past in a seafoam of sand. When something large and silver swam by his face, he jammed his eyes closed to avoid getting hit.

He sucked in air, feeling the metallic taste of blood in his mouth. Dust filled his throat, making it burn. The sensation of concrete under his fingers had him pressing his cheek to its surface. Pulses pounded in his ears too fast, too fast. He wanted to scream, but he knew it was useless. Nothing would warn her in time.

"Did you drop something?"

That voice. It didn't belong in the cage. He couldn't place it.

"Rock? I have a broom with a long handle, and it will reach to the back. Maybe we can sweep it out."

Vanilla. Something smelled like cookies, the kind Ma used to make when they were kids. They'd have them with milk after school, something to help them keep their energy up during their afternoon chores, she liked to say. Another memory of vanilla on a cold winter afternoon crushed him with confusion.

"Here's the broom."

A tap hit the back of his hand once, then again, and reflexively, his fingers reached out and closed around it.

"What did you drop? I can help you look for it."

A body lowered next to him with a heat he could feel through the cold invading every cell of his body. Breathe in, breathe out. Breathe in, breathe out.

"Mrs. Ferris really was upset that she couldn't pick up her tray now, but I think I have her calmed down. She said someone from your family does her accounting. Who is that? Oh, never mind. I'm being nosey again. Darn, I'm not finding anything under here. Can you see it?"

The body pressed up against him, jarring him out of the dust and back into the present. The smell coming to him wasn't blood but cheese. He was here to do a job, one he volunteered for, and then he was leaving, and he was never coming close to this place again. Vanilla crept back stronger, and it made his mouth water.

He turned his head and found himself nose to nose with wide-eyed woman. But it wasn't who he expected. Brown eyes hit his with open curiosity, flicking over his face. At this distance, they looked more like chocolate, mixing with the vanilla in his scrambled brain. The warmth of her flooded through him, leaving him sweaty and irritable.

Pressing his hands into the floor gave him quick leverage to leap into a crouch. The woman moved more slowly, wincing as she prepared to stand. Jenn. Jenn of long ago. Jenn who fell down his mountain.

The reach to help her to her feet was automatic. Her hand burned in his, and before he could react, she withdrew it and shoved it into a pocket of the blue shop apron. Fluster replaced every other expression as her eyes darted everywhere but at him, and she pulled the hand out of her pocket and put it to her hair.

He turned with an abrupt jerk back to the fridge. He tried the trick the shrink suggested back at the army hospital. Day. Date. Time. Name. Location. Ground himself in the facts.

"Did you say something?"

He'd been mumbling the litany to himself, and she'd heard him. She probably thought he was crazy. Hell, he was crazy. She just didn't know it. It would be better if she did, because then she'd leave him alone.

He fiddled with the locking mechanism, keeping his hands busy while his brain repeated the phrases. It emptied his mind, which it was designed to do, until he wasn't thinking about anything. Prying the door open was easy with the right tool. Pulling the handle from his pocket, he held it in place and wiggled the screw into the hole. It wasn't more than a minute before he had it back in place, and he swung the door shut. He pulled it open, and the latch worked without protest.

"You saved me again, my hero. You fixed it. How can I repay you?"

Hero? She'd called him that before. He was no hero. Heroes saved people. He hadn't been one when it counted.

He shoved to his feet, returning the tools to the bag. He didn't respond. What was the point? She'd learn soon enough, and then she'd understand.

But Jenn wasn't next to him. She stood at the back counter, her huge bag open and a wallet in her hand. When she turned around, dismay paled her face.

"I'm sorry. I never paid you for the tree. I only have enough to pay you for the tools today. I, ah, don't have anything to give you for your time and trouble. Unless you take plastic?"

The disconnect in that had him blinking rapidly, trying to keep up. He shook his head, lifting the bag of minor tools and extending them to her. She accepted the bag, but when she tried to hand him a stack of singles and some loose change, he pushed his fists back into his pockets.

His fingers closed on things, things that weren't his. He pulled out her keys and hung those on a single finger, reaching toward her. She seemed determined to hand him the money first, and he shook his head. They stood like that for what felt like minutes, before he raised his eyes and met her wide eyes.

Damn, more like a proud doe than a timid fawn, and about as determined as his Ma. He liked that about her, the confidence that she was doing the right thing overwhelming the fact that she probably didn't have the money to spare in the first place. Didn't she tell him she really needed this job?

"No charge. My pleasure." His words sounded raw to his own ears, but she didn't seem to notice. Doubt chased the determination, and quick on those heels, the bright smile beamed at him.

"Thank you, Rock. I'll find a way to repay you, I promise. Can I send you home with some cheese in the mean time?"

Why did he suddenly feel reluctant to pull the leash out of his pocket as he should? She accepted the keys with a grimace and a glance at the ceiling before returning her gaze to his with a hesitant half-smile. When his hand came out of his jacket again in slow motion, her eyes widened.

"Oh, I wondered where that went. You found it. See, my hero again. That's Sweet Pea's favorite leash."

Her fingers slipped around the red leather, brushing his. He fought the urge to close his hand around hers and trap them together. He knew better, though. Traps were deadly, and she was too nice a person to be trapped in anything with a man like him.

Still, his grip tightened for a moment when she tugged, before letting go and spinning for the door.

Chapter 8

"Ranger, come."

The dog didn't lift his head off his plaid bed. Rock swore the animal looked anywhere but at him. He recognized that sign. Never look your enemy in the eye unless you were willing to challenge him. The dog carried painful memories to be that afraid.

"Ranger, truck ride. You like to ride in the truck."

The dog's big brown eyes flicked up for a brief second, then examined the floor in front of his nose. Rock couldn't leave him alone. He didn't want to, an emotion he didn't want to examine, not tonight. If he planned to use the dog as a crutch, it was no one's business but his and Ranger's.

Desperate times, extreme measures. He knew this wasn't the way to win the dog's respect or affection, but he'd do it in a pinch. He lifted the bag of treats, the ones marked with a statement that no dog could resist their bacon flavor and shook it. Ranger's eyes settled on the bag with brief interest, then dropped once more.

Being late to dinner at the ranch was not the way to keep Ma off his back, and if he was too late, Deke and Jake would probably arrive on his doorstep to drag him over. Under the radar meant toeing the line enough to satisfy everyone. The dog wasn't helping.

"Treat?"

Eyes snapped between the bag and Rock, a shimmer of interest showing where none had been before. Rock waved a strip close to the floor, and Ranger lifted his head. His nose twitched, and he flashed his eyes between the man and the meat like he didn't trust his good fortune.

"Come on. Truck ride. Treat. And I promise you'll be smothered in love for the rest of the evening. Nothing gets my family going like an animal in need."

That was something he should remember for his own situation.

On cautious paws, Ranger crawled forward, nose sniffing madly and eyes glowing. His body and coat hinted at German Shepherd with a cocktail of other breeds thrown in. The shelter said he was found skinny and dehydrated, and while he looked better now, Rock knew that kind of suffering wasn't something man or beast forgot quickly.

With a delicate grasp belying his huge jaws, Ranger closed his teeth on the end of the treat, as far from Rock's fingertips as he could get, and pulled with a gentle tug. Releasing the meat as soon as he felt the tug, Rock tried not to feel satisfaction that he might be able to earn the dog's trust. Food would only be the beginning, but then in a few months' time, where would Ranger be?

Leading with another bacon strip, they got as far as the door. Ranger surveyed the outdoors with apparent misgivings, trying to duck back inside. The call of the treat was too much, though, and he jumped over the step and to the ground. After he gobbled up another piece, he trotted over to a nearby bush and anointed it.

"Bet that feels better too, huh?" Why was he talking out loud to the dog? It wouldn't understand his words. For that matter, why did he talk to anyone?

Rock eased the driver door open. Ranger approached with neck outstretched and active snorts. He cowered back, looking longingly at the treat Rock wiggled as enticement. "One leap, boy, and you're home free. I won't even make you get out at the ranch, I promise."

It would be a great excuse, having to take the traumatized dog home. Do the minimum amount of socializing, enough to satisfy his family he was well on the road to readjustment, and make tracks. There was nothing wrong with retreat under certain circumstances. If only he'd listened to that lesson in the past.

He tossed the treat across the front seat, and it thumped against the passenger door before landing on the seat. A moment later, a flash of blond-brown fur covered the distance and lifted airborne, grabbing the meat up before his haunches hit vinyl. Rock didn't waste time on congratulations, slipping behind the steering wheel and starting the engine.

Still chewing, the dog appeared to regard the passing terrain with a shred of interest. His nose twitched at a rapid pace, and Rock kicked himself for not cracking the side window open. He hadn't been around a dog as a pet since his high school days. He was out of practice. When he rolled his driver side down to compensate, the dog sniffed faster.

Of course, he couldn't get too comfortable with any of this. He had plans, big plans, important plans, and by the time he was prepared to execute them, he hoped Ranger had settled in well enough to find a home on the ranch.

The ride went by too fast, the dog maintaining a companionable silence and looking at the sights. Rock found himself wanting to give the guy a tour, a trip down memory lane, like pointing out the old grocery store where he got in trouble for buying beer with a fake ID, and the road leading to the make-out spot where he finally got to third base. He zipped his lips shut, though, because the dog wouldn't understand.

When they reached the sign arching over the drive, Ranger let out a single bark. It surprised Rock so much, he took his foot off the accelerator. The dog hadn't barked before, so he wasn't sure if this was an expression of fear or joy. He put out a hand to pat the guy's fuzzy head, and the dog immediately shrank against the side door. Rock froze.

"It's okay, guy. I get it. You're not the touchy-feely type."

He took it as a good sign when Ranger sat up again. His head followed the cows in the pasture, then the horses. Or maybe he looked at freedom. Rock understood the sentiment and glanced in the rear view mirror down the last curve of the drive where the county road beckoned.

"You and me, we're more alike than you might think, Rang, old buddy. I guess that means we were meant to be."

Damn it, he was talking to the dog again. This was probably why Ed took him to the pound in the first place. If he wasn't going to talk in counseling or group, he might talk to an animal that couldn't ask questions or fire back.

"There you are. Ma was about to send out a search party."

His oldest brother stood at the open window, resting his palms on the door like he thought Rock might throw it into reverse for a quick escape. Deke's genial expression didn't hide the worry crinkling the corners of his eyes as he stared into Rock's face. It was only after he must have seen enough to satisfy himself things would be okay that he glanced over at the dog. A hint of a smile came to the corners of his mouth.

"Who's this?"

"This is Ranger. He came from the pound. He wants to stay in the truck."

Double damn, why was he talking like he knew what the dog thought?

"Don't let the women see him. Amber wants a dog. The baby would love to ride on his back. And Ma would probably find him a steak to compensate for his hard luck story. He must have had one."

Perceptive as ever, Deke looked to Rock for confirmation as Ranger turned his muzzle to the back seat and his broad butt to the two brothers. If he could cower into a smaller beast, this is what it would look like. Rock fought a new urge, the one to comfort the animal and assure him things were going to be all right.

Deke swung the door open and extended a hand inside to Rock. After a brief hesitation, Rock grabbed it for a fast shake, but his brother was faster. He seized him in a big hug and yanked him out of the vehicle, all in one smooth move. Rock didn't have a choice but to quick step up the path to the house as Deke dragged him along.

"There you are. I was getting concerned, and I was about to have the boys come and fetch you. How are you, my son?"

Ma's hug around his waist was a clutch, making Rock suck in a surprised inhale at its ferociousness. Patting her back seemed to lessen the grip, and by the time she'd let go, Rock's remorse about not coming by more often had grown to match the lump in his throat. Pinwheels of light curled at the edge of his line of sight.

Not now. Not here.

People pressed in on him, Jake next, then his uncle, and then the sisters-in-law with babies and a few of the hands who'd been around for as long as he could remember. Handing him from person to person brought his feet to the steps up to the big porch, as wide and welcoming as it had been when he was a kid. Too bad he didn't deserve that welcome.

He focused on breathing, on the feeling of air pulling into his lungs and pushing back out again. His pulse accelerated into a pounding beat in his ears, making it harder to hear. People said things, but he wasn't sure what they were. He couldn't stop blinking. Every cell in his body wanted to duck to the ground and roll into a ball.

"Here, I made cookies for later. Vanilla sugar cookies, like you used to love when you were little. I don't think having one or two will hurt your appetite, will it?"

Vanilla, warm and fragrant, waved under his nose. That feature twitched hard enough to rival Ranger's, Rock bet, but the aroma didn't bring him back to childhood afternoons. His internal vision locked on big brown eyes and a killer smile, and thoughts of Jenn eased him back into the present and loosened the clutch on his heart.

A couple of hours later, Rock found dinner wasn't as bad as he'd feared. His brothers weren't fools, and they made sure the conversation didn't focus on him or linger on any topic that might cause him to panic. Most of the talk was about the ranch. Heritage cattle herds. A new breeding line of hogs fed on oak acorns. The likelihood of a rainy season worth mentioning. It wasn't until dessert that Marlee, Jake's wife, grinned over her coffee mug with a single lifted eyebrow.

"It was good that you got the door fixed."

He halted mid-move, his fork full of pie and ice cream poised for a quick bite.

"Fix what? Did something break down at the cabin? Tell me it wasn't the baler. I swear, that new machine isn't worth the metal it's made of." Uncle Ronan's grousing lasted long enough to cover Rock's return of the fork to the plate. He'd lost his appetite.

"No, he was helping the cheese lady." Marlee's eyes sparkled with mischief as she took a sip of coffee. He vaguely remembered Jake saying his wife was the quiet type, and Rock sincerely wished she'd live up to that right now.

"You were helping the cheese lady? I couldn't get you to go inside the place the other day." Ma's eagle eye settled on him with an uptick of interest he found discouraging. Dogs with fresh bones had nothing on her. He dropped his eyes to the puddling mess on his plate, unable to find an explanation that made sense.

"He's probably going to be too modest to share it, but Jenn, that's the new woman working at the shop, had a problem with the refrigerator. The handle broke off, and Rock fixed it for her. I heard all about it from Mrs. Ferris after Jenn delivered her captive cheese."

"Oh, that Jennifer. She seems very nice, and new in town. Rock, maybe you can invite her to dinner next time. She probably doesn't know many people yet, and you two are friends already." Ma's benign expression didn't fool him.

He stood fast enough to tilt his chair back on two legs. It clattered to the floor, and he spun around to lift it into place. With four feet firmly planted on the ground, it mocked him. Everything seemed to give him away today.

He turned once more and grabbed his plate, reaching for the ones next to him in rapid fire. "I'll clear," he muttered, hoping the offer would break him away before he was pinned in the line of questioning.

"I'll help," Jake said, and Deke rose too. Great.

Stacking plates in silence, he moved around the table. It wasn't until he neared the kitchen door that Ma said, "Rock, did you return that nice leash to Jenn? Such a cute little thing, that leash. Must belong to a cute little dog."

He didn't miss the quick exchange of glances between his brothers. Jake's mouth twitched like he fought off a laugh. Deke was not nearly as discreet. By the time the three of them were behind the kitchen door, both openly grinned.

"She has a dog? And now you have a dog? Is this a coincidence?" Jake shook his head like he couldn't believe it.

Rock put the plates on the counter and began the hot water in the sink. At the ranch, there was no such thing as women's work or men's work. It was just work, and they were all expected to do whatever was required from the time they were old enough to carry a bucket. Rinsing the dishes and loading the dishwasher seemed like light duty now.

"He's ignoring us." Trust Jake to state the obvious. He wished they'd catch the hint.

Deke leaned into his field of vision, effectively blocking the dishwasher's door. His expression had sobered as he examined Rock's face with too much analysis.

"It might be too soon, you know. Too early to get involved with someone, I mean. What do you think?"

His brother waited like he expected an answer, so Rock gave him one, the only one that mattered. "I'm not getting involved with anyone. Ma didn't raise animals, and I was doing the gentlemanly thing and helping her out with a problem. She's a city girl." Like that explained everything. He pushed Deke out of the way and opened the appliance hard enough to make the door bounce down and rise once more.

"I heard you carried her down the mountain at the farm," Jake said.

Rock said nothing.

"And I heard that you carried her up the stairs to her apartment and set up her tree," Deke added. "And you met her dog."

"And now you have a dog too." Jake lifted his hands like this explained everything.

This would be a good time for Ranger to howl or bark. Anything to give him an excuse to flat out run from this inquisition, because all it did was remind him of those grateful wide eyes, a smile that opened his soul, and the promise on that winter day long ago.

Chapter 9

Jenn flipped between websites, examining their services with the studious attention she brought to every project. This was no different than learning about any other business. It was the least she could do for Rock. He'd saved her life again this week.

Did he remember who she was? That day long ago remained magical in her memory.

"This is the most beautiful place on the planet. You must come here all the time."

He'd shaken his head, shoving his hands deep into his pockets. Hers still glowed from the warmth when it was folded in his. He kicked at the untrampled snow. She couldn't understand why he wasn't staring at the lake in front of them. She had a hard time taking her eyes off it.

"It's a special place, a magical place. I know it must be. It's the kind of place where, whatever you wish for, it will come true. Don't you think?"

He shook his head again, but she caught him glancing her way with a puzzled expression.

"I think we should make this our special place," she'd said. His mouth dropped open, but at least he didn't shake his head this time.

The feeling of magic made her feel like dancing, whirling in the snow and laughing while Rock watched her, his mouth agape. That was probably why he could move so fast when she slipped, headed on a downward slope to the icy edge of the water.

"Got ya." She hadn't even had time to scream. His hands closed on her coat and grabbed her, bringing her crazy ride to a halt. He helped her up, and she threw her arms around his neck.

"My hero."

He blushed, but he had that nice goofy sideways smile and his eyes seemed to flash different colors.

Jenn wondered if the lake was still there. Rock had probably forgotten about that day, but she hadn't, taking out the memory from time to time with a fondness that bordered on obsessive. She knew it, but it gave her comfort, particularly this past year.

Remembering the past wasn't going to get her anywhere now, however. She doodled on her legal pad, thinking about how she could repay him. Rock was handy at fixing things. He was a gentleman, or he wouldn't have carried her up the stairs which, she admitted, still made her feel undeniably soft inside. He ran a Christmas tree farm. What did he do for the rest of the year? Internet searches brought up a lot of information about the family, but little about him.

All of that would have to wait until later. Shelley expected her downstairs bright and early today, given that it was Saturday and holiday parties were in full swing. Maybe she'd take a drive past the tree farm tomorrow, just to see how it was doing in the holiday rush.

"Sweet Pea, please be a princess today and don't tear up anything, okay?"

The dog's head popped out from a pile of plush toys. Jenn sincerely hoped that mound kept the dog busy today. She'd need to research a cut-rate source of dog toys next, because the toys didn't fare much better than pillows. It was a mystery how a tiny dog could create such fleece and fluff havoc all by herself.

A single bark, more like a yip, responded to her statement. She was out of options on how to control Princess, because she yowled when caged and she peed on things when confined in a single room and she chewed when given free rein. Jenn lifted her eyes to the Christmas tree, its bottom foot devoid of ornaments because she knew those would be goners too, and wished she could sit here all day, staring at its sparkles and thinking about the man who brought it to her. But she needed the job more than she could afford to daydream, especially to keep one Yorkie in plushies.

The shop door was already unlocked with its lights on. Her boss sat with her back to the room and ran a rapid finger down the computer screen, glasses perched on the end of her nose. Shelley was about fifty, Jenn guessed, and had been running this shop for more than a decade. She seemed to know every local who walked in. Jenn tried to mimic the woman's best attributes, including getting to know the townies and what they liked.

"Oh good, you're here early. Good morning, by the way. I'll need you to run these products over to the bakery. They'll have bread for you to bring back. Do you know what happened to that order from the producer in Cloverdale, Oregon? I can't find it anywhere."

"I reorganized the fridges yesterday. I hope you don't mind. I thought it would be easier to sort things alphabetically. You know, so we can find things faster."

Shelley stared at her, removing the glasses in a slow sweep of unpainted fingertips. A blinking frown came next. "Alphabetically? But then, how will we know what we need to reorder?"

"Using the inventory levels. I set up that function on your computer system. You didn't have that turned on, so I took care of it. Now you know how much you have of everything, and I entered possible reorder points, based on past sales."

Jenn tied the apron with a sharp tug, giving Shelley her best convincing smile. It made perfect sense. Why invest in a sophisticated system if you weren't going to use its best features? This would make it easy to identify what orders to place every day. It seemed Shelley spent long hours puzzling over what she needed and more hours on the phone with her distributors to fill those needs. The next step would be automating that process too.

"But I order certain cheeses from certain distributors. Sometimes two or three different places for a single kind. How will we know who to call?"

Grabbing a damp rag, Jenn wiped down the counters she'd cleaned with diligence last night.

"We're going to need to put the cheeses back in their places, Jenn, and you can turn off that ordering thingie. I won't use it."

Now would be a good time to make her pitch. "Oh, I could take care of that for you, Shelley. Honestly, it's no trouble, and once I've worked out any kinks in the system, I can show you how to run the reports. Really, it will save you tons of time."

The woman blanched. "Kinks? Jenn, I don't think you understand. It's the holidays, our busiest time of the year. I can't afford any kinks."

"Don't worry, I have it covered. I checked the inventory when I moved it. The balances in the system are real. I checked the sales for the past twelve months and used that to create average inventory levels and reorder points. This is the kind of thing I do for a living." Did for a living. She kept the cringe to herself.

Shelley waved a hand, then pressed fingers to her temples. "Yes, I remember you used to be a consultant of some kind, but I've been running this place for years. I know what I need, and I know who to call to get it. And sometimes, they might not have what I need, so I order something else. You can't put that in a system, Jenn. Honestly, I don't know why you didn't discuss this with me beforehand. I appreciate your initiative, but it needs to be tempered with consideration."

By lunchtime, it was clear her efforts to make things more efficient weren't going to be met with happiness. Shelley asked her with a sharpening tone where this chevre or that cheddar was now, emphasis on the final word. Jenn thought perhaps Shelley would see the value of her new system when she located the item quickly, but the deep sighs and temple-rubbing continued.

It didn't help her peace of mind when she checked on Princess during her lunch break. The hide of a purple rhino that had been as big as the dog littered the carpet from the sofa to the dining table. Fleece pieces scattered around like snow.

"You can't keep doing this, Princess. Why can I convince the CEO of a multinational company to embrace my system changes, but I can't change the habits of a dog?" Or convince her current boss to try a new method, for that matter. Disheartened didn't even begin to describe her feeling as she returned to the shop, meek and quiet and trying to stay out of Shelley's way.

In the lull after the lunch rush, her employer gave her a stern warning not to change anything else while she did the banking and ran other errands. The tinkling tone marking her exit even sounded disapproving. Jenn thought that bell needed work too, but far be it for her to change it. Shelley would fire her for sure.

She sat at the computer researching the vendors the shop used for its purchases when the bell rang again, accompanied by the sounds of two women engaged in an animated conversation.

"But he is different. Deke said as much."

"I don't know. I'm not convinced, and I think we need to keep an eye on him, just in case."

One voice carried a lilting French accent Jenn immediately found delightful. The other women's tone marked her worry more than her words did. Hopping off the stool, Jenn hurried forward to greet the customers.

"Welcome. My name is Jenn. How can I help you today?"

Both women turned to face her with slow swivels. Jenn felt the hard intensity of their stares like a bug on the end of a pin might. She didn't want to twitch.

The French accent said, "Pardon me, but did you say Jenn?" When she nodded, open curiosity lit the woman's features as she examined Jenn from head to foot and back to her face. "You are not what I imagined."

Beside her, the other woman bit off a laugh. "No one is what you imagine, Marguerite."

"But this is true. Yes, you are, shall we say, considerably more upscale than I would have thought of for a woman who attracted his attention."

"Who's attention?" She hadn't been in town to garner any attention, except the kind she'd rather forget.

The other woman nodded with an understanding smile. "Why, Miss Emie's son. She tends to be part lioness and part matchmaker when it comes to her sons."

The French woman nodded her agreement, continuing her speculative assessment.

"You're talking about Rock's mother."

More enthusiastic nodding. "Yes, our formidable mother-in-law speaks highly of you." Emphasis placed on the French pronunciation of formidable snapped through the air.

"We decided to check you out ourselves. You see, we've grown kind of protective of Rock too." The other woman narrowed her eyes, and her quick scan had Jenn wishing she'd dressed in something more Flynn's Crossing today, rather than Bay Area.

That was her problem. She didn't fit in here. She wanted to, but her heeled boots and dressy shirts stood out on Main Street.

When flustered, pass muster, that was her motto, and it had served her more than one unflattering situation when a consulting client looked her up and down with that expression speaking louder than words about her probable inexperience or unsuitability for a project. She lifted her hand and stepped forward.

"I guess formal introductions are therefore in order. I'm Jennifer Stanton. I just moved to Flynn's Crossing. I've been coming to the area since I was a kid, and when I had an opportunity to move here, I had to grab it. Miss Emie was kind enough to introduce herself the other day. She's a very sweet lady."

The French woman offered a firm handshake and wide smile. "Only just moved here, and already causing quite a stir. Tell me, how did you come to be working for Shelley?"

The other woman shouldered her out of the way and gave Jenn's hand a quick pump. "We're delighted to meet you. I'm Marlee Kermarrec, and this is my sister-in-law, Marguerite Kermarrec."

Her research efforts saved her once more. Jenn turned to the Frenchwoman with an enthusiastic smile. "You're the winemaker. And you're married to the rancher. I read about you."

A chuckle held indulgence. "You probably also read about the heritage cattle and such my husband raises. I am happy to say our press has all been good these last few years."

Marlee shook her head. "Marketing. That's almost all you talk about."

A shrug looked exaggerated as Marguerite rolled her eyes. The twinkle in them as they returned to Jenn had her liking the woman even more. "But of course. It is better than talk, talk, talk about the numbers. The numbers come from the marketing."

It sounded like a tussle the two had more than once, and Jenn smiled at their friendly bickering. Despite the obvious disagreement, they sounded like close friends. She missed having that, not that she was sure she ever did have it. Too many years climbing the career ladder didn't translate well into time to build solid friendships.

"Meanwhile, down here where real people live, I do the books for the ranch and the winery, and oh yes, this shop, along with many other small businesses in town. Numbers aren't boring, they're fascinating."

Jenn grinned back at Marlee. She could absolutely agree, since she was fond of spreadsheets and flow processes herself. Nothing like a good system reorganization to get the juices flowing. Except when the client – or the boss – didn't like the outcome.

"Oh, your wonderful grin has faded. I am so sorry Marlee bored you to tears. What time do you get off work?"

On reflex, Jenn said, "Six o'clock."

"Good. We will then share a glass of wine together, maybe two. And we will all get to know one another quite well." Marguerite nodded as if this was a given.

"But, I can't." Going out for a glass of wine wasn't in her budget, at least not until she knew for sure Shelley wasn't going to can her as soon as the holiday rush was over. She had bills to pay and a monster dog to support.

"Nonsense. Please, it would be our pleasure. In the interest of our mutual, how shall I put this, interests?" Marguerite tipped her head to the side, regarding her gravely.

Marlee nodded. "We'll dish dirt on all things Kermarrec and particularly, Kermarrec men. They are pretty formidable," she put the French spin on it, "so you'll understand what you're getting yourself in to."

"But, I'm not getting myself into anything. You misunderstood."

Jenn didn't have a chance to say more, not when Marlee shook her head with vehement insistence and Marguerite muttered a low string of denials. The door's bell announced Shelley's return, and talk quickly turned to business. It wasn't long before Jenn was rushing between the fridges in the back stockroom to the storage in the shop proper as Shelley listed out cheeses Marguerite needed for a winery event.

Discussions punctuated by occasional laughter and deep conversations went on as Jenn wrapped and labeled. Marlee sat at the computer, flipping between screens and tapping notes into an electronic tablet she'd retrieved from her purse. When Shelley said something to her in a low voice, both women looked in Jenn's direction. Curiosity colored Marlee's expression.

Jenn's cheeks warmed, and she turned away on the premise of finding more paper. It would be obvious for her boss to share with her accountant that her newly hired help decided to revamp the program and take on the task of reorganizing inventory. It would also be within her rights to share that she hadn't approved the change, and she wasn't pleased with it. Jenn had to admit she'd handled it with a heavier touch than she should have used.

Shelley wasn't her client but her boss. She hadn't had buy-in or permission. This was a job, not a career, and she'd better remember that before she became too enamored with making other changes.

"You turned on the reorder module."

Jenn blinked a couple of times, trying to clear a sideways view of Marlee's face. The woman's focus was on the cheese being wrapped, which was just as well. If she looked at Jenn, she'd see the sting of tears she tried not to let fall.

"How did you do it?"

Pausing in her wrapping, Jenn glanced up quickly, then back down. "It's in the settings. You click the option from off to on."

Marlee waved a hand dismissively. "No, I understand that part. I have this same system installed in the back offices of many of my retail clients. Each business uses various features, and few use them all. I mean, how did you convince her to do it?"

This time, Jenn had to look up. Marlee's frank gaze held no censure.

"I, ah, didn't. She was gone yesterday, and I thought I could help by reorganizing the inventory. You know, so it would be more efficient. I ran an inventory while I did it, and that's when I noticed reordering was turned off, so I ran a report to show – "

She bit off the rest of her explanation. Marlee wouldn't care how she did it. She wondered how long it would take the accountant to tell her not to change anything else in the system without express approval.

"You did all that in one day?"

Jenn nodded, reaching for another piece of cheese as a reason not to meet the woman's eyes.

"She said you used to be some kind of management consultant."

Used to be. She couldn't even help a cheese shop with her skills. Too bad she'd been fooling herself into thinking she'd ever have a future in that field again. She'd have to learn to make this retail gig stick, and Princess was going to have to make do with torn up toys.

Marlee glanced over her shoulder across the shop, where Marguerite and Shelley examined jars of pickled vegetables. Leaning closer, she lowered her voice to a whisper. "Good job, Jenn. I've been trying to get her to use more of this program's features for a year. For what it's worth, she said she might be able to see the benefit of it now, though she's not convinced she could work it."

Jenn's attention snapped up and her mouth opened. At the congratulatory regard she encountered, she shut her mouth. She didn't need to defend herself or her actions, at least not here. Marlee's smile held as much curiosity as glee.

"I think I've found a new best bud in town. We have things to discuss over drinks tonight, sister, so bring your best brainstorming mode. Let's meet up a little after six, at the wine shop. Also one of my clients, I should add, so be prepared to be grilled a little if this goes as I think it will."

"As what goes?" Jenn didn't want to believe anything was turning around, not when things had looked dark for long enough to even set her optimistic spirit into the doldrums.

Marlee winked at her as Marguerite asked the other woman's opinion about a selection. A final hard glance from them as they pulled open the door told Jenn she'd better show up tonight, or she had no doubt they'd come and find her.

>>>>>

It wasn't until the end of the day that Jenn could reflect on the afternoon's visit and the promise she never made to the women. She hadn't exactly said she would join them. Then again, she hadn't said she wouldn't, either. It would be impolite to stand them up. The wine bar was only a block away.

"What do you think, Princess? Buzz in, tell them thanks again for the invitation but no can do, and then we'll take a walk. What do you say to that?"

The dog watched her pick up the plush cover of a toy, a bright holiday red this time, and shake out the remaining fleece into a trash bag. Forget her own penchant for boots. She'd need her retail job plus more to keep the creature in fuzzies.

Two quick yips Jenn took for agreement came next, and she washed her hands and checked her reflection in the mirror, happy to see she looked none the worse for the busy day. Shelley had been markedly kinder to her that afternoon, and while she hadn't said she thought Jenn's changes had been good ones, she didn't seem to be as disappointed in her anymore. Marlee had liked the changes, though, and Jenn decided to hang on to that.

Dusk had fallen some time ago, and the gaslight-styled streetlamps cast a warm glow on the sidewalk. Sweet Pea trotted in front of Jenn at the end of her red leash with a snooty importance. Usually, she found it endearing in the dog, but today, she was more concerned about how she could keep her quiet inside her bag.

"Come on, kiddo. In you go. You need to mind your manners, so no barking. That will get us thrown out for sure."

Jenn pushed open the door to the wine shop, scanning the area by the bar for the women. The stab of disappointment when she didn't see them surprised her. She'd talked herself out of feeling this was important with so much determination, she thought she'd be fine turning around and heading out.

"Are you Jenn? They're out back."

The man behind the bar waved at a door Jenn hadn't noticed. Hanging on the window, a sign said, 'patio open'. In the middle of winter? At least her explanation about why she needed to leave wouldn't take long in the cold.

A low growl sounded from her bag as she walked through the store. If anyone heard Princess, they gave no sign of it. Jenn paused long enough to shush the dog in a low voice at the outer door. Taking a moment to mentally prepare her planned words to decline the drinks invitation, she pasted a smile on her face and pushed through.

If she'd had any expectations about what the world looked like behind the wine shop, this certainly wouldn't have been it. Two steps down led to a brick walkway, and beyond that, bistro tables dotted a brick-walled patio. Heaters made the exterior toasty. Strings of old-fashioned bulb lights ran between the surrounding bare trees, making the dark enclosure festive. Jazz music played at a low volume from hidden speakers, and a warm fragrant smell made Jenn's mouth water.

"There she is. Jenn, we've been waiting for you."

Marguerite waved her over to their table. That enticing aroma wafted by once more, and Jenn's stomach grumbled in response. As if she heard it, Princess growled from the confines of leather. Jostling her to send a message, Jenn moved forward once more.

"Needing a snack before dinner? I know the feeling. We're having roasted chestnuts. They are amazing. And these truffled almonds are to die for. Plus, olives, a weakness of mine." Marguerite waved a hand over the foods on the table.

Marlee patted the open chair. "Take a load off. You must be tired after being on your feet all day in those boots. Which are gorgeous, by the way."

"Are you a wine drinker? Red or white? I ordered both. I'm happy to pour." The Frenchwoman lifted an empty wineglass and wiggled it in Jenn's direction.

As if she could read Jenn's indecision and took exception to it, Princess barked at full volume from her purse. Leather muffled the bark, but not enough to keep her from being noticed.

"Your purse is barking," Marlee said.

Princess barked in response.

"Yes, about that. It's my dog. You see, I was about to give her a long walk."

She never had a chance to get further. "Emie told us about her. Did you know Rock now has a dog too? I want to hear about the whole tote and carry thing, both at the tree farm and at your apartment. Those were very Kermarrec male things to do. Plus, we want to know what you think of Rock."

At Marlee's pronouncement, two sets of eyes settled on Jenn with varying levels of curiosity. Another set of barks came from the bag over her shoulder as if Princess would also like to know what she thought. When her stomach rumbled its empty displeasure, the matter was settled.

Jenn sank into the chair. At the questioning tap of bottles from Marguerite, she pointed to the red with a muffled thank you. And when Princess yipped her reminder, the others laughed with good humor.

Marguerite said, "I think you should let the doggie out of the bag, so to speak, and then, my dear, you must tell us everything."

Chapter 10

"I'm going to work on the roof so we don't have a repeat of the flood from last night, okay? You can come outside with me. Or you can stay in here. Your call."

He was having a discussion with a dog. What was wrong with him? Rock could only imagine what his therapist would say if he told him. If only dogs could talk, he might learn why Ranger's anguish existed on par with his own.

"What's your story, boy?"

The dog gave a deep sigh and closed his eyes, as if his memories were too painful to contemplate.

"I hear you. Enough said."

Rock glanced outside as the afternoon light faded further. If he wanted to stay dry tonight, he'd have to hurry. The old cabin showed its age, and the leak last night left the interior humid and musty. That sent him back up the ladder, intent on his task, hammering in nails to pin a tarp in place even if winds came up.

The pound of the hammer echoed in rhythm around the clearing. Nothing like a little physical labor to make your mind wander, and his, though it should know better, wandered into dangerous territory. His brothers' razzing about Jenny and her dog and him and his dog didn't end when he swore at them in language as colorful as Ma's favorite outfits. They'd laughed, then they got serious, and asked him if he was serious too. Serious about Jenny was not going to come into the picture.

She'd called him a hero, and he was about as far from one on the spectrum as humanly possible. He'd failed his unit, and he'd failed their charges, and now, he stood poised to fail his family in the worst way possible. Jenny wouldn't be calling him a hero then.

Ranger slunk out of the cabin and circled the clearing, sniffing with occasional glances at Rock as he moved the ladder. Rock paused and watched the dog's earnest examination of a bush before giving it a watering. A single glance after that, the dog returned to the cabin and laid down in the doorway, his eyes on Rock.

Why had he adopted that dog? He knew better. Now he'd have to arrange for him too. Ranger didn't seem to be the cuddly social type, but Rock's brothers would never abandon an animal, even one as shy and scared as this dog. The fact that they'd be grieving wasn't lost on him. He'd added another layer to their burden.

Half an hour later, he was close to finishing, and no closer to answers. Ranger, the cabin, Jenn, his family, himself. Nothing was clearer. Ed had encouraged him to think about options for his life beyond the tree farm or working with his brothers. On Monday, he'd said, "What about going back to school? Or maybe volunteering with a group that means something to you? Your situation means you have a ticket to almost anything you want to do."

The only ticket he needed was the one he punched himself. The counselor didn't understand, and Rock only felt a minor discomfort that the reason he didn't was because he didn't know the whole story. And Rock wasn't going to enlighten him, just as he hadn't told his brothers or his mother or anyone else about it.

Except Ranger. That dog proved to be a good listener when Rock needed to talk himself down. Maybe Ranger's nightmares were as gruesome as his own.

Without warning, the faded afternoon turned to glaring sunlight. Dust and heat penetrated the corners of his consciousness, unrelenting in their need to crawl into every crevice of his body. Someone played a musical note, a sharp contrast to their stark conditions. The stale taste of vomit in his mouth reminded him he'd been unable to hold down the meager gruel they'd given him for the day's single meal. But that wasn't the worst part. That was reserved for his eyes only, and it was something he'd never forget seeing. He wished it was him, he prayed for that release, even as he'd –

"Oh, there you are. Did you know there's a chain across your driveway? I saw the lights on, though, so I assumed – "

The cheery voice carried a hint of breathlessness, one that snapped him back to a colder but better place so fast, his head spun. Rock reached for the top of the ladder with shaking hands. He'd been so deep in the hole of his personal hell, he never saw daylight. His toes twisted in his boots, trying to cling to the nearest rung of the ladder as it swayed under his weight. The voice continued, distracting him, and his hands slipped again.

It was like that time he fell out of the tree long ago. The sensation of flying without control as time elongated from seconds into hours. The heady feeling of being weightless before gravity did its thing. The knowledge that the elation he felt in the moment was about to turn into something he was going to hate. And then, the jarring pause that preceded blackness.

Nighttime passed quickly, not that he could always discern the difference between day and night in the hole. Darkness never lasted long enough. Anything was better than the daily searing torture and gruesome reminders of his failures.

"Wake up, please, wake up. Not now, doggie. I have to wake him up. Damn it, why is there no cell coverage here? Is there a phone inside, boy? Is there?"

Where was he? The air felt cool and crisp, so this might be heaven. Then again, he didn't think there were frantic sounding women in heaven. It could be hell, in which case the religious types got it wrong, because the drops of welcomed dampness on his skin made his burning hellhole a distant memory. Something wet wiped across his face once, then again.

"Stop licking him. Oh, go ahead. Maybe it will help. Maybe I should splash water on his face. That's what they do in movies. Damn it all, why didn't I pay closer attention in those safety courses?"

Another wet coating, and he lifted his hand in a vague wave to stop it, because it was suffocating him. But wait, how could he feel like he's suffocating if he was dead?

"Oh look, thank god, he's moving. Rock? Can you hear me? Rock?"

Insistent shaking jostled his brain, as along with that, a sharp lance pierced through his arm and up into his shoulder. It didn't matter anymore if this was heaven or hell or someplace in between. Rock moaned against the excruciating pain.

"Rock, you're waking up. He's waking up, boy, look. You fell, Rock, and you hit your head and you passed out. Are you listening to me? I need to call for an ambulance. You're hurt."

"No. 'Lance.'" He said the words with determined force, or at least he thought he did. It was hard to say what came out of his mouth.

"What was that? Oh bother, never mind. Rock, I'm going inside to look for a landline phone, because the cell connection isn't working. You stay right there and don't move."

Move? He couldn't even bring himself to open his eyes. Another wet warmth bathed his face.

He pushed an eye open, prepared to tell the angel or devil to stop with the waterworks, and forced himself to still when he focused on a big gold eye. He didn't think spirits at either end of the spectrum came with gold eyes.

A whine hit him along with the next spear of pain. Was the noise his? Something put weight on his chest as if to hold him down, and he tried to push it off. Another whine, more determined this time, followed, and he knew it wasn't him.

"What the hell?"

It sounded like his voice. He blinked rapidly, trying to breathe through the pain. It didn't abate. A pulse sounded in his ears. He was alive. Damn it all.

He strained to focus as details came in slowly. Hard ground under his back. A warm wet sensation under his head. Shooting pain down his right arm. Towering over him, a large dog crouched protectively.

"Are you still awake? Good. I can't find a phone inside. Where is it?"

"No. Phone." Shit, his voice sounded weak. A pale face swam in his vision, and he squinted at it. A girl.

A pretty girl. Brown curls of hair under a red and green knit cap. Wide eyes and milky skin and a mouth that never stopped moving. A soft hand in his, like it was now. That funny feeling in his stomach.

"You. Here before."

The head nodded with apparent relief. "Yes, I was here before. I cut my tree here, remember? And then I fell, and you took me and my tree up to my apartment. And you fixed the door handle at the cheese shop and found Princess's leash. Jenn. My name's Jenn. Do you remember your name?"

"Frederic."

Eyebrows pulled together in the pale face, and the girl stopped moving. Other details were coming in clearer. Not a girl but a woman. A big dog. His dog, Ranger, who not only sat here amid commotion but allowed the woman to put her arm around him. The woman wore a hat that would have looked more appropriate on Santa's elves.

"So Rock is short for Frederic?"

He nodded, immediately sorry he did it.

"Help me up," he said.

Happy his voice sounded stronger, he waited. The woman, Jenn, shook her head in disagreement and he started to push himself upright alone. With a frustrated sigh, she put an arm around his shoulders and hoisted him. When he saw two Rangers instead of one, he wished he hadn't been so insistent.

"I have to call an ambulance. Will you be okay here if I drive down the road to get a signal?"

"No ambulance."

Jenn looked like she was going to argue.

"I'm fine." Ooo-kayyy. The world hadn't quite resolved into single vision yet, but it was coming closer. He shut his eyes.

"Either I call an ambulance, or I drive you to the emergency room. What were you doing up on the roof, anyway? I sang to get your attention because I didn't want to startle you. Didn't you hear me?"

Didn't she ever shut the hell up?

Hands patted him down, starting at his jacket and going south, and he grabbed them before they invaded his privacy further.

"Stop. Go away. I'm fine."

She looked at him like he'd lost his mind. A hand wrapped around his head and he felt the light touch like a saber's blade. He couldn't stop the wince, and Jenn looked vindicated as she held up a bloody hand in front of his face.

"You have a head wound. You were unconscious for three minutes. I timed it. I think something's wrong with your arm, based on the way you're holding it."

He glanced down at his left arm cradling his right, and he couldn't argue. As if to emphasize the point, his shoulder took the opportunity to offer a jolt of pain. He was about to say he could drive himself to the hospital if he felt the need, when he remembered his old truck was a stick shift.

>>>>>

When he'd tumbled off the roof and flown through the air, Jenn's feet were already moving. If her instinct was to try to catch him, she'd never know. He landed with a crunch of hard body on hard dirt. Blood coming from the back of his skull made a rapid appearance. Her glance at her phone told her she had no service. Three fifty-four in the afternoon. It was useful to know that, since he didn't wake up until three fifty-seven.

He didn't say much on the drive to town, holding a towel to the back of his head and wincing with each bump in the road. She put her foot down as far as she dared, given the twisting, unfamiliar road. The little car shimmied a few times, forcing her to slow down as Rock gripped a hand on her dash. He held his injured arm tucked into his waist, and by the grimaces on his face, pain had set in.

"I guess I should tell you why I was there, since we have this time together. I did some research for you, about goats. For your farm. They eat the bramble, so they'll clean up the place, and if you want, you can raise them as dairy goats. You can make cheese. There's a big market for goat cheeses, goat milk too. And if you have poison oak and the goats eat it, you can sell the milk to wildland firefighters. They like to drink it to inoculate them against poison oak, so when they're fighting fires, they don't have to worry about that. I couldn't verify that last part, but it makes sense, doesn't it?"

Oh hell, why couldn't she stop the nervous babbling? Why would he care about goats at a time like this? If his pinched eyes and the contortions of his face were any indication, the pain was severe. That, or he really wished she'd shut up too.

He'd been in the back of the emergency department for three hours. She'd asked about his condition, only to be met with a kind but firm declination of information. She wasn't family, so she wouldn't learn more. He didn't ask for her. She'd considered calling his mother or brothers, but that wasn't her place either.

"Excuse me. Are you here for Rock?"

The man in the long white coat wore a kind grin and an understanding look in his eyes. When she nodded, he offered her his hand.

"I'm Dr. Kinkead, but please, call me Noah. I've been taking care of Rock. Before you ask, he's doing fine. We're going to hold him overnight for observation. Are you a close friend?"

She shook her head, standing too. "I found him. He fell, and I tried to get him to take an ambulance, but there was no cell phone coverage." Babbling again. She bit her lip to stop the flow.

She wanted to ask if she could see him, because she really wanted to apologize. She was the reason he fell off his roof. Plus, she needed to take care of his dog. She hadn't had to do more than close him inside the cabin where he howled before subsiding into a long whine.

The doctor nodded again. "As I said, Rock is doing fine, and we're holding him overnight for observation."

"No."

The voice held both conviction and pain. She lifted her eyes and encountered the man himself, dressed as well as possible with his coat on his uninjured arm and a blanket wrapped around the other. He struggled to jam a knit cap over his head and flinched with the action.

The doctor shook his head. "Rock, no. I told you, you had a concussion. Someone should watch you for the next twenty-four hours. You already said I can't call your family. You have to stay here."

"I'll watch him."

Why the words popped out of her mouth, she wasn't sure. Probably guilt, or maybe it was the stricken look that flashed across Rock's face as the doctor insisted he was worse off than he wanted to believe.

The man she felt such sympathy for grimaced again. "No." He paused, then seemed to reconsider how that sounded. "Thank you."

"Really, it's no trouble. I don't have to work again until Thursday, so I have tomorrow free. Plus, I need to make sure your dog is okay. He howled when we left. I had to lock him in your house, you see. He's worried about you."

Rock gave her a confused look. "He howled?"

She nodded.

"Are you sure you want to check yourself out, Rock? Against your doctor's recommendation? I can still call your brothers."

Jenn saw a flash of sadness cross the man's face at the mention of his brothers. She thought they were close, according to their wives, but maybe she'd gotten that part wrong. When he shook his head and took a few tottering steps toward the door, the doctor put a hand on his uninjured shoulder and guided him into a chair.

"I have a form you need to sign." He turned back to her, regarding her carefully. "You'll watch him?" She nodded. "Then there are discharge orders for you to review before you go."

She sank into the opposite chair. She watched Rock. Rock watched her.

"I have to make a stop, a quick one."

He nodded, looking sleepy but still watching.

"You have to stay awake while I do."

He nodded with more force this time. He had no comment when she stopped at her apartment. When she put the big bag in the back seat, she prayed he'd have no comment on that, either. Man, did she pray.

She forced herself to stay quiet as she drove back to the tree farm at a much more sedate pace. The slower rate was necessary, since rain pelted down and night had long since fallen with a density you never found in the city. She slowed as she approached the area where she thought the driveway joined the road. Without the holiday tree farm signs to mark it, she'd driven past earlier. That felt like days ago.

"There." Rock pointed, just in time for her to slow further and take the turn. By the time she got the chain pulled aside, her wool coat had rivers running down the sides.

Lights blazed in the cabin, since she hadn't taken the time to turn them off. As if the sight of that surprised him, Rock sat still and stared at the place when she parked and turned off her ignition.

"You've been here before."

Maybe that knock on the noggin was worse than it seemed. They'd covered that before, unless he'd forgotten his knightly rescues.

"Yes, Rock, I got my tree here." Agreeing seemed like the safest thing to do. Anything to get him inside. She hoped the heat was on, because drops of rain had found their way down her neck and she was cold.

He waved an impatient hand and shoved the car door open with surprising speed. Bolting out of the car, he wavered on his feet, and she matched his speed to get next to him and put herself under his good shoulder.

He glanced down at her, though with the rain and darkness, she couldn't read his expression. He glanced at the ring of stones marking the firepit, then back at her. When his request came, it seemed strange.

"Hold my hand."

"Can you walk?"

He nodded. She moved away from his body, wishing she didn't have to do so. He felt so solid, like a strong column, and he smelled good, like pine sap and wood smoke. When his fingers entwined with hers, he tightened his hand, like he didn't want to let go.

They walked slowly to the cabin. She hadn't found a way to lock it, and she hoped he wouldn't be upset by that. He pushed the door like he expected it to be unlocked, though, and as soon as he did, a deep woof sounded from inside.

"What the hell?"

His dog bounded out of the house and jumped up on the man's chest with surprisingly gentle paws.

"Ranger?"

He probably should have stayed at the hospital. He didn't seem to remember his own dog. Her nerves kicked into higher gear.

The man put a tentative hand on the dog's head, scratching slowly and then with more speed. The dog's tongue came out and lolled to the side, a canine smile on his face, and Rock grinned back.

Man, what a grin did to those stern features. Jenn stood transfixed as that nudge of remembrance came without warning. He'd smiled that day by the lake. She hadn't seen him smile again since. A shiver moved through her, and the cold penetrated her body at the same time the feeling of it penetrated her mind.

Cold. The cabin was cold. No heat came from the woodstove, and as she glanced around, she didn't see any other sign of warmth either.

Rock seemed to realize this about the time she did, and he frowned at the dog, then the stove. "Sorry I left you so cold today. I promise it won't happen in the future."

The dog dropped down, moved to the bed by the stove, and circled once before laying down with a deep sigh. He wound himself into a little ball, one surprisingly tiny for such a big animal, and his eyes when they flashed to Jenn's held a question.

"I'll start a fire," Rock said, shifting like he searched for balance on unsteady legs.

Jenn grabbed his arm and guided him to the sofa, pushing him into it. "I'll do it. As soon as I, ah, get my bag from the car."

Her bag. Her problem. She hoped it wouldn't be a big one.

Rock turned to examine her, starting at her boots, which admittedly, weren't the most woods-worthy. She hadn't planned on hiking up his drive. Nor had she thought she'd need to go outside in the middle of the rainy night to hunt up firewood. She busied herself with her keys and spun away to bite her lip. She should tell him, but she was afraid that would put a new wall between them.

"I'll be right back," she said, not waiting to see what his reaction would be. When she opened the car door and pulled out her bag, she wondered what else the night would bring. Then she remembered the warmth in his humorous look, and she wondered if that was more of a threat than the bag would be.

Chapter 11

Jenn set the bag on the floor in the furthest corner with a soft touch. Most women Rock knew dumped their purses, particularly one as large as hers. Her gaze darted to him, then Ranger, then back at the bag, and she twisted her hands until her knuckles shown white. Ranger's nose worked overtime, his eyes glancing between Rock and Jenn, and finally settling on the bag too.

"I'll get firewood," she said.

"I'll get it." He stood, only to have his arm protest. He'd refused the pain killers Noah wanted to shove into him. He didn't need them, never wanted them, and wasn't going to begin now.

"Tell me where it is and I'll get it. Please, before we have to drive back to the hospital tonight because your stubbornness makes you pass out."

When she put it that way, it made sense. She bent over close to her bag, and despite his intentions to remain distant, he enjoyed the view of the rain-soaked coat riding up her hips. He knew he should stop gawking, but he'd lost the power to turn away.

She hustled wood from the lean-to, followed his instructions on how to lay the fire in the old stove and set a match to kindling. Delight bloomed on her face when it lit, and as the wood caught, she clapped her hands. It was clear she'd never lit a wood fire before. He had to give her points for bravely taking charge.

When she stood up, she examined the interior of the cabin again. "Where's the bathroom? I'd like to freshen up." She glanced at the bag again.

"Outhouse is outside. Turn left, then left again. There's a flashlight by the front door."

Her mouth opened and closed a couple of times before she set her lips in a firm line. A forced smile came to her face, and she hefted the big bag to her shoulder. "Left, left. Right. I'll be back in a few."

He had to admire the false bravado on her face and give her points for willingness to embrace the unfamiliar. Only a minute passed before his thoughts strayed to another woman, and another kind of false bravery in the face of greater danger. By the time Jenn came back, again setting that bag down gently, his mood was dark as he gazed into the woodstove's glass door.

Rubbing her hands together as she drew close to the stove, she said, "Where do you keep your coffee? Not for you, but for me."

No stimulants for him. It would be a good thing to stay awake all night. At least the monsters of his dreams wouldn't show up that way.

"And water? Please tell me you have running water inside."

The quiet desperation in her tone pulled him out of the dark place. She probably wasn't aware she was ringing her hands, or that the pleading on her face was so damned enticing. He wished he was a better man to offer her whatever she needed to make that worry go away.

"I have indoor water, at that sink. It's not hot, but it's wet. Coffee's in the grinder on the counter."

If that surprised her, she didn't show it. It wasn't until she stepped across the room and found his hidden treasure that she quite literally squealed. Ranger lifted his big head and tilted it to one side as if he didn't know what to make of the sound either.

"You have an espresso machine. I love this model. I had one like it before." Her voice trailed off. He turned to see what stopped her words and found her face drawn into a morose expression as she stroked the metal.

Damn it, he wanted her to talk. Gab like crazy, as she'd been prone to do every time they shared breathing space. The silent woman who moved quietly around his kitchen was an anomaly. Her nervous glances between him, the dog, and her purse continued like another strange tick.

What had she babbled about before? Goats. Cheese. God help him, she'd mentioned a business plan.

She probably had it tucked into that big purse and couldn't wait to spring it on him. He couldn't draw his eyes away from it, thinking it would probably go off like a bomb any minute. As if it responded to his thoughts, the purse moved. He only stopped himself from jumping by sheer will.

"Did I tell you about the client I had who insisted that anyone who worked there had to know how to make coffee? I mean, not just any kind of coffee, but like fancy espresso drinks. That kind?"

She must have noticed him looking at her bag, because as the coffee brewed, she moved into his line of sight and blocked any view of it. She hissed, then shot him an apologetic look.

"Sorry, nerves. Anyway, what was I saying?"

A rustling noise he couldn't identify sounded in the room. Ranger heard it too, and the dog's attention immediately focused on the big bag. Jenn turned as well, and when it moved this time, there was no mistaking it. All three of them stared at it, and Ranger was already on his feet, taking cautious steps forward.

"Um, my, you must be hungry. Can I make you something to eat? Do you have a radio, you know, to play music? Or I could sing."

She started to slam out a show tune he recognized, slightly offkey, but there was no mistaking the sound that she tried to cover.

A distinct growl, high and excited, sounded from the bag. Ranger sniffed the leather from one end to the other, then focused on the middle. A yip sounded next, and he leaped back, looking at Rock as if he awaited orders.

Jenn jumped too, straight at Rock. She landed on the sofa next to him, wrapped two arms around his neck, and pulled his face down. When she planted her lips on his, he forgot about the sounds coming from her bag, too busy listening to the sounds coming from the woman with such interesting distraction techniques.

The initial shock of it froze him in place. Her hands slipped to his face and held firm, even when he attempted to ease out of her grasp. His lips tightened on instinct, fending off her attack, while his brain attempted to process the mix of sensations. She pressed against him, and the softness of her curves met his hard planes with an eagerness his body recognized.

His mind had other ideas, reciting the many reasons why this was a very bad idea. As if she could hear his thoughts, her kisses gentled. Her warmth lured him deeper, as she tilted her head for a better angle. The objections he should have been voicing faded away, and in their place, something snapped.

His lips suddenly grew persuasive without conscious direction. A hand tangled in her coat, pulling her closer. Rock couldn't keep the groan of pleasure from rumbling against her mouth, and his tongue pierced through her boundaries on full attack. Her deep lusty whimper sent tingling to his fingertips and toes. His body came alive as if it hibernated in a deep sleep for a decade.

Rock knew he had to stop this. If he didn't, who knows what would happen next. When he leaned away, the reluctance he felt scaled into full-blown regret. That didn't keep him from framing her face and staring at it in wonder.

"You did that to me before."

Jenn shook her head once, then slowly began to nod.

"Years ago, by the pond."

Another nod. She bit her lip, which only made him want to bite it too. Better yet, pull her in close and keep kissing her for hours.

A high-pitched rumble added to the ringing in his ears. A whine followed, punctuated by a yip. Through the fog of lust, he vaguely registered the noises, even as feelings clouded his self-discipline.

"We have to talk about this," he said.

Her gulp in response did wonderful things to the rise and fall of her chest. Her glance at her bag once more had him turning for it slowly too. At that moment, the bag growled fiercely.

"What was that?"

She shook her head. Embarrassment began a crawl across her features.

He shook his head and winced. A growl came again, muffled and squeaky. The whimpering continued, and for a moment, he thought it might be coming from her. Another bark cleared the haze of lust faster than a barrage of gunfire.

"I can explain." Jenn was already on her feet, making fast work of closing the distance to her bag. Yipping reached a new crescendo from its leather depths. As realization struck, he wasn't sure what he was more upset about, the noises from the bag, or missing the woman who left his arms too easily.

"You brought your dog."

"But you see, I never leave her alone overnight. I couldn't, and since you have to stay awake, I figured I could keep an eye on her, you know, so she doesn't make a mess or anything."

It took a second for him to identify the source of the whimpering, which came from Ranger huddled in the opposite corner of the room, making as small a mound as he could.

"I have a dog."

"They're going to get along fine, you'll see." Her fingers reached for the zippered top.

"Keep it in the bag." Rock wobbled to his feet, not sure if his loss of balance was the concussion or the kisses or both. He crouched down and spoke to Ranger in a calming tone. "I'm not sure how this is going to work out, bud, but let's put up a brave front."

Gold eyes flicked up to him and over to Jenn in rapid succession. They landed last on the bag, where the frequency and volume of yips and growls intensified. When Rock looked back at Jenn, whatever admonition had been on his lips fell silent. Aching desire and the urge to protect her lanced through him at the worry in her large eyes.

"I can't keep her in there forever. You'll see, they'll get along. We'll introduce them, and they'll sniff each other, and all will be well."

Rock heard the uncertainty in her tone, but acting on her words, Jenn went back to opening her bag. The heaving breaths she took reminded him of what she felt like as her body pressed against his. He felt her warmth even with layers of coats and clothes between them.

Yes, the kisses surprised him. What shocked him more was that he wanted them to continue, and that was something he never expected. That part of him should be dead, as dead as the bodies back in that bunker. His soul, his feelings and emotions, died that day too. Or that's what he'd thought, until this moment.

"Help me out here, bud." The dog responded to his whisper with a twitch of his ears and lifted eyes. Then the animal's attention switched to the woman. "Yeah, I get that. Hard to keep eyes on the prize. I have a bad feeling about this."

Ranger whined as if in agreement, and Rock stood. It was only when he tried to plant his hands on his hips that he remembered he wasn't operating at full capacity. That bonk on his head had to be the reason the vanilla scent of this warm female was something he couldn't get out of his mind.

The dog alerted suddenly, rising to stand and leaning forward with his eyes narrowing. Rock turned in time to see Jenn with her hand outstretched, and in it, a handful of dog treats.

"Ranger, would you like to make a new friend? Come on over, big boy. She'll be happy to see you."

He didn't expect the sudden surge of jealousy as the woman crooned to his dog. Jenn, on her knees and bending low, whispered suggestive words into the heating air. The woodstove must be an inferno to make the room this hot. Rock slid his coat off the single shoulder. When he yanked off the knit cap, his sutures pulled hard, but even that didn't knock any sense into him.

He wanted to slink forward like Ranger was doing, sniffing wildly and excited beyond belief at his good fortune. Sinking to his knees, he'd pull her into another round of those kisses, and let time and their circumstances melt into oblivion. If only it was that easy to forget it all. At least he knew he'd have no nightmares tonight. He knew he wouldn't sleep, even if she left him alone.

"Good boy. Look who is such a good, good boy. You are a gentle giant, aren't you, Ranger? Guess what? I have a friend for you to meet. Her name is Princess Sweet Pea. You'll have to be careful, though, because next to you, she looks like a fly."

Ranger sat with his head cocked, and bright interest shown in his eyes. He'd never given so much attention to anything before, and Rock didn't think it was the promised treats, now all gobbled down. Ranger watched Jenn with cautious adoration.

"Princess, this is Ranger. He lives with Rock, but you know Rock already. He's the nice man who brought back the leash you lost. I know you and Ranger will be great friends, Princess. Say hello."

Ranger sat with polite attentiveness, his head cocked to the side as Jenn revealed what was in her arms. The little dog wore a red coat with a matching bow in the hair on top of its head. The yipping didn't stop, not when Jenn leaned forward to Ranger, her dog in her hands, and Ranger extended his nose for a sniff.

She was so lovely, a determined expression on her face as if she could will the dogs to be friends. Her lips were almost as red as her dog's coat, no doubt from that fine mouth-to-mouth time. Rock didn't want to think about it, which meant it was all he could think about. His head ached, and he couldn't attribute it to his fall.

Jenn's eyes met his as a triumphant smile filled her face. The pure joy he saw made a funny tremble come to his stomach. It was a feeling he remembered from long ago like it was yesterday.

"Friends?" She asked the question with a hesitation in her voice. Rock wasn't sure if she talked about the dogs, or them. Without responding, he looked back at the dogs. He only had a second to react when he saw the moment unfolding.

Toy dog growled. Big dog drew back and opened his jaw as if ready to bite its little fool head off. Rock's feet were already moving as Ranger leaned forward. Damn it, why was he never fast enough when it counted?

Toy dog squirmed its body like a snake in Jenn's hands, and it leaned forward too, its mouth open. Ranger stretched closer, and little mutt's teeth closed on the tip of Ranger's nose.

Ranger yelped, not moving for a moment and then nothing but motion. He dropped to his belly and whined, backing away from Jenn and the little monster as fast as he could. When his tail hit the corner, he rolled himself into a ball and cried pathetically. Rock dropped to a knee and put out a consoling hand, but the dog didn't want his sympathy.

"Oh my god. Oh my god, I'm so sorry. Princess, say you're sorry. Damn you, what am I going to do with you? Princess, I'm going to change your name to bitch dog."

The tirade was so out of character with everything he'd heard from Jenn to date that Rock could only gape in silence. Jenn crouched down on her elbows, bringing her almost low enough to be nose to nose with the beast, and Rock had a fleeting thought that perhaps he should yank her up, in case the dog had more nasty ideas. Said creature looked damned pleased with itself, like biting other dogs thirty times its size was a fun gig. It bounced on its four paws and wiggled its behind, its stump of a tail waving madly.

Troubled lines filled Jenn's face as she got up quickly, coming toward Ranger with a hand outstretched. "I'm sorry, Ranger. I don't know what to tell you. I can't explain why she acts this way. It's like the devil's gotten into her, ever since I lost my job and my condo."

Rock held himself very still as Jen cooed at the big wuss in the corner. The dog's whimpers faded away, but his eyes remained sorrowful and teary. Jenn extended a tentative finger to his nose, and the dog tried to cross his eyes to watch it approach.

"You're not bleeding. Thank the doggie god for that. I know it probably hurt at the time, and it was a shock to get nipped like that, but do you think you could forgive her, Ranger? Princess isn't a bad dog, not really."

Across the room, Princess laid down on the corner of the rug and had the braiding in her treacherous teeth. She growled as if she was one bad ass dog the size of a bag of bullets, and she wasn't going to let anyone forget it.

Jenn stood, and remorse swam along with apologies in eyes gone teary too. "I'm sorry, Rock. Sorry you fell off the ladder because I startled you. And sorry you're stuck with me tonight as your guardian. And sorry about Princess and Ranger. I thought maybe I could return the favors, since after all, you rescued me so many times this past month. You've already seen what a poor job I did with that."

He noted she didn't apologize for the one thing he couldn't stop thinking about, and for some reason, that made him want to grin. If she had said she was sorry she'd kissed him, disappointment wouldn't even begin to describe how he would feel.

"It's going to be a long night, I'm afraid," she said, glancing between the dogs.

He didn't voice his agreement. It was going to be a long night, but for completely different reasons than the ones she thought.

Chapter 12

Why hadn't she listened to her common sense, the voice that said retrieving Princess and bringing her along was going to be a bad idea? Why couldn't she do a better job of controlling the dog? She was able to direct important people in ways to improve their companies, and yet a tiny pile of fur defeated her every attempt.

The stove's door stood open, allowing its light to bring a friendly glow to the room out to its corners. In one, Ranger still curled up, though now it was less a ball and more a sprawl. He snored ever so softly, and every once in a while, he had a puppy dream, legs paddling wildly. She didn't think those dreams were happy ones.

The man, on the other hand, stayed very still, so still that from time to time, she felt like she needed to poke him to make sure he hadn't drifted off. He sure hadn't been still when she'd kissed him, his lips as persistent and hot as the fire was now. It would be best to not think about that now, because all it did was make her want to kiss him again. If she did, she could claim it was to make sure he was awake, because she wasn't sure his eyes were open. Reaching across the space between them, she tapped the back of his uninjured hand.

As fast as she imagined a snake would strike, his hand flipped over and engulfed hers in a grip that crunched tendons. She grimaced, not because it hurt so much as the surprise of it, and he immediately lessened the clasp but did not let her go. Lifting her eyes to meet his, she noticed those lids still drooped. His jaw clenched, though, as if tension had him in its unforgiving hold.

"Never touch an animal you aren't familiar with."

The conversational tone for such a dangerous message made her pause, regarding him steadily. He didn't frighten her, because for some reason she couldn't identify, she trusted him.

She glanced over at Ranger, now on his back and sleeping without the bad doggie dreams.

"I didn't mean him. I meant me."

Blinking rapidly, she turned back. While his expression gave nothing away, she detected a hint of sadness in the line of his mouth. That mouth. She wouldn't be able to stop thinking about the brief experience she'd had with it.

He tugged on her hand, and she attempted to wiggle it free. He held on a moment longer, watching her as if he wanted to make sure she got the message. She did, all right. When he let her go, she immediately threaded her fingers through his and made sure her clasp was as tight as his had been.

This time, his eyes opened wide. Such unusual eyes, colors that seemed to kaleidoscope between green and blue and gray. She blamed the flickering firelight and the distraction every time she got close to Rock for the tumble of emotions racing through her every time they got near each other.

If she wanted to, she could lean forward and put her lips on his. If he wanted to, he could kiss her back. His close examination of her face, ticking between features as if he planned to describe her to a police sketch artist, made her want to babble from her growing tension. The night grew longer by the minute.

"Are you hungry? We didn't eat anything. You should eat, you know, to keep up your strength." Why she said that, she wasn't sure. Even with the cast on his arm and sutures in his scalp, he looked like a mountain lion at rest. She'd seen one at the zoo once, draped over rocks in the shade. When a bird flew into the enclosure, the animal went from sleepy relaxation to active predator in a blink. The bird never stood a chance.

She guessed any prey around Rock would be the same. A shiver she attributed to the nerves of the evening ran through her, making the hairs on the back of her neck lift. Being the subject of an attack of a sexy personal nature wouldn't be a bad thing with this man. He didn't move away, and she forced herself not to spin into his arms.

"We have to talk about it."

"Food? Sure. Do you have any cereal? Or maybe some canned soup? We could make sandwiches." She felt powerless to stop the idiotic torrent raining from her lips as she stared into his mesmerizing gaze.

He shook his head and grimaced. "Why you keep kissing me."

"I didn't kiss you. I was trying to distract you from Princess. I know, it was a mistake to bring her here without asking you first, and I am sorry for that." The distraction technique, not so much.

His eyes dropped and lingered on her lips once more, and she swore they tingled in response to his sharpening expression.

"You did kiss me. Now, and back then."

"I – ." She stumbled to a stop. Denial would be a lie. Besides, she'd enjoyed the results far too much.

Lifting her chin, she returned his laser stare. "I did kiss you. I'm not ashamed to own up to that. Besides, you kissed me back."

A muscle twitched next to his mouth, derailing her attention. "Kissing someone back is a normal adult response. I've grown up a bit over the last few years."

As if she hadn't noticed. It was all she could do not to drop her eyes to the broad shoulders and muscled chest, obvious despite the sweatshirt he'd wrestled over his cast.

"And you did kiss me back when we were kids too."

Another twitch, this one lifting a side of his mouth enough to qualify as a smile, had her answering with a grin. "I did not."

"Did too."

The welcomed sound of a single chuckle rumbled out of him, along with a denying shake of his head. That brought another twist of pain as his expression grew solemn. She wanted that smile back. He lit up the room when he smiled.

"It can't happen again."

Now he was just being stubborn. "Why not?"

He disentangled from her fingers and dropped her hand. A quiver of new tension curled her toes in her boots. Those hot kisses before hinted at off-the-charts chemistry. When her fingers closed into fists, she realized she didn't need another for verification. He felt it as much as she did.

"Because it can't."

She wanted to do it, and not only because he said she couldn't. She'd never done well with people throwing roadblocks in her path. Add to that the spine-shivering desire to experience the heat of his lips again, and she was ready to prove him wrong.

Except she needed to stop thinking about that. She was his monitor for the night, and then she had no reason to stay. The memory of that day long ago rammed into her with a force that had her inhaling fast.

She should probably tell him. He had to remember that day like she did, or he wouldn't have mentioned it. It was a highlight in her young life, until it faded from prominence in the wake of other, less innocent days. If she brought it up, though, she'd attach more importance to it now, like those kisses.

To distract them both, she stood and turned to the sparse shelves in the kitchen with her hands on her hips, more to keep from reaching for him than any other reason. "What do you have for us to eat?"

An hour later, they forked in mac and cheese in a hush only broken by periodic downpours of rain. She'd tried every opening gambit she could think of. The man did not waver from his steady pace of eating or his monk-like vow of silence, sitting like the proverbial rock on the old couch. She almost wished for the roof to fall in, if only to have something they could both talk about.

Setting his fork in his bowl, he eyed her with sudden attention. The gaze made her want to babble once more. Goats. They could talk about goats. But before she could launch in, he asked the one question she didn't want to discuss above all else.

"What did you mean before, about losing your job and your home?"

Jenn went still. With exaggerated care, she put the fork down in her bowl and set the whole thing aside. She lifted a paper towel to her lips and dabbed delicately. He would recognize the delaying tactics. Hell, he probably invented them.

"Why do you ask?" Her tone fell shy of nonchalant.

"You told Ranger about it. Why not tell me?"

"I just – " She bit off whatever she was going to say next and chewed on her lower lip to keep the words in. When she shifted her eyes to meet his, she found him studying her movement with a narrowed gaze still showing a brilliant blue.

A harsh sigh accompanied his reply. "If we're going to stay up all night, we need to discuss something. Otherwise, we're both going to nod off."

She bobbed her head before he even finished. All this nervous energy she kept bottled up inside made her feel like fireworks ready to explode. When she got the rapid movement under control she said, "If I answer this for you, can I ask a question in return? And you have to answer?"

He sat back and nodded in slow motion.

Jenn bit the bullet, wondering why explaining this to Rock felt so embarrassing. He'd never understand the position she was put in. If she danced around the details, perhaps he'd let it go.

"I am, or was, a management consultant. It was a dream job. I helped clients fix their problems, like streamlining processes or selecting systems or addressing the weak points in their organizations. A little bit of everything for companies in the small to midsized range, an ideal gig for someone like me. I hated having to quit."

He picked at the discrepancy like Princess would a fleecy toy. "You said you lost the job."

Her gaze darted away this time, focusing back on her dog where she sprawled on Ranger's bed, taking up as much of the landscape as possible. Ranger lay on the other side of the woodstove, with its metal bulk between him and his nemesis. If Rock's dog slept with one eye open and focused on the little terror, Jenn could understand why.

"Yeah, about that. Technically, I was fired, but I prefer to think that I made the choice."

He sank deeper into the couch, giving the seat next to him a pat. Accepting his invitation would be so easy. Jenn popped off the dining chair and took her bowl to the sink. Her head swiveled as she looked at the shelves. "Where are your storage containers?"

"I don't have any."

She shrugged, shoving the pan with the leftovers into the fridge. Retrieving his empty bowl, she kept her eyes averted and her body angled away from him. Washing the bowls took no time, and by the time she was finished, Rock hadn't said anything more. She was at a loss about how to change the subject.

When he patted again with a determined slap, she sighed and sank down, sitting on the edge of the faded leather as far from him as she could. Temptation, thy name is Rock.

"Can we talk about something else?"

"One for you, one for me. That's how our deal works."

"Fine, whatever." She fell silent, seeing no way to wiggle out of this, not when they had hours ahead of them to stay awake. She turned toward him with a furrowed frown. "They should never have asked me to do it. It was unethical and immoral, and perhaps borderline illegal."

"Asked you what, and agreed to what?"

She sighed again, knowing the ringing fingers twisting in her lap gave away her turmoil. Before she could stop the agitated action, Rock reached over and put his hand on hers. He squeezed and kept up the pressure until she searched his features.

"You have a sympathetic face. It's easy to talk to you."

His question came a touch above a whisper. "What happened?"

"They asked me to hold back on revealing some data, so the numbers looked better than they were. It was a financial analysis to support a buy-out, and the client, the seller, wanted me to pick and choose between data points. Only use what supports our strengths, they insisted, and if something looks bad, ignore it."

She paused, letting that sink in. Rock didn't know her well enough to understand how far this went against everything she believed in.

"Didn't your bosses support you?"

She shook her head. Looking down at his hand on hers, she realized she'd turned and laced their fingers together once more. And he'd allowed it.

"You left because your ethical code didn't align with theirs, and you didn't get the support from your company that you should have. I don't know you very well, but I can understand how that hurt you. I'm proud of you for leaving, Jenny."

She focused on him in disbelief. Tears in her eyes made his face wavery. When he reached out his good arm and pulled her in, relief had her leaning on him and inhaling his rich, woodsy aroma.

"Thank you." Her voice cracked. Few people, even her family, had been this accepting.

"For?"

"For believing me and understanding so easily. Many people didn't."

She listened to his steady breathing, the rise and fall of his chest under her cheek. He was almost a stranger, and yet she felt closer to him than she had anyone in a very long time. The weeping she felt powerless to stop continued as a fresh wave of rain pelted the roof. Her tears wet his sweatshirt, but he didn't budge. His voice sounded sad and distant when he finally replied.

"Most people don't understand the ethical dilemmas they're faced with, not until it's too late. When the world is at its worst, people like to bargain or provide excuses. Doing the right thing is often hard, harder than any of us imagine."

She wanted to ask him what he meant, using her tit-for-tat question to encourage him to open up. For a reason she couldn't identify, though, she stayed quiet. The restlessness she'd felt since they entered the cabin tonight faded, and for the first time in months, peace washed over her.

Chapter 13

She stretched into the warmth, the completeness of it luring her back into a drowsy place. There was an elusive something she was supposed to be doing, but Jenn couldn't grasp what it was. She wanted to dive deeper into the fading dreams where everything was rosy, her life felt complete, and the worries that marked her days dissipated.

Snuggling in, she encountered a hard mass of heat. She must have slept with the electric blanket on high last night. A niggling out of reach thought stopped her slide back into nothingness. Remembering the pelting rain on the roof last night, she listened with more intention. The only sound she registered was a steady wind blowing in a consistent tempo not far from where she lay.

Her brain wouldn't clear. If she could rid herself of the memory of that elusive important task, she knew she could go back to sleep. She usually woke bright eyed and ready to face the day, though lately, she felt more compelled to sleep late, like she was in a coma she couldn't shake.

Coma. The wiggling came again, this time accompanied by a growl. Shifting against the rock she lay against, her brain snapped into gear about the same time she remembered.

Rock. She was supposed to keep him awake for the night to make sure his head injury didn't cause him to slip into a coma and lose consciousness, and what did she do? Passed out on him. And not only on him, but literally on him. Her fingers enjoyed their mindless leisurely stroll across granite abs and a chest made for exploring.

She pushed up with a start, trying to make out his face in the dim light. It must be morning, though she wasn't sure how late. The rain drumming the roof overnight no longer made a sound. The wiggling and growling proved to be Princess, who wore the affronted look of a prima donna whose beauty rest had been interrupted. The dog jumped off the sofa and sulked to a corner, but Jenn ignored her.

"Rock. Wake up. You're supposed to stay awake."

She shook him but received no response. Probing her fingers on his neck, she tried to find a pulse. What she noticed instead was how hot his skin felt to her touch, and how much he was sweating. He was drenched. Was a fever a side effect of losing consciousness or a head wound? She frantically tried to remember every word on his discharge instructions but couldn't clear her cobwebs fast enough.

Shaking him again, she pleaded, "Rock, you have to wake up. Please. Damn it, this is my fault. I should have had more coffee."

This time when she shook him, he moaned, and the sound of it ran a tremble up her spine. His body quaked like a fever racked him and his shallow rapid breathing wrenched her heart. She had to call an ambulance. Damn, that's right, no reception. How did he stay connected with the world without a phone?

"No, no, please." His words slurred and ran over one another as his agitation increased. "Not them. Please, no, no, no."

"Rock, honey, you need to wake up. I think you have a fever and you're delusional. You're home now, but I'm going to get you back to the hospital." Though how she was going to do that was a mystery.

A large hand closed on her forearm and tightened to the point of pain. His moaning increased in volume and his words jumbled in a desperate tone. Jenn didn't know what to do, because her useless cell phone was across the room on the table, and the man writhing next to her would not let her go.

Warmth pressed up against her back. It took her mind a moment to process that it was Ranger, leaning against her as if he shared her concern. She tried to wrap a free arm around him, thinking maybe he'd understand commands like 'go find help'. It had worked with Lassie.

"Ranger, what are we going to do?"

The dog jumped off the couch in response, and Jenn missed his support immediately. He circled the room and stood on Rock's other side. When he jumped up with big paws landing on the man's chest, she tried to push him off, but he ignored her.

"Ranger, get down. You'll hurt him." The dog's bowl-sized paws kneaded Rock's chest in a steady rhythm, and he leaned forward with a whine to lick Rock's face.

"I don't think that's a good – " She was about to say idea, when Rock suddenly stilled. His breathing became a greater struggle. She was about to jam her elbow into the dog to shove him off when Rock's eyes popped, open wide enough to show white circled around swirling fear, and his gaze darted around in panicked confusion.

"Rock, oh thank god. Do you know where you are? Do you know who you are? Do you know who I am?" She waved her hand in front of his face. "How many fingers am I holding up? Who is the President of the United States?"

Eyes colored a turbulent dark gray blinked rapidly. They flitted around the room before settling on her. The blinking continued, and as it did, the grip on her arm lessened. When he removed his hand, she shook her arm to ward off the sharp tingling of returning circulation.

In an abrupt movement, Rock stood, dumping the dog and her to the sides. Ranger recovered more quickly than she did, sitting at his master's feet with a lolling tongue in a muzzle that looked like it grinned in relief.

"What are you still doing here?"

The harsh tone registered about a moment before his words did. He was breathing more normally now, though his face appeared unnaturally pale. He examined the cast on his arm like he'd forgotten it was there. He put a hand to the back of his head but without a grimace this time. He grabbed the knit cap he'd discarded at some point overnight and yanked it down to his ears.

"I'm sure you can find your way off the property without my directions." He didn't turn back to her with the rude words.

"But, Rock, you have a concussion. You need to go back to the hospital, because you had some kind of episode just now. It must be because of the concussion. They need to figure out what's wrong."

A bitter laugh barked out of him, making Princess growl in response. A slow turn of his head in the little dog's direction had Jenn thinking she needed to scoop up her girl before he ground her under his heel.

She stood, wanting to help him understand how serious this was. "You have to go to the doctor. Something's wrong. They can figure it out, and they'll be able to fix it."

A chuckle holding no humor marked his slow turn to her. The eyes looking back at her were ice cold blue and empty now, as if they'd shared no stories overnight, as if they hadn't laughed over dinner preparations, as if he hadn't comforted her, as if those kisses had never happened. A sneer cut across his face.

"Little girl, what's wrong with me is something no one can fix. Not a doctor, and certainly not you with your simplistic way of looking at life. Right or wrong, crystal clear, rose colored glasses. No, the one thing that's wrong with me right now is the fact that you're still here. I'm heading out. Be gone when I get back."

The door slammed on his retreating footsteps, and Jenn stared at it, unable to process what had happened. She would not cry, though as she had that thought, the tears were already making tracks on her face. Why he blew up at her was a mystery she didn't want to linger on, not here.

It wasn't until much later that she'd dried her tears and told herself she would let it go. As if it could be that easy. The rose street glow lighting her apartment walls brought her no comfort. She squeezed the needles on the fir, surprised when they gave and bent under her fingers. Nothing was like a freshly cut tree. The years she'd bought pre-cut ones at a boy scouts' lot near her condo had nothing to compare.

Even if her decorations consisted of paper chains and cheap plastic shiny things from the discount store, it was pretty. Her nice ornaments sat in a box in that storage center, waiting for her to have a real home again.

"And we will, Princess, as soon as I can figure out how to do it."

The dog never looked up from the rope toy she currently molested. Jenn had found them at the feed store, and so far, they were the only ones that could withstand the gnashing attacks of the tea cup monster.

The man who brought the tree up for her lingered on her mind too. Why did she think she could help him? She couldn't even take care of her own business crisis. She was in no position to advise someone else. His easy dismissal of her in the light of morning wasn't something she understood. You never knew when that rug was going to be pulled out from under you. Life wasn't fair.

Like it hadn't been fair that cold winter day long ago, when she'd kissed a boy for the very first time. It was stupid, really, to want to have a blood bond. She'd read about it in a book she'd taken from her oldest sister's hidden stash, and she thought it was so wonderful. The girl would soon be moving far away. She'd grown up with the boy, her best friend, and they swore a blood oath to always be true to each other until they were old enough to leave their parents and wander the world together. They'd sealed the oath with a kiss. It was so romantic. She wanted a romance like that.

Besides, she was twelve, and her girlfriends were all finding boyfriends. Jenn didn't have one, and she wasn't sure why. They didn't like her, she supposed, even though she tried to act weak and needy and silly. It wasn't long before her true nature came out, though, and she couldn't help herself. She had to tell them what they should do.

"My curse in life, I guess, eh, Sweet Pea?"

The dog growled in response and ripped a clump of threads from the rope. Doggie, one, and rope, zero.

But that day, she'd lived a little of that book. A blood bond was a silly idea, given that she'd probably never see him again, but they'd done it. She'd kissed a boy, and she thought he'd kissed her back. The slight pressure and quick movement made her toes tingle and her breath come fast. It wasn't slimy, like she expected, and even in the cold, his lips had been warm.

After they pulled back, he'd done a nice thing. He'd taken her thumb where the blood hadn't yet dried and he wiped it on his jacket. There wasn't enough there to leave a mark, but she felt better when he did it. Then he kept her hand in his, and together, they turned toward the path down the hill. When they got to the parking area, her family was already tying the tree to the top of the van.

"There you are, Jennifer. Where did you wander to?"

"Rock, what have you been up to? You're supposed to be greeting customers. Are you sure you didn't hit your head when you fell out of that tree?"

The adults rapidly lost interest in them now that they were in sight, but two other boys, older and taller but with the same features as Rock, pointed to their joined hands and whispered. Then they snickered and laughed, elbowing each other. Rock dropped her hand like it stung him, and he kicked at the trampled snow underfoot. His face turned redder than the cold had made it. That didn't make the kiss any less real.

Was that why she'd been drawn to search out that tree farm, because of that magical day long ago? There'd been no guarantee it was even in the same family, and yet, it had been. Anyone could have been there the day she went, but it was Rock. And he saved her, like he'd promised long ago. Maybe the universe wanted them to have another chance.

That should have made her feel grateful, but loneliness ruled instead. Rock didn't remember that day long ago with the same joy she did. It burned brighter than Christmas lights in her memory.

"I'm heading out. Be gone when I get back." He punctuated the hard words by slamming the door on his way out. In the silence of the cabin, even Sweet Pea kept her comments to herself. Every time Jenn thought they grew a little closer, he did his best to push her even further away.

With a fresh wave of nostalgia and grief, she wondered how she could make things right again between them. Gathering a pillow that had survived her dog's attacks, Jenn curled up and wondered about the man and his resolution to keep her at a distance.

Chapter 14

He hiked up the mountain, breathing the cold morning air in and out in rapid puffs. The magnet of the past drew him forward, on the path leading up the mountain in the opposite direction of the trees customers fancied. His feet shuffled through layers of underbrush littering the long-forgotten trail. Beside him, Ranger trudged along without so much as a sniff at a bush, though Rock told him more than once to go back to the cabin.

His surroundings registered with him as his feet called an unconscious halt to his march. The pond shimmered before him, releasing its warmer steam into the air as sun pierced between clouds and glittered its surface. He sucked in a breath, pine and damp earth mingling with the memory of vanilla. It had happened here, right here where he stood now. His life changed in that one idiot moment.

He shook his head, looking down at the layer of dead leaves and thick ties of bare blackberries. The lake was still the same, though it looked smaller today than it had back then. Experience and time made everything shrink in comparison. Everything, that is, but his memory of that day.

In his mind, he could see her elf ears wiggling with each step. She never let go of his hand, carrying her cider in the other and blowing on it before each sip. "Have you ever visited a cider mill? I have. They're amazing places. Messy, but they smell wonderful. You should visit one someday, since you serve cider and all. I wonder who first thought about crushing apples to make juice?"

He didn't care, not then, and not now, and no, he'd never made it to a cider mill. When they reached the top of the hill, he wanted to let go, but she wouldn't let him. She pulled even with him and let out a gasp. The little lake, its surface still unfrozen but flat as glass, reflected bare trees and pines and the clouds above.

"Oh, it's beautiful. I never imagined there'd be a place like this up here. Where does the water come from? I don't see a river. Is there a spring? I bet there is a spring. We should explore and find out."

She carefully folded the paper cup and put it in her pocket, then reclaimed his hand and tugged to lead the way. He didn't move.

"Come on. We should figure this out. If it's a spring, maybe it's hot, and the lake never freezes, even when it's the middle of winter. You could have one of those spas, you know, where people go to soak in hot springs. Then you'd have a tourist attraction for the times you can't sell trees."

She never stopped talking.

"But then this place wouldn't be a secret, like only you and I know about it. I like having secrets with special friends. You are my new special friend. We should have a blood bond."

Blood bond. Now she was talking about something he could understand. He had blood bonds with his brothers, the older ones anyway because the twins were too little, and with his best friends from school. He'd never known a girl to want that, though. In his experience, girls didn't like a little blood.

"What could we use?" She dropped his hand, and he wanted to grab hers back. Something about her comforted him, and he didn't even know he was hurting. She scoured the ground, and her grin turned to a giggle when she pointed to a blackberry bramble.

"We should use that. I bet no one has ever had a blood bond with a spiny vine before. Have you heard of anyone using it?"

He shook his head, and before he could say a word, she grabbed it between two fingers. He heard her cry of ouch as the spine pierced her thumb, but her face when she turned back to him was triumphant.

"Here, now you do it."

Who knows why he did it, but he did. It didn't hurt nearly as much as his arm had when he broke it, more like a sting from a bad bug bite. When a drop of blood oozed out of his thumb to match hers, he might have gotten a little woozy.

"Here, now we rub our blood together."

She took his thumb and pressed it to hers and rubbed, and the sting of pain disappeared.

"And now what?" His voice squeaked on the words.

"And now, we're blood. Whenever you need rescuing, I'll help you. And when I need it, ditto for you. This is so much fun. We should seal the deal."

Where did she get these weird ways of talking? It didn't matter. He'd seal it, because he couldn't bring himself to call her a stupid girl, which would make him a dumb guy for following along.

She leaned forward and closed her eyes. Her lips twisted into a tiny circle and stuck out like a calf's did when it was searching for milk.

"Come on, we need to seal the deal." She made that face again.

"How?"

Exasperation came out of her like a swoosh and she put her hands on her hips. "We seal the deal with a kiss. That's what they do in books, anyway. We have to kiss. On the lips."

It was over fast, like a shot in the arm. He'd felt his face heat back then and told himself it was because she probably had cooties or something else icky. The thought today made him smile. Jenny's kisses were anything but icky. He sobered as he relived the past few minutes.

He felt like shit. It wasn't the throb of his broken arm or the twinges of stitches pulling on the back of his head. Even the memory of the nightmare that still gripped him at the edges of consciousness didn't faze him. He was used to it.

No, his stomach churned and his blood pounded because he'd said nasty things to a woman who was only trying to help him. While she might have startled him off the ladder, it wasn't her fault he hadn't been paying attention, lost in the past as he'd been. She didn't know about the demons he fought every night.

He owed her an apology. She deserved an explanation, but nothing he was willing to give would satisfy her, he feared. And she'd go right on trying to fix things, because that was her way.

Pacing up the land, his anger abated fully, and shame took its place. He wasn't mad at her. The anger he felt was all on him. What had the counselor said? The first step he needed to take was to forgive himself for something he had no control over.

Except he did.

Like last night. He'd avoided opening up to her in a way she wouldn't recognize the importance of, because she didn't know his story. Thank god they'd dozed off before she got a chance to ask her one question. He bet it would have been a doozy, and even more so now. For whatever reason, he found it impossible to lie to her, so vague prevarications would have to do.

She was smart, and she'd figure it out. It wasn't a product of his accident but a flashback. Soon, she'd put two and two together and come up with a solution she thought would be the answer. It was only a matter of time. Jenny would invade his space with his best interests in her heart. When he turned her away without further explanations, she'd feel honor-bound to go to his family and tell them. Too damned ethical for his peace of mind.

He'd overreacted this morning like he had back then. It didn't seem he had any more control over himself or his emotions now than he had back then.

"You're just a stupid girl." He remembered his words cutting through the cold mountain air as his brothers hissed and simpered in the background. Jenny stood gaping at him, her mouth hanging open on her last words of protest and a suspicious shiny brightness to her eyes.

"That was completely gross. You're gross and I don't like you. Go away."

He'd spun on his heels and gave his brothers a satisfied nod, but inside, he was so embarrassed, he almost hoped Aunt Debbie or Ma saw the exchange and made him apologize. He really didn't think she was stupid. Jenny was kind of neat, for a girl.

He'd pushed her away today because she got too close to his truth, just as he had back then. He was no better off for it, and neither was she.

Except maybe this would drive her away for good.

He stopped and listened, hearing no engine noise. She wasn't leaving like he'd demanded, probably planning to play housekeeper and nurse and who knew what else. Or she'd want to hogtie him in her little hybrid and spirit him back to the hospital, where she'd call his brothers and his mother and tell them all about his nightmares.

Not if he disappeared first. He looked down at Ranger. The dog gazed up at him with doggie worry and sat with a low whine. Rock couldn't do it. He hadn't planned for things to be on this path. He wasn't ready, or at least that's what he would tell himself.

"No, not yet. Don't worry, I'll make sure you're taken care of. You'll have a warm bed and nice life in a forever home. I promise you, buddy."

Ranger barked, then bounded off to water a tree. He trotted back when he finished and sat again, his interest shifting to the cabin below them. His ears went up, and the lolling tongue retracted into his head. When his body stilled, those big ears drooped.

Rock heard it then, the slam of a car door. No engine sound came next, but that was expected. It was a hybrid, after all. It wasn't until her tires hit the road that he confirmed it. She was gone, feelings hurt, just as they were decades ago.

He forced himself not to think about anything, a skill he'd mastered during the darkest days, and focused instead on putting his feet down without making a sound. Ranger slunk at his side as if he too tried to be silent. The curl of smoke from the chimney told him she'd taken the time to stoke the fire before she departed.

When Rock pushed open the cabin door, he half expected to see evidence of her presence, even though the car was gone. She always seemed to leave something of herself behind.

He found it in under a minute. On the couch where they'd wrapped around each other in sleep, there was a folder. A sticky note in bright yellow lit its drab color. He didn't want to read it, thinking throwing the folder into the roaring woodstove without looking at it would be the best approach, but he couldn't bring himself to release it.

'Rock, this is for you. I never got to ask you the question last night, and now I have twenty others. But I'll stay out of your way. Just thought you would want to look at these ideas. I wish you the best of luck with your endeavors. I don't know what happened, but I'm sorry. J.'

Chapter 15

The damn cast got in his way all day, making his patch job even more frustrating than it already would be. Monotony in the climbs up and down the ladder should hold his full attention. Rock had successful avoided thinking about his foul treatment of Jenny for most of the day, except for those times when his hands were busy but his brain was not. That would be most of the day, frankly.

His umpteenth trip down the ladder coincided with a vehicle's tires spitting gravel as it pulled off the road. It stopped long enough to move the chain, and Rock's heart did a funny off-tempo beat. The rumble of an engine clearly not a hybrid's brought twin sensations of relief and regret. She was better off angry with him and far away. "And that's what it has to be." He muttered the admonishment and tried to look busy poking through the toolbox.

Deke's truck pulled into the yard, not bothering to line up with the faded parking markers worn out by the tree farm's customers. Rock wouldn't have to worry about them again. Funny, this thought didn't bring him the solace it usually did. When his uncle pushed open the passenger door in time with his brother's exit on the other side, he figured it was too late to disappear into the woods to hide.

He couldn't exactly conceal the strange position of his arm, either, which he held at an angle at his waist. The sweatshirt was the only thing he could manage over the cast. At least it wasn't plaster. He remembered the clumsy weight of that from before.

"What happened to you?" Uncle Rowan walked up and tapped on the blue exposed by sleeves he'd pushed up to work.

Deke glanced at Rock, the ladder, up at the roof, and back again. "Is that how you broke it?"

His uncle was easier to distract. "Darnedest thing." More tapping. "It's made of plastic and it's like a net. Deke, come look at this."

Rock pulled his arm out of his uncle's reach and hid his face from his brother's prying eyes. He knew he looked like he hadn't slept. He hadn't, not since the woman who'd caused this mess left behind that note yesterday morning. He'd half expected her to arrive at some point to check on him. He told himself he wasn't disappointed that she hadn't shown up.

His nightmares when he did doze had taken on a new gruesomeness, and their subject morphed into modern times, when the face he watched take its last breath was one he tried hard not to think about when he was awake. Ranger laid over him and licked his face when he woke from that one. Since then, he forced his eyes to stay open, hoping exhaustion would guarantee tonight he'd sleep like the dead.

Like he deserved to be. That brief foray into uncharted territory with kisses that reminded him he wasn't a ghost were an anomaly he couldn't afford to repeat.

Deke's piercing gaze, so like his own that he sometimes felt like he looked in a mirror, ignored the cast. The worry wasn't hard to see. His brother did that a lot when it came to Rock. He had all his life, he and Jake both. Soon, they wouldn't have to worry any more. It was better that way.

"You want to talk about it?"

Rock shook his head, the movement reminding him of the shaved patch on the back of his head. If Deke saw that, there'd be no question of him being carted off to the ranch to recuperate. All it would take is Ma finding out, and his agony would be complete.

"You didn't mention the roof needed patching." Uncle Rowan stood up on the ladder, examining the old structure.

"Did you fix it?"

Rock nodded to answer his sibling, not wanting to explain the particulars.

Deke shook his head with a snort. "Still trying to do it all yourself. It's okay to ask for help, and to accept it. Will you ever learn?"

Without warning, the flashback bled over him like it was yesterday. *'Why do you have to try to do it all yourself? Aren't you ever going to learn?'*

The voice was a woman's, angry and snapping with the urge to fight. She'd been like that, always ready for a confrontation. He was the peacemaker, always ready to negotiate. At the end, their roles reversed, they'd each struggled to survive.

It was the innocent ones who'd been hurt the most, though. The two of them had skin in the game and the ability to affect the outcome, for better or worse. The others were pawns, sacrificed because there was no other way. Their screams were his, every night since then.

"Rock? Damn it, you're white as snow and you're sweating. Let's get him inside." His brother's voice came across an ocean's distance away and more.

"He's crying." A weathered hand on his arm accompanied Uncle Rowan's mystified tone.

Rock couldn't stop. Sobs shook him, coming from a void so dark, it swallowed any light shined its way. Hands guided him, but he couldn't see where they took him. When he fell to the ground, he wrapped his arms around his belly to protect soft tissue and waited for the kicks and blows to come.

Please, no. Not again. Let them go. Let her go. No, take me.

"What the hell's he saying, Deke? I can't understand it over the weeping. You think he's having a nervous breakdown?"

Arms pinned him in place, and he didn't have the strength to fight against them. One more time, he'd failed. He could hear their screams lifted over the laughter of their tormentors.

Something hot and wet hit his face. A low growl followed, then a high-pitched whine. Again and again the heat came, until his tears stopped. He opened eyes he wasn't aware he'd screwed closed and came nose to nose with Ranger's muzzle, and the cage in his mind morphed into the cabin in the open clearing.

"Well I'll be damned. The dog knew just what to do. Is he some kind of service dog, you reckon?"

A vibration of words in response felt through the arms holding him in a tight embrace drew his attention to his brother. Deke's eyes reflected the darker turbulence Rock was sure marred his own.

"Are you ever going to tell me what happened?"

Rock shook his head, trying to loosen Deke's hold at the same time. His brother didn't budge.

"I think you should go to the doctor."

His negative was undeniable.

"Not the medical one. The psychiatrist."

Not only no, but a thousand hell no's. With a low string of curses, Deke withdrew his support and rose sharply. His back said more about his disappointment than words would have as he paced to the cabin. Rock rose with a hand on Ranger's supporting back and trudged behind his brother. His parched throat made him believe he could drink the well dry. All he needed to do was convince his family to leave.

"Hey, what's this? You thinking about goats? I always thought they'd make interesting livestock."

Deke flashed a curious glance between Rock and the folder in their uncle's hands. "Goats?"

Uncle Rowan answered before Rock could say a word. "You know, to eat the weeds you don't want to choke out the trees. Like that blackberry, which I have to say, you've done a piss-poor job of chopping out this year. You'll be working all winter on that and well into next spring and summer if you're not careful."

Deke sidled over to read along with Rowan. The glances he shot in Rock's direction hadn't shaken its apprehension completely, but a glimmer of hope shown there too. He hated lying like this, but Rock nodded, as if he'd been planning this new addition all along.

"Hey and look. Cheese-making too. Always thought your ma teaching you all to cook was a good idea, despite what your dad said. Proves she's a wise woman, just like I always knew."

It didn't take him more than a moment to read the expression on Deke's face now. Yes, Ma would hear about it, and yes, she'd love it. And yes, once she found out, Rock wasn't going to have any peace.

>>>>>

"Sure, Shelley. I have things covered, don't you worry. No, I won't reorganize anything. I'll check expiration dates and dust the shelves and fill the orders and help the customers. I promise, that's all I'll do."

When she hung up the cordless phone, she sighed. Her boss clearly didn't trust her to stay out of trouble for the day. While Shelley wasn't happy about it, her doctor insisted on more tests. Jenn suspected fear about the results played a role in her sharp tone. Promising to be on her best behavior today was the least she could do.

Not five minutes went by before her personal phone rang. She lifted it from her back pocket and noted the display. Kate. Her sister would keep calling until she answered, so it was always better to get it out of the way quickly. She answered with a cheery greeting, suspecting what was to come wouldn't be pleasant.

"Jennifer, when are you coming home?"

She rolled her eyes. Kate might be a handful of years older, but she'd assigned herself the role of mother hen and guardian ever since Jenn had moved in. Well, those days were over. At least, that's what Jenn wanted to assure herself.

"Katherine? I am home."

Silence met her statement. When her sister spoke again, it was with the long-aggrieved notes of someone who's patience was worn thin.

"Come on, we both know there aren't big consulting companies in the foothills. You're working at a little shop, a nice temporary gig, but come the new year, you need to get serious about finding a real job. It's been too long."

Like she hadn't spent the last year doing just that. Jenn feared she might be blacklisted for her attempt to do what she considered right. At least here in Flynn's Crossing, she might find small projects, without the tarnish of being fired hanging over her head.

"I have a job, and I like it just fine. In fact, I'm helping my boss upgrade the computer system." She crossed her fingers, the ones holding the phone. "And I have leads on other projects." Did leaving the goat husbandry folder at Rock's count?

"They won't be enough for you to make a living wage, I'll bet." Her sister sounded almost triumphant about that.

"In case you don't realize it, sister dearest, the cost of living is much lower in the mountains. Princess and I are doing fine, great, as a matter of fact."

The sound her sister made was a cross between raspberries and a snort. "Whatever you need to tell yourself, Jenn. We can talk about as soon as you come back."

Jenn would bet the value of every item she'd ever bought for Princess ten times over that her sister didn't realize how smug she sounded, as if Jenn's return was a given.

"I'm not coming back."

Kate fell silent long enough for Jenn to think she might have hung up. When she finally spoke, a softer voice said, "When you change your mind, know that your room is still yours. I'm happy to help you, Jenn, and no strings attached. Don't you miss your old life?"

Jenn considered this. She found she was doing fine with the contents of her small apartment and her job. There was little she missed about the grinding hours and constant push to go further faster from her consulting years. She felt like she was on the brink of something amazing, an independence she'd never had before. Her greatest fear was that if she went back, she'd never have the guts to strike out on her own again.

"I'll call you when I'm not at work, okay? Love you." She hung up as her sister stuttered a similar surprised reply.

She was afraid. Afraid she would never find the kind of work she truly loved. Afraid she'd lost all momentum in having her own home and her own life. Afraid that despite her best efforts, she wasn't going to be able to provide for herself and keep Princess in kibble and toys. And if she was honest with herself, afraid that the growing feelings she had for a man who clearly didn't want anything else to do with her were going to distract her for life.

Yes, Rock had been hurtful and rude. When he stormed out of the cabin, she had a five minute pity party before the real reason for his gruffness dawned on her. He was embarrassed she'd been there to witness his nightmare. She dried her eyes and stoked the fire, moving around the cabin to fold blankets and straighten the meager kitchen to fill the time. When he still hadn't returned, she thought about leaving him the note to tell him she understood.

In the end, though, she didn't understand, not really, just like she hadn't all those years ago. There was no way to sugar coat that part.

"You're just a stupid girl." He'd thrown off their linked hands the minute they heard giggling hidden in the trees along the path. Two boys came out of the forest, pointed at them, and laughed outright. Rock had blushed a deep red and continued to yell at her until she turned and ran for her family's van, tears wetting her face like rain. She told her parents she'd tripped and fallen and that made her cry. It took her longer to understand back then that he'd been ashamed of getting caught holding hands with a girl.

There was nothing she could do about their parting now and dwelling on it would only distract her from what was important. Shelley needed her to mind the shop today without incident, and she'd do her absolute best to earn back the trust she'd miscued before.

She straightened displays and restocked nonperishable items, assisting the customers as they arrived for scheduled pick-ups and spur of the moment selections. When she sold extras with every transaction today, she felt proud of herself for finding a way to grow business. She checked the orders for the next day and filled them. When a customer complimented her on the tray she toiled over, she felt vindicated. She could totally rock this.

Rock. He was never far from her thoughts. She tried to set him aside as she had her sister's concerns, but with much less luck.

Jenn was nibbling on cheese and crackers for her late lunch when the chiming doorbell announced another set of visitors. Miss Emie came in with Marlee and Marguerite in tow, and the three of them grinned hugely as soon as they set eyes on her.

Emie swept Jenn into an embrace that surprised her. "Well aren't you as pretty as a picture show on Sunday." The younger women exchanged an amused glance as Jenn sought out their take on what that meant.

"Jenn, how are you? How is the job?"

"And how is that sweet little dog of yours?"

Questions rolled one on top of the next, and Jenn wasn't sure how to answer everything so fast. She expected to receive a chilly shoulder instead of this intense personal interest. By now, they had to know about Rock's injuries and the role she played in causing them.

The three women watched her expectantly. Her gaze traveled over them, noting no hint of animosity or worry. Relaxing a little, she figured they hadn't seen Rock yet or heard about his fall. But it had been two days. Should she worry he'd drifted off into a coma and no one knew about it?

"We're here to pick up our order for the ranch gathering," Marguerite said.

"And to plan for the New Year's Eve party we've decided to throw." Marlee grinned and wiggled her brows.

"And to tell you that Rock fell off a ladder and broke his arm," Miss Ellie added.

Jenn sucked in a breath.

The older woman continued, "He was working on his leaky roof, you see, and he must not have been paying attention to his footing. He fell out of a tree when he was a child and broke that same arm. And then when he was in the military, on some hush-hush mission he can't tell us about, he broke it again. Same arm, and the Army doctor said it was a blessing he broke it as a kid. If it hadn't reset the way it did back then, he wouldn't be able to use it after that secret injury. And now, again." She shook her head like it was a puzzle she couldn't solve.

"About that," Jenn started to say, then stopped. "I'm sorry."

Emie waved a dismissive hand. "Oh, don't worry, dear. Boys will be boys and all that. They've been kicked by bulls and trampled by horses and fallen out of or into just about everything you can imagine. They always survive."

Smiles continued as Jenn tried to comprehend how Rock's mother could be so understanding. After all, it was her fault he fell in the first place.

"I'm sorry," she said again.

"Don't worry, Jenn. It will mend," Marlee assured her.

"Now, about our orders," Marguerite said.

Jenn retrieved the trays for the winemaker, then wrote down the specifics Marlee dictated for a party for the extended Kermarrec clan plus families. Emie examined the jars of mustards and selected a dozen, saying they would be perfect compliments to the holiday baskets she was assembling for her close friends. As they gathered belongings and purchases, Emie paused once more.

"I'll show the baskets to you when we see you on Sunday, dear."

Jenn shook her head. "I'm not sure what you mean."

"Why, for dinner, dear. You have to eat. Sunday dinner is a big deal in our family. It's always big and noisy and fun. Say you'll come." She squeezed Jenn's hand for emphasis in a surprisingly strong grip for a woman of her years.

"Oh, but I'm not sure – " She was about to say she wasn't sure Rock would like her to be there.

"Nonsense. You're new in town, but I already consider you family, and we roll out the red carpet for new folks. Bring that sweet little doggie too."

They didn't know. That realization arrived, followed rapidly by the knowledge that she'd have to tell them. She hated the thought of killing off the delight on their faces.

"I'm the reason he got hurt."

Silence greeted her statement, loud enough to have her wishing for the phone to ring as an excuse to turn away. Momentary confusion cleared faster on Emie's face than the others. "Well, isn't that interesting?" Her eyes narrowed in sharp assessment while her smile grew wider.

"Interesting?" Jenn wouldn't call it that. "I didn't mean to do it. I startled him, you see, and he was up on the ladder, and he fell, and there's no cell service there, and he doesn't have a landline. I did the best I could."

Emie beamed as if this was the best news she'd heard in decades. The younger women exchanged glances and looked between Jenn and their mother-in-law with growing grins of their own.

Marguerite said, "Did you know?"

Emie shook her head, still looking pleased.

"Well, this is interesting." Marlee nodded with a chuckle and a shake of her head.

"That's what I think. Now, you'll come, and I won't take no. And if you're worried about Rock, don't be. If he doesn't mind his manners, I'll take things into my own two hands. He isn't big enough to frighten his Ma. Or as I like to tell the boys, I brought 'em into the world, and I can take them out of it."

The older woman laughed with a hearty guffaw, and reluctantly, Jenn smiled. The grinning threesome headed for the door, heads already bent in an intense discussion. Marlee turned and gave her a bright smile with a thumbs-up. "Five o'clock at the Three Rivers Ranch. I'll text you the address."

"I know where it is," she replied, then bit her tongue.

Emie did a little dance and gave Jenn a pert glance over her shoulder. "Well now, isn't that interesting too?"

Jenn stood without moving and pondered what she'd gotten into long after the tinkling of the door chime faded away.

Chapter 16

Rock rubbed the bridge of his nose, willing back the tension that threatened to turn into a full-blown headache or worse. Ranger pushed against his leg, settling his butt on the floor with a profound sigh. Across the desk, Ed grinned and leaned back in his chair.

"You and Ranger seemed to have established a major bond."

At the sound of his name, the dog perked up his ears, but he didn't lift his head from its place on Rock's knee. His eyes stayed pinned on him too, a point he noted as he tried to avoid meeting the counselor's direct gaze, only to run into the dog's.

"And what happened to your arm?"

"I fell." It seemed simpler to avoid explanations about that too. Like he did with his uncle and older brothers, he didn't make a big deal out of it. But it had put a definite crimp in his plans.

Uncle Rowan wouldn't let him forget the whole goats issue, saying maybe it was an idea worth exploring. Deke clucked over him like a mother hen, insisting he visit a doctor to make sure things weren't going down a slippery slope. And Jake, once he learned of the fall, stopped in whenever he was in the tree farm's part of county.

"Is there no crime or mayhem elsewhere for you to deal with?" Rock's words bit out of him when Jake made his third appearance in forty-eight hours.

"Nope, you're pretty much all the mayhem I have to handle these days." His brother grinned.

"Are you in pain?" The same question Jake asked him as he drove Rock to his appointment this morning didn't sound any better coming from the counselor.

Rock shrugged. "Been here before."

Ed leaned back and tapped a finger to his chin. "Physical pain or mental?"

Ranger slapped his chin on Rock's knee with a pointed whine, as if he understood the question. "Both," Rock grumbled.

"Want to tell me about it?"

No, he did not. He knew from experience, though, that Ed would keep the same inquisitive expression on his face until Rock explained. The man mastered the silences as well as he probed with his penetrating questions.

He used to be able to do silences too, pregnant pauses in touchy negotiations meant to disarm the other party and force them to babble. Now, they made him nervous. If he said nothing, he felt like he was letting someone down.

"I broke this arm when I was a kid."

Memory of that fall, the pain of the break and the lecture he endured from his father, while Ma fussed and iced and bundled him off to the hospital, still feeling fresh after the decades in between. Something else lit up his brain cells. If it wasn't for his broken arm, that afternoon at the tree farm when a pretty girl wearing elf ears and talking a mile a minute took his other hand would never have happened. That day had been an epiphany. It seemed some things were no different now.

"So, you're no stranger to the routine, or the itching that undoubtedly awaits you," the counselor said with a smile.

That hadn't been the worst of it when he was twelve. It might not be the worst of it now, either, unless he could barricade the road and hide.

"How are you sleeping?"

"Fine."

As if he intended to call him on his shit, Ranger gave his leg a nudge and rumbled, his expressive golden eyes focused on Rock. That dog pulled him out of the nightmares without fail, as if he had appointed himself Rock's personal guardian. Dumb dog, getting attached to someone like him. Still, he put a hand on big furry ears and scratched, and he swore the animal hummed in response.

"So, not so fine. Is Ranger helping?"

Rock wouldn't put it past the counselor to have planted the dog at the pound and introduced them, all the while knowing Ranger was trained to assist people with post-traumatic stress. Ranger put a paw on Rock's knee with a grinning pant. Damn dog could probably read minds too.

"He's sure become devoted to you. No one knows what his story is. They found him on a remote county road, wandering and scared and skinny. He'd been skittish in the cage, but it seems like he's found a kindred spirit in you."

Rock nodded. How would Ranger adjust when he wasn't around anymore? He hadn't thought this through.

The rest of his hour passed too quickly. Ed's questions barely distracted him from the place where his mind wandered too easily. A grown up version of the girl who could never stop talking, except for a brief few seconds that turned Rock's twelve year old world upside down. Since she had repeated her distracting performance twenty years later, he couldn't stop thinking about it, back then or now.

His mind was still on Jenny when he and Ranger left the counseling center, stepping into bright winter sunshine with a picture perfect blue sky. He expected to see Jake lounging on his regulation SUV cruiser, sunglasses hiding the direction of his eyes and hands resting gently on his equipment belt at the ready, but instead, he got an eyeful of Ma in full holiday regalia.

Today's ensemble consisted of a red and green tie-dyed skirt, popping red stocking cap, and an equally bright green fleecy jacket. Her barn boots stuck out under the hem of the skirt as she rested one heel on the running board of the ranch-logoed truck. She looked like a hippie version of Santa's elf. The thud of white mitten-covered hands clapping when she saw Rock was hard to miss, even over the town noise.

"There's my boy. How is your arm today? Jake had to go on a call, and I was in the area, so I came right on over." She tapped her cheek, and Rock leaned down to give her a peck, because whatever else happened in his life, he could never seem to tell her no. Best to get the acceptance over with and not fight it.

"And how is my gorgeous boy today? How are you, Ranger? Ready for some love yet?"

The dog slunk behind Rock and whined pathetically. He found it hard to imagine this was the same creature he awoke to when the darkness clutched at him, only to find the dog draped bravely over his chest, licking his face madly.

Ma stood with a stoic expression on her face. "Well, at least one of you is happy to see your old Ma. I'm usually the animal whisperer, so whatever hurt that dog, hurt him bad." Her eyes lifted to pin Rock's in an assessing stare. He knew the look. The comparison she made wasn't far off the mark.

A horn blared on the street, and despite his will to show no reaction, Rock jumped. Ranger whined again and pressed so close, it felt like the dog wanted to crawl inside his skin. He put a hand down on the dog's head to calm them both. Ranger's haunting memories might be as bad as his.

"Let's get a move on, son. Your chariot awaits. I've got a stop to make, and then we're on our way."

Rock groaned inwardly. Ma's single stop would never be just that. She'd called Flynn's Crossing home her whole adult life, and no matter where she went, she ran into someone she knew. That meant a gab session was in order, and Rock would be left twiddling his thumbs until she was good and ready to move on.

"Why don't you pick me up when you're done?"

"And how will you stay out of trouble?"

He had a single stop he should make too.

"Ranger and I are going to take a walk." A walk down to Main Street, and past a certain shop. If someone happened to be working today, he might even stop in. Closure. That's what this was. That's what it had to be. He'd been abominably rude to Jenny, and he never liked to leave business unfinished.

Ranger gave a huge yawn, and the sound he made with it came out like a disbelieving snort. He could almost hear the dog's thoughts. *'Whatever you need to tell yourself to make it through the day, dude.'* He wouldn't be far from wrong, either.

"We'll wait for you at the park."

Ma nodded, but sly delight came to her face. "Great view from the park," she said, nodding faster. By the time Rock had an opportunity to process her words, she was gone in a squeal of tires.

>>>>>

Jenn adjusted the crackers and stepped back, finally satisfied with the tray laid out in front of her. She was going to show Shelley she was indispensable, damn it. She was not going to lose this job.

The morning hadn't gone well. Her boss wore a serious expression in response to Jenn's cheery hello, and her eyes stayed troubled as Jenn recounted something she'd read last night about pairings of cheese and jams. The silence was enough to make her nervous that she'd done something to again overstep her boundaries. She wasn't sure what it could be. She'd been diligent to the letter in following the woman's instructions.

Without warning, Shelley launched in. "Jenn, I appreciate everything you do and what you're trying to learn about this business. I know this isn't the kind of work you're used to. I want to make sure we're clear. I may or may not be able to keep you on after the holidays."

Shelley continued, explaining that tourist traffic died down during the winter. Weekends remained busy, so she might need a little help then, but full time wasn't going to be an option.

Jenn's heart hammered in her chest as she absorbed the news. Being frugal was the only way she got by on a forty-hour workweek at her current hourly rate. Part time wouldn't cover her rent and basic expenses. If Shelley didn't need help, chances were other retail owners wouldn't either. She really didn't want to go back to Kate's with her tail between her legs.

Had she done the right thing, over a year ago? At the time, she was convinced her actions were sound. She'd had plenty of time since then to second-guess herself. If she'd kept her mouth shut, she might not be in this predicament today. But then she wouldn't be able to live with herself, either.

Nope, not going to worry about it anymore. She would focus, doubling down on her work and letting Shelley see how much she was worth. There was just no other solution. When the older woman received a call and hurried out with a distracted wave, Jenn vowed to have every single order ready to go by the time she returned. She'd be super-cheese-woman. Shelley wouldn't want to fire her after that.

She blinked rapidly, realizing she'd teared up without warning. She needed this job. She needed this town. A little voice whispered inside her head that she needed someone here too.

The picture of Rock flashed in her mind's eye. Not the angry, sneering man who'd kicked her off his property, but the one who occasionally seemed amused by her stories during the night. There was no denying their easy discussions, or the appreciation she noted in his warm gaze. The simple word 'like' didn't begin to cover the sparks in the air between them after their kisses.

If it was a side effect of the knock on his head or regret in the reality of daylight, she had no way of knowing, but Jenn knew one thing for sure. His kisses were not lame, and if they were any indication, everything that could follow would be amazing and toe-tingling too.

The bell tinkled and Jenn sniffed, moving to the sink to wash her hands as she called over her shoulder, "I'll be right with you."

The person who came in didn't move. Jenn turned with a shiver of apprehension, only to find Shelley standing inside the door with her cell phone clutched in the resting over her heart, her face paler than the paper wrapping her cheeses.

"Shelley? What's wrong?"

The older woman raised her face, exposing tracks of tears on her cheeks and fear in her eyes. Jenn rushed forward, her arms already outstretched, and she grasped Shelley's ice cold hands in her own. "What can I get for you? Would you like to sit down?"

The older woman shook her head. "I'll have to close the shop."

"But why? Shelley, what's wrong? You look like paler than a fresh chevre." She felt rewarded when Shelley gave a watery half-smile and a chuckle, even as her own heart pounded, and an instinctive churning began in her gut.

"I've had bad news, and I'm still trying to make sense of it. I have a tumor, you see, and the doctor wants to operate immediately to take it out." She gave a choked gasp. "Only when they have it out will they be able to tell if it's cancer, you see."

"Oh my god, Shelley, that's awful. Please, what can I do for you?" Jenn rubbed the woman's hands in hers. She couldn't imagine the terror of it.

"I have a sister, and I need to call her. She'll come, of course, at least for a while. She has a job in Chicago and won't be able to stay for the whole time." The woman's voice trailed off, and she picked up a jar of mustard and stared at it as if she didn't recognize what it was.

"I'll have to close the shop, and cancel the orders, and throw out the perishables." Her voice had fallen into a low register.

"But Shelley, you don't. I can run things until you come back after your surgery."

Jenn heard the mechanical whir of the refrigerators in the dead air that followed her words. The genuine fear she felt for Shelly coupled with the hope this could be her way out made the gut churn speed into full-blown agitation.

Shelley spun in a slow circle, her eyes moving from shelf to display around the shop. By the time she'd turned back, her tears stopped, and her body quit its restless movements. Her focus turned sharp, and Jenn tried not to fidget under the intense regard.

"I can't make any promises, Jennifer. I don't know what's going to happen, what they'll find. Even if things turn out well and it's nothing, that's no guarantee your job will continue long term. I might not be able to afford it."

Jenn was nodding even before she finished. "I understand. All I'm saying is that you have a choice. I can run things until you get back. I've learned which distributors bring us products, and while my trays aren't anywhere as outstanding as yours, I can manage. Everyone will understand, and your customers will be supportive. They're your friends, Shelley." She tightened her hands, finding her boss's warmer than they had been moments before.

"Are you sure? I'd hate to keep you from a legitimate job that you want, if – "

Jenn shook her head quickly. She wanted to reassure the woman there would be no legitimate job she'd be following. She'd overstepped boundaries and burned bridges and every other catch phrase in the book. Jenn had nowhere else to go.

A level of relieved resolve came to Shelley's features. "All right then. You have a deal."

Jenn tried not to let her relief show, because she hated benefiting from something so awful. She moved to the window and busied herself rearranging perfectly wonderful displays as Shelley spoke in a low voice in the back. Not wanting to intrude, she examined the traffic on Main Street. At least she'd get to stay here for a while longer. After that, she'd figure things out. She'd always been good at achieving her goals in the past. Now it was time to make a new plan.

It wasn't until her eyes roamed over the bench in the little park that she recognized him. His hunched posture and the big dog sitting at his feet were unmistakable. Her heart kicked up its heels, even as she told herself it didn't matter. Distance hid his expression, but his face seemed to be turned toward the shop as he sat in the afternoon sunshine.

She raised a hand and waved, then dropped it, embarrassed. Rock had plenty of reasons to be sitting in the park. It wasn't as if he was here to watch her. He swung a foot, kicking at the gravel, and it sprayed further on the walkway. He wasn't here because of her.

As if to underscore that thought, a truck with a logo on it pulled up at the curb, and man and dog rose. They got inside, the dog in back and the man in the passenger seat. The driver's identity was hidden in the cab's interior. He'd been waiting for his ride, that's all.

Jenn was about to fade back into the shop, her eyes still following the truck as it drove past. As it did, the man put an arm along the back of the seat, and this time, his face turned directly toward her. Then his glance drifted up to her apartment.

"Jenn, I'll need to go over the outstanding orders with you."

"Coming," she said, still watching until the truck with the man she couldn't stop thinking about was out of sight.

Chapter 17

"How's the arm?"

While Deke drove with the same intense attention to detail he used on everything else, Rock didn't see a way to avoid making conversation.

"Okay."

A quick glance told him Deke was looking for more. Stubbornly, he didn't want to provide it.

"Ma's really happy you're coming to dinner. Jake thought he might have to take you home in handcuffs, but I assured him that whatever you do, you wouldn't disappoint Ma."

The brothers stood united on that score.

"Marlee and Marguerite are pretty excited you'll be there too, though why, we can't figure. They sent Jake to the store for more bread, though we both know there's enough to feed a small army, and Uncle Rowan grumbled about his errand to the winery, even though Marguerite has a cellar full at our house to choose from. That left me to pick you up, and Ma told me in no uncertain terms that you needed to be presentable."

Presentable? He'd washed the grime away and dressed in clean clothes, and he'd even trimmed his beard and hair. None of this was easy to accomplish with one arm in a cast, but he knew this mattered to Ma, so he did it.

"Anyway, Jake and I are glad you'll be there. It will be as close to old times as we can make it."

That stabbed at him. The last time they'd all been together was when the twins graduated from college. Rock had gotten leave to come home for seventy-two hours, the shortest three days of his life. After that, he rarely had time to contact his family, much less visit.

He'd missed so many things, major events in their lives. Deke and Jake, both married and fathers. Disasters, injuries, celebrations, moments of tearful joy. He could never get those times back. The important work he'd told himself mattered more than the passing years didn't seem so all damned essential now.

No, the best he could do now was keep them all happy. Soon enough, they'd be disappointed in him one last time.

"Uncle Rowan's all fired up to discuss the goats. He says he thinks it's a damned great idea, and he wants to buy the beginnings of a herd after the new year. I have to say, I think it's sound too. You created a good business model, and those services are sorely needed by landowners around here."

Rock didn't know. He'd never read it, and when his uncle whisked the folder away, he put it out of his mind. That is, except for reminding himself a dozen times an hour that he still needed to apologize to the woman who came up with it.

It wouldn't be enough, not as an apology and not to satisfy the insistent memories. It didn't pay to compare the kisses from way back when and the recent past. When they were kids, that kiss was more a peck of smashed teeth to lips. The firestorm a few days ago had been a hundred times more intimate.

And her body, pressed over his as he came out of that nightmare, brought on a whole new set of issues. These were the kind he wouldn't even discuss with the closest friend he had. At this point, that was the dog.

Ranger must have heard his thoughts and sat up in the back seat. On reflex, Rock fondled the furry muzzle and got his hand licked in response.

"What kind of dog is Ranger, anyway?"

Deke's eyes strayed to the rearview mirror before glancing at Rock.

"No idea."

"He sure seems to be taken with you, though why, I couldn't say."

Rock thought he knew why. He'd rescued Ranger, taken him out of that steel cage and offered him a warm bed and a place where he was welcome. And a purpose. Rock was coming to expect he'd wake up with the dog's big body across him, panting and licking if he'd wakened him from a nightmare, and snoring dead weight if Rock woke peacefully. It wasn't the same as having Jenny's body draped over his, but it was as good as he was going to get.

Damn, there she was again. Fresh on his mind and vivid, despite his better efforts to block her from his memory.

He didn't even notice the turn under the big ranch sign. He was too busy berating himself for not being able to let it go. He wouldn't be able to, not until he said he was sorry.

"Hey, come take a look at the new bull. I think he's going to be a great breeder, which means by next year, the ranch can begin selling shares in the steers."

Next year. He wouldn't be here next year to see it. A pang made him gasp in a breath and for a reason he couldn't fathom, a vision of Jenny's tear-streaked face raced through his mind.

>>>>>

She wasn't sure which way to look, trying to take it all in and stay on the driveway. Pastures with neat rail fences lined the road, and in the distance, she saw cattle with big horns grazing peacefully. Closer in, horses trotted alongside her car. In her carrier on the front seat, Princess must have seen them too. She growled, of course.

"Those are horses. They're big, and they could trample you under one hoof. Promise me you'll behave yourself today."

The dog swung her gaze at Jenn with a look that might have been a doggie version of 'who, me?'. It lasted only a handful of seconds before the Yorkie's attention pulled outside to a pack of dogs of different breeds approaching the parking area.

"Stay out of trouble, Princess please? If you bite any more dogs, the nice people of Flynn's Crossing are going to shun us."

In response, the little dog growled. Jenn hoped the dogs were friendly as she pulled in between a shiny truck with the ranch logo and a minivan. By the time she retrieved the bag of goodies from the backseat, a knock sounded on the window. She was wrapped up in Miss Emie's strong embrace before her boots hit gravel.

"Oh, you made it. I'm so happy you're here. Did you find us all right?"

She never got a chance to respond, because Princess decided the attention should all be directed her way, and she set up a string of agitated barks. That drew the gang of lose dogs closer.

"Oh, don't worry. We're used to a ruckus around here. You got here just in time. Why don't we bring your little darling inside?"

She barely got the car door closed before Miss Emie sailed into the house, the dog carrier in her arms and talking nonstop to a suddenly silent Princess. Jenn followed along up the big front steps and the wide porch.

"I'll introduce you around to everyone in a bit. I hope you like pot roast, dear, because that's what we're having. It's a favorite of my sons."

Emie hummed as she turned away, a big grin on her face. Jenn took in the wide entry leading off to a living room on one side and a big kitchen on the other, all of it looking like something out of a midcentury ranch magazine. The appliances were new, though, and the place was pristine.

"Looks like almost everyone's going to make it tonight, dear. Just family, but we're a big one. I hope you don't mind that I consider you family too, dear."

Jenn knew she should set the record straight. The older woman must not have listened to her explanation the other day. She should tell her now, before things went further.

"Miss Emie, about that. I'm not sure you heard me the other day."

The woman waved a hand and shook her head. "Oh, I heard you all right. You scared that poor boy of mine right off the roof. I got that part."

That made Jenn stop her covert scrutiny of family photos on the wall.

"Do you want to discuss it before or after dinner?"

A man's voice she didn't recognize came from an alcove at the back of the kitchen. The sound of boots and other rustling followed, along with a thud of something on wood.

The same voice said, "Don't shake your head at me. You know we have to talk about it. Now, or later?"

Princess made a strange sound, a cross between a whimper and a growl, as scratching approached the kitchen. Emie turned toward the sound too, a wide smile on her face as she wiped her hands on a towel. She had those arms open once more as three men entered the room.

Jenn had a scant second to process what she was seeing, and about a second more to realize this wasn't going to turn out well. She didn't know the man in front or the man in back, but the one they flanked had been the subject of her overheated dreams.

"There's my middle favorite. Rock, how are you? And Ranger. Good boy, you know how to shake now. Look, Rock, we have a new friend at the family table. And I do consider her family already."

Jenn couldn't stop the heaving breath when Rock locked eyes on her. His eyes widened, and he mouth gaped open.

"You," he said.

"Rock."

It was all she could manage. His face was different, and it took her a moment to realize his hair and beard were shorter. Surprise in his eyes faded to anger. Jenn wanted to explain, but for once, she had no words.

Princess chose that moment to try to leap free of her constraining arms and in response, Ranger yelped and took off for parts unknown. By the time she could tighten her grip on the dog, the man had disappeared too.

The dog took her moment of distraction, her eyes on Rock's retreating back and the arguments raised by the other men, to break free and scamper on eager paws in the same general direction Ranger had taken, red leash streaming behind her.

"I'm sorry, I'll get Princess. Maybe it would be better if I left."

Emie looked unfazed by the commotion. The two men had followed in Rock's trail. Emie stirred something in a bubbling pot and wiped her hands again.

"Nonsense, dear. Family, remember? Now, I'll go after your cute little dog. She won't be a bother. And you go after my stubborn boy and talk some sense into him."

"What?"

Emie patted her arm as she removed her apron and hung it on a peg. "That's what I call him. My Rock. Oh, the boys think that nickname came from something else, but I know differently. Stubborn as a rock, that boy is and always has been. Now, you go after him. He'll listen to you."

Torn between finding the dog and fleeing the ranch or following Rock, Jenn took in the sounds of peace in the house. No yelping dog, no growling little monster. It might be her only chance, her last chance, to apologize to Rock.

She headed out the same door Rock had taken moments before. She saw him walking at a rapid pace across the parking area, the two men behind him. Their voices raised in worried words, and Rock waved his arm back at them as if he wanted them to leave him alone. He put his good hand on the top rail of the fence and jumped it in one easy leap as if he did this all the time. In a streak of brown fur, his dog leaped over too, trotting to stay at the man's heels.

Jenn rushed along to catch up, happy that for once, she seemed to have made a better footwear choice. The low heels at a jog ate up the ground quickly, and she soon drew even with the two men watching Rock pace away across the open field.

"What is his problem?" The thinner of the two shook his head and rested his hands on his belt.

"I am."

Her words brought them both to stare at her. The other man spoke first, extending a hand with a half-smile. "Deke Kermarrec, ma'am. This is my brother, Jake, and that idiot racing away is Rock."

"I know."

If they were surprised, neither one of them showed it. They exchanged a glance, and Jake gave a slight grin too.

"So, it looks like you and Rock have already made each other's acquaintance."

Jenn nodded, watching him grow farther away with each passing minute. She eyed the fence, knowing there was no way she could climb across it gracefully.

"I need to go after him and apologize. You see, I'm the reason he fell off the roof, and then he got mad at me later when I was supposed to keep him awake. In between, I thought things were okay. I should have handled things differently."

Another glance passed between the brothers, then they looked back at her. "How fast can you run?"

She looked at Deke in confusion. Was he telling her to run back to her car and drive away? She bit back the tears threatening to fall and lifted her chin in defiance as she let her words take over.

"You cannot make me run away."

Deke shook his head, and Jake chuckled. "Not away, after him. We haven't seen that much real emotion from Rock since he got back. All that feeling is a good thing for him. If you're the reason, then we say go for it."

Jake took her hand and pulled her, and when she was about to protest, he put his hand on a gate latch and swung it open. She didn't wait for answers or directions.

Jenn ran.

Chapter 18

Of all the stupid things. He wasn't sure who he was angriest with, his family for trying to put the one woman he needed to ignore in his path, or her for going along with it, or himself for saying he'd be here. A little voice in his head, the sensible one, said of course he was angry with himself, because the first thing he did when faced with an opportunity to say what needed to be said to the woman he wanted to avoid was run.

Rock continued across the field, not lessening his pace and not feeling any better about things as his self-loathing grew. The expression of shock and dismay on Jenn's face when she saw him said it all. She hated him, and he couldn't blame her. He'd been brutally rude to her, and she'd only been trying to rescue him from the pain of the past.

The blood pounding in his ears turning into a high-pitched ringing, and he shook his head to throw it off. As the ground began to rise, his feet slowed. It had been ages since he'd been up this hill. He forgot how long ago. Why this direction drew him now wasn't a mystery. The past met the present with a clash of staccato fire.

The heritage oak stood at the top, silhouetted against the sky but still bold in the dusky light. Branches hugged low to the ground, an unusual configuration for such a tree, and that was what made it special. As boys, each of them had climbed it more than once. He was the only one who fell out of it. He could still feel the slippery sheen of ice on the rough bark under his fingers. His foot landed on a patch thicker than most, and he lost his balance faster than he could grab for another hold.

His arm ached in memory. That same arm had suffered repeated injuries since then. This latest wasn't as bad as the last time, and not as bad as the first. Every time he wanted to be bigger and better than he had a right to be, he fell.

Remembrances had a strange way of distorting the past too. His reach to climb that lowest limb wasn't nearly as extreme as it had been that day. The blue oak didn't seem as massive, just as his temptation and determination to scale it as Deke and Jake had done didn't seem as important. He could probably climb it today, even one-handed, and with an ease that years of experience had taught him.

"Rock."

He spun to find Jenny bent over, hands on knees, pulling in deep breaths as if her life depended on it. She raised a hand and pressed it to her side. Ranger's lolling tongue tried to swipe at her face. Rock swore the dog narrowed his eyes on him in reprimand when he did nothing.

"What are you doing here?" Here could be a lot of things. Here, on his family's ranch. Here, at the family dinner. Here, in his life, where he couldn't ignore her.

She waved a hand and returned it to press her side. Her breathing slowed, but it did nothing to temper the bright red spots in her cheeks. She lifted troubled eyes to his. When gasps were no longer the only thing coming from her, the questions began.

"Why did you run away? Is this the tree? I know you hate me, but can I please apologize?"

The last one stopped his own mind from whirling. Hate wasn't something he had time for in his life, unless it was directed inside.

"I walked." That question seemed safest to answer.

Jenn waved a hand again. "Walked, ran, whatever. You felt the need to escape."

"Maybe I wanted to visit this tree."

"So, this is the tree."

He narrowed his eyes. "Who told you?"

"I was – " Whatever she was going to say next got lost when she bit her lower lip. "It must have been your mother."

Ma would be like that, clucking over him and telling a stranger how he'd broken this arm before. And Jenny wasn't a stranger, not any more.

"It must have been a fun climbing tree," she said, gazing upwards. "Where were you?"

He didn't want to be having this conversation. At some point, she'd connect the past with the present, and embarrassment would begin in earnest.

Still examining the tree, she said, "Why do you hate me?"

"I don't hate you."

Her eyes snapped to his. "Then why?"

Ranger whined, putting his big head on his paws and gazing at his master too. Rock paced away, unwilling to meet the pain and confusion in the woman's gaze. Like he had every time he'd tried to be better, he'd failed once more. Why did she have to keep asking questions?

"Rock, please, tell me. I feel like we were becoming friends, and now, you hate me."

"I don't hate you."

The explosion of words echoed off the tree's sturdy trunk. Ranger rose on another whine and came to lean against denim, pushing his considerable strength into Rock. The pressure offered both comfort and warning.

"I don't understand."

He spun again to face her and took a step closer. "Who said I'm in the market for new friends?"

Her eyes shifted away. He'd seen that same tell countless times, over too many negotiations to name. When it counted, he hadn't read it. All hell was to pay.

His hell. The hell he deserved and the price he had to pay. At least the worst of it would be over soon.

"We're already old friends." Back to looking at the tree, she evaded his direct stare.

She had to understand. If she became attached to him, it would hurt the more when the inevitable happened. New friend, old friend, it didn't matter. He had to make her listen to sense.

He took a step closer, close enough to catch the heated scent of vanilla. He shut his eyes. She'd even smelled of vanilla then. He recalled the aroma, reminding him of his aunt's cookies cooling in the cabin.

"Jennifer."

If his use of her full name surprised her, she didn't show it. Her face turned, revealing tears tracing rivers down her cheeks. The color from her running had faded and the pale left behind was as out of place as the exertion had been.

"I guess you really meant what you said back then. I was a stupid girl then, and I'm a stupid woman now to think those kisses meant something," she said, her voice muffled and watery.

He grimaced. All he could think about was how perfect their kisses had been, and how the idea that it could never happen again brought a twist to his gut.

"Don't cry."

She swiped hands over her face and lifted her chin, and he remembered that touch of defiance in her. That day, her sisters had nodded and giggled behind their hands, just as his brothers razed him. She'd pulled a queenly haughtiness out of somewhere. She'd turned toward him as her family loaded into the van and paused. When she lifted her palm to her mouth and threw him a kiss, he felt it hit him like a caress on his cheek. To say he had been shocked by that was an understatement without end.

Emotion he didn't want to call regret pulled the words out of him. "Blood bond. You and me. We'll always rescue each other." Except he was beyond rescue now, and the sooner she knew that, the better. "I shouldn't have kissed you. I'm sorry about the other day."

If his softer voice made an impact, Jenny gave no sign. She watched him for a moment before lifting her chin with a defiant glare.

"Well I'm not."

She spun on her heels and retraced their steps to the old tree. A sniff carried across the cold air to him, drawing him forward. Asking her forgiveness would solve nothing, because then she'd believe his redemption was possible. That would never be. If only it had been another time and another place, they would stand a chance. His chest ached with a swelling feeling he knew he shouldn't have.

He didn't see if Jenny's tears stopped as each firm plant of one foot after the other marched her down the hill. His gut heaved, as if her emotional pain was physical for him. Ranger stood and looked down at her, giving a strange squeak until Rock's feet began moving too. He stalked at his human's side with barely concealed eagerness to move them faster, glancing up at him from time to time with the same wounded expression Rock imagined colored his own face.

At the fence, his brothers glanced between the two of them and shut their mouths in matching firm lines. Jake held the gate open for Jenny. Deke offered her his arm, as if the courtly gesture was the least he could do to apologize for his brother's actions. Together, they filed along the path to the ranch house.

He expected recriminations, or at least questions. Instead, Emie informed the group dinner was on the table and they should wash up, pronto. She herded Jenn to a powder room and handed off Princess, who, for once, seemed subdued. By the time she entered the dining area, all seats were taken except for the one directly across from Rock. When Jenny dropped into it and eyed him with that same determined glint, he didn't want to look anywhere but at his plate.

"How are you enjoying our town, Jenn?"

Marlee's question opened a barrage around the table. Uncle Rowan shared a series of homespun sayings, timed to correspond with others from Miss Emie, and the group laughed more than once at their repartee. More than once, Rock glanced up to find Jenny examining him with a serious expression, despite her pleasant responses to his family.

By the time dessert was done, Rock felt like he was sitting on a bomb about to blow. He sprang out of the chair as soon as the last fork hit a plate and began to clear. When he reached across to take hers, she grabbed his hand, and he couldn't avoid looking into her wide eyes. The shake of his head had her loosening her clutch and turning away.

"So, are we talking about those goats now or what?"

Uncle Rowan glanced between Deke and Rock with an expectant nod.

"No."

The single word from someone who'd said nothing for over an hour froze his brother and uncle in their seats. Rock noticed Jenny's puzzled frown and the mouth he wanted to kiss more than anything opening to chide him. He couldn't do this anymore. The harder he tried to push her away, the closer she drew him into her orbit. He turned abruptly and clattered the plates back onto the table. He walked out the front door with Deke's heaved sigh and Rowan's sputtering following him.

He expected someone to follow him. In fact, he deserved it. Whether it was Ma's twist of his ear or Jenny calling him a fraud, he waited to see who it would be. When the minutes ticked by and only Ranger showed any interest in his abandonment of the table, his ill-ease grew.

Rock stood rigid next to the ranch truck, waiting. He knew Deke wouldn't be long, because he was sure his brother was ready to read him the riot act and call him a hundred kinds of names for his behavior. He had it coming. He would take it without complaint, because the woman who kept putting herself in his way didn't deserve his unfair treatment.

No one appeared to follow him, letting him stew in his misery for long enough to make him think he needed to go inside and let the apology burst out of him. It was odd that they were leaving him alone. Usually, his behavior alone would bring a brother or Ma on his heels to remind him of his manners.

He'd almost convinced himself to move when Jenny emerged on the porch, getting a hug from Ma and the women. When his brothers and uncle offered the same, he straightened. They were all too cozy, so something was up. As if he knew it too, Ranger gave a whine at his side.

It wasn't until she turned and spotted him that he could see her smile fade and indecision take over on her face. He should take this opportunity to apologize for his actions, both that morning and tonight, like he should have done on the hilltop. Rock wasn't sure why he couldn't, other than the moment had been ripe with other emotions. Now he had even more to apologize for and an audience on top of it.

'Blood bond. You and me. We'll always rescue each other.'

The words came back to him. Something about the lift to her chin as she marched across the parking area gave him a sinking feeling.

"Will Ranger be okay in the back?"

He blinked, not processing. In the big purse on her shoulder, Princess growled, but she quieted the moment Jenny told her to hush.

"The back of what?"

"My car. I'm your ride home."

As if emphasizing the point, the porch lights went out, leaving them highlighted by the barn spotlights. She didn't wait for his response but beeped the hybrid open. She slid her bag on to the backseat floor with more whispered words, then came around and opened the back door on the passenger side.

"Come on, Ranger. Up inside. We're going home."

The dog didn't hesitate, not even when the yippie little monster let out another round of high tones. He sat on the seat as far from the purse as possible and glanced back at Rock. His message was clear. *I'm willing to brave this if you are. Coming?'*

It wasn't that far. He could do this. It offered him the chance to tell her he was sorry and inform her, in no uncertain terms, that he would never see her again. That was non-negotiable. She got behind the wheel without looking at him, as if she too expected him to hop inside.

A curtain flickered over a dark first floor window in the house. He was sure half a dozen pairs of curious eyes watched their actions. Why Ma was doing this was no mystery. Ma had matchmaking on the brain. His brothers, though, were another story.

He didn't want to draw this out. The sooner he was back at the cabin, the better. With a determined step, he crossed to the car and slid inside.

If his action surprised her, Jenny didn't show it. She didn't say anything either, except to correct the little beastie dog whenever it growled. Ranger whined once, then stopped, as if realizing it showed his fear.

Never let them see your hand, and never show weakness. Those were rules he'd learned early on in his training. They served him well over the years. Now was one more of those times.

"You showed the goats project to your family."

Her statement was said in a matter-the-fact manner that was more conversation than question.

"They think it's a wonderful idea," she continued.

He didn't need to answer her. He kept reminding himself of that when her tires quieted on the main road.

"I'm sorry."

Her words forced him to turn to her, staring. She had nothing to apologize for, except being a caring person.

"I want to help you with the farm because then at least I know I can still make a difference for people. This past year has been difficult for me. I thought I had the world in the palm of my hand, and instead, I had shit."

He coughed on her words, because the curse was said in such a heartfelt manner.

She turned on her blinker at the stop sign. The pause she took was longer than necessary, since no cars came from any direction. When she glanced his way, he read the sorrow in her face.

The speed of her words accelerated with the vehicle. "I lost my job, because I did what I thought was the right thing. I compounded that by doing more of what I felt was the right thing, and now I'm blacklisted. If I lose the cheese shop job and I go back to my sister's, I'm not sure I can take it. I want something, anything, to work out right."

Blacklisted? He knew how that hurt when you were trying to do the ethical thing, the honorable thing. She didn't deserve this.

He didn't argue when she took the turn up his rutted drive. Only when she turned to him and reached out a hand did he meet her eyes. His hand rose automatically to grasp hers.

"Remember the blood bond, Rock? If either one of us needed rescuing, the other would come running? I think that's why I came here to the tree farm. I need rescuing, and in the worst possible way. Can you help me?"

Her hand was warm and small in his. Her grip tightened as if in appreciation of his quiet understanding, and her weak smile held both humor and bravery. Behind them, the dogs stayed eerily silent, as if they too were absorbing the moment.

The shift was subtle, so below his radar that he didn't realize it at first. Rescuing was his specialty. His chest expanded with the weight of responsibility. He needed to help her. He'd promised, long ago.

"It's late." His voice forced its way past a throat constricted with the moment.

Her expression fell into sadness as she attempted to pull her hand away. She shook her head, and that watery glow reappeared in her eyes. She misunderstood him.

"It's late, so if you'd rather not drive back into town in the dark, you can stay here. You and your dog." With silent apologies to Ranger.

She blinked, and a sunny smile came to her features one by one as if she couldn't believe her luck. "Thank you."

This was probably a bad idea, but once it took hold, Rock couldn't let it go. One more chance for vindication. One more opportunity to fight the wrongs of the world. One more person to save, successfully this time. One more time to show a woman who mattered to him what he felt, even if he couldn't say the words.

And then he could die in peace.

Chapter 19

The fire gave the small room a cozy serenity, and her eyes drooped. Jenn fought off sleep, determined to explain things to this stubborn man and make him understand. Snuggling deeper into the blanket, she tried again.

"But don't you see? I violated a client's trust by telling the other side they needed to look closer. I even pointed out where they needed to look. I shouldn't have done that."

She argued against her position and she knew it, but the man stretched out on the narrow bed shook his head.

"You righted a wrong. If that deal had gone through without the truth coming out, think of all of the people who would have been hurt." He already knew the deal fell apart, and it had everything to do with her. The situation primed her company and her client to denounce her in the process.

Rock said, "Jenny, look at me. I've been on all sides of nasty negotiations. If someone trustworthy took me aside and said I needed to look deeper at a promise the other side was making, I damned well would listen and be grateful for it."

"You called me Jenny."

He looked uncomfortable. "Sorry. You seem more like a Jenny to me than a Jenn or a Jennifer."

Sidetracked by this, Jenn sat up straighter. "What does that mean?"

Rock shrugged. The crackling fire was the only sound in the room other than snoring dogs. Princess and Ranger seemed to have reached an uneasy truce for the night.

"Warm, and friendly, and fun."

She bit off a chuckle. Those weren't the words anyone would have used to describe her in the past few years. Driven, cutthroat and obstinate was more like it.

She had to ask, because she'd wondered about it for years. "Why did you kiss me all those years ago?"

Those unusual eyes swung to her. It was hard to tell what color they were now in the dancing light. A flicker of some emotion she couldn't name crossed his face, then a mask dropped into place. "You kissed me, if I remember correctly."

"You kissed me back."

He said nothing.

She sighed and settled back in. She wanted to know why he'd allowed it, not when they were kids, but days ago. She'd blamed the head injury, but she had a feeling he didn't do anything without a purpose.

Drifting, she thought about that winter day long ago. The walk to the lake had been magical. She'd never seem so many tall trees or heard snow crunch underfoot. He'd held her hand and guided her around tree stumps hiding in the layers of white. Even the cider tasted magical, unlike anything she'd had since.

What would it be like to have that magic now? His kisses proved he'd grown up, but then, so had she. They could fix up this little cabin, making it a cozy retreat from the outside world. She'd help him heal the wounds he wouldn't share, and together, they'd run this farm and buy goats and make cheese. And at night, they'd wrap around each other for hours on end. If only she could get him to open up to her.

"Jenny."

The single word filled the darkness with longing. This mountain and this man were interconnected, and she was tied to him.

"Jenny."

Her name came with urgency. She shifted closer into his embrace and lifted her face. When his lips settled on hers, she heard music in the blood pounding in her ears. The confusion she felt in the kiss dissipated when she felt the press of his tongue. Opening for him was automatic, like a flower opening to the sun.

Too many layers separated them, and she shed the blanket wrapped around her and pulled at his. His hand, callused and rough, slid under her sweater and lifted it higher. A muffled oath as he struggled to remove his sweatshirt over the cast on his arm made her giggle, and his lips came back with an answering smile. The heat between them sparked like the wood in the stove, and it crackled in growing intensity as something cold nuzzled against her back.

Something cold and insistent. She tried to push it away, but it whined and became more determined. Then it vanished, and a curse came from the man she was wrapped around.

"Jenny? What the hell?"

She blinked at the confused tone. Trying to pull him back to her didn't work. Forcing her eyes open, she encountered confusion and dismay on the face above her.

She sat up fast, looking around. The cold wet something was Ranger's nose. The man looked anything but enraptured, his jaw pulled into a hard line like the granite boulders on his mountain.

Their situation said it all. Her shirt was gone. His was unbuttoned, leaving a tempting view of hard abs and a smattering of hair on his chest. The bulge marking denim wasn't something she could mistake. How had they gotten this way?

A dream. She'd been having a dream, and she'd acted on it. What the hell indeed.

She jumped off the man and the bed and looked around wildly for her shirt. Shivering from head to toe with embarrassed reaction, she grabbed a blanket from the floor, but it did nothing to drive away the coldness she felt inside.

"Jenny." Weariness sounded in Rock's tone. She sought out his eyes in the darkness and found him staring at her with an unidentifiable expression.

"I'm sorry. I'm so sorry. I must have been dreaming. Have you ever acted on a dream and didn't realize it was one? And then you find out and it's so mortifying? I'll leave. I'm sorry."

The man didn't move, other than heaving out a huge sigh. His dog lay down on the floor across the front door. Where had she left Princess? Oh yes, curled up in her bag on the table, so she wouldn't attack the big dog in his sleep. Unlike her mistress, who attacked the nice, big man.

"Jenny, come here."

She glanced up at him as she tried to find her boots. She had a vague memory of slipping them off by the door.

"Jenny, please, come here. It's okay. You did nothing wrong."

She waved a hand at him. "I just attacked you in your sleep. That's wrong."

He sighed once more and rose. The open shirt remained a temptation she might not be able to fight. Her eyes ranged lower and stopped there, unable to look away.

"It wasn't wrong, Jenny, not when I awoke and realized the wonderful dream I was having was real."

She froze, her eyes darting up to meet his. It must have been a trick of the fire, the change in color so marked, it took her breath away. He paced within a breath of her and stopped.

"I need rescuing, remember?" She gave a chuckle that choked in her chest.

His nod was solemn. "Maybe I need rescuing too."

This time, when his hand came out and tugged at the blanket, she let go.

>>>>>

If it had been a dream, he didn't want to wake up. It was better than anything his brain could make up and certainly more uplifting than any others he'd had in the past two years. The warm skin pressed against him was real, and that made him smile.

He had to give her credit. When Jenny committed to something, she gave her whole heart and soul to it. Her kisses were open-mouthed and as hungry as his. Her body wrapped around him so completely, he wasn't sure where she ended and he began. When she cried out in passion, the sound brought a light to his heart, a light he hadn't felt in a decade. When he entered her in a single stroke, he knew he'd come home.

This made lying next to her with peace in his body the hardest thing he'd ever done. Peace of the body was no substitute for peace in his mind.

The heat increased, and the press of flesh grew unbearable. Crammed together as they were, there was no mistaking the sweat of fear or the unwashed blood. His arm ached like fire, and the hallucinations of infection drifted in and out of his consciousness. A blackout would be a blessing, but he wasn't sure he'd come back from it this time.

"Talk to them. You can do this. You know how. Say the magic words to get us out of here."

The tone in the soldier's voice underscored his desperate pleading. Anger pulsed at the edge of it, anger because Rock wasn't doing what they thought he should. He couldn't, not when the risk to others was so great.

"Fuck you, Kermarrec. You're supposed to fight for us, not them. They'll back off once they know. Why won't you tell them? You know where they are."

Except he was afraid he'd already told them and his arm with its multiple cracks and tears was his reward. The pain of torture was like that, and he wasn't sure if he'd dreamed the unwilling disclosure or said it out loud in his delirium. Even at the price they'd all have to pay, he couldn't say more.

The first blow from his angered buddy came without warning, and he prayed it would be enough to knock him out. The physical agony was bad. The mental screams were a thousand times worse. When the true beating began, he didn't care about defending himself. He let them rain blows over him like the blessed showers of fall at home.

"Come on, fight, you fucker. Fight, so when I kill you for getting us into this mess, I know it was worth it. If we die, you deserve to die a hundred times over."

And he did. But he still couldn't tell them.

He must have passed out, because his next memory was being dragged through the sand by his feet. Bare skin peeled away. It wasn't even specific pain anymore. He was beyond feeling, beyond caring. He wished he'd taken the time to call Ma one more time before this mission.

The rumble of laughter marked the end of his journey. He didn't need a translator to understand the finer points of what the enemy said. They kicked him, and he couldn't bring himself to curl up. They kicked again, and he finally saw their purpose. When they rolled him on his side, he saw why they cackled with glee.

"No!" His scream split his parched throat. He couldn't hold it back. "No, please god no."

"Rock. Rock, sweetie, wake up. It's a dream, Rock. You're safe. Ranger, tell him he's safe. See, your doggie's here and I'm here and Princess is here. Rock, it's Jenny. Wake up."

He fought against the tight bands around him and the wet that teased his dried wounds. Nothing could wash away his guilt or his sorrow. They lay beside him like corpses as vivid reminders of why he had a final mission to complete.

The burst of ice hit him with an electric shock. He couldn't breathe through it. Shrieks as earsplitting as the scream of jets overhead rang through his surroundings. They came again, and when they passed, the empty void of silence was even more terrifying.

"Oh God, Rock. What did they do to you?"

He was dead. He had to be. He felt no sensations. This must be the moment when his soul left his body and began its journey into sure hell.

"Damn it, who do I call? How can I call? I can't leave him like this. Yes, Ranger, I know, you'll protect him, but I can't leave him alone. Rock, are you breathing? Say something, anything. Wake up, damn you."

He stumbled over the word. "Dead."

"No, you're not. You're breathing. You're alive. Here, feel your heart beat."

Something pressed hard to his chest, and it took time for him to recognize the shape of a hand. But maybe that was part of the devil's torture, allowing you to believe you were alive until reality hit you.

"Open your eyes. Look at me. If you don't open them, I'm going to toss another bucket of water on you."

He wasn't sure about much about hell and the afterlife, but he was certain it didn't involve buckets of ice being available to its inhabitants. Peeking one eye open to confirm this intelligence seemed a prudent course of action.

The sight that greeted him made him cry out. An ethereal woman rose over him in naked splendor, her mass of hair the color of newly hewn wood tumbling over her shoulders and reaching out to him. Next to her, a beast of an animal panted and whined in agitation. Somewhere else, another dog barked.

"There you are. Rock, do you know where you are? Do you know who Ranger is? Do you know me?"

She sure as hell wasn't the devil. Bits and pieces returned, then flooded his mind, and he gasped to control his panic. How much had he said? What had he done?

"Are you all right?"

She seemed stunned that he asked the question.

"I am fine, other than scared out of my wits. I didn't know how to help you. What happened to you?"

He dumped her aside but had no luck sitting up on his own. She shoved back with more force and waved an admonishing finger in front of his face as she straddled him, hot flesh to hot flesh despite the cold water bath.

"No, that is not going to happen. You pushed me away before, and it didn't work, did it? No, I'm staying right here like this until you tell me what happened."

Since right there like this included miles of pale skin and perky breasts that already had him getting hard despite the situation, he couldn't truthfully complain. He settled back against the bed, noting the soaked sheets and blankets beneath him.

"Sorry, you weren't waking up and you seemed so tortured, so I threw water on you. The bed's not going to dry quickly."

She didn't look in the least bit sorry, though. Her arms crossed in a move more defiant than protective of the gorgeous breasts he remembered loving a short time ago. Jenny's eyes flashed, communicating her commitment to keeping him in this position until she got answers. Ranger nuzzled his hand and he scratched the dog's ears absently. The wet underneath his back began to translate into cold.

"Are you going to tell me?" If she could have tapped the feet she had wrapped underneath her, she probably would have. Something about her expression of boundless determination brought the beginning of a grin to his face.

"Rock, come on. It helps if you talk about bad dreams. They lose their power over you then."

That sobered him up faster than a bucket of ice would have.

"Not dreams. I have nightmares."

When she replied, her voice had softened. "I know."

He shrugged, willing to wait her out. She'd lose interest at some point, and she'd start talking, and once he got her going on a new subject, she'd forget about this.

He wasn't sure how many minutes had passed. They continued their staring contest. No crackling warmth extended from the fire, and his body grew cold enough to make even the thought of hot sex with the demon woman in front of him inadequate to keep his libido burning. It wasn't until he noticed the sheen of goosebumps covering her skin that he relented.

"We can't stay like this."

"Then tell me what happened."

Stubborn, almost as stubborn as him. His grudging admiration for that was something he'd keep to himself.

"Let's find dry clothes," he said, hoping to distract her.

She glanced around, guilt crossing her face. "I think I soaked them all."

He stopped in the act of rising. "All of them?"

"Well, what I was wearing, and what you were wearing. They were on the floor by the bed, you see, and the water went everywhere, including the bed and the floor." She looked away. "And the sofa."

That covered every square inch where someone could sit in the cabin. Jenn's shivers grew in intensity, and she rubbed her hands on her arms. Her teeth might be chattering.

"We can't stay here."

Already striding toward the fire, he froze when a hand closed on his bicep. Looking down at it, the force of emotions hit him again, like another hard kick to the ribs. He liked the way her fingers wrapped around his arm, like they were never going to let go. He followed the hand to the arm and the face.

"We're not done with this conversation, Rock Kermarrec. But if we don't get someplace warm, we're going to freeze to death."

Freezing was not the way he planned to go.

Chapter 20

Jenn's heater blasted on high, raising the humidity in the car enough to fog the windows inside. Her teeth finally stopped chattering about five miles into their drive. He didn't want to break her concentration, not when she drove the dark road with precise care, as if every turn hid a nightmare. There would be time enough to talk when they were both warm.

Ranger pressed against the outer door of the back seat, as far as he could get from a growling Sweet Pea. Other than her dog's vocals, the only sound was the harsh exhaust of hot air. Jenny's unusual silence made him wonder what was going on in her head. He was sure her list of questions grew with each passing minute. First, their shared passion had been off the charts amazing. What did she think of his lapse into terror on the heels of that? He ached to ask but wasn't sure he wanted to know.

When they dashed through the cold for her apartment, he said nothing. When they got inside, she mumbled about dry clothes and closed the door to her bedroom. By the time she'd changed and reappeared, he still stood inside the door wearing his coat and staring at the Christmas tree.

"It turned out well, don't you think?"

It was a pretty tree, even if it had no ornaments for the first foot and a half. She crossed and hit a button on a remote, lighting up the twinkling lights. A beautiful tree, but the woman glancing between him and the fir was even more amazing.

He nodded. He didn't meet her eyes or turn her way but paced over to the window and looked down on Main Street. Ranger followed, tying himself around his legs. The dog's agitation wasn't too much different from his own. This might have been a bad idea, but he craved these few hours of solace in Jenny's presence instead of considering the past or what was to come. The burning torture of the last nightmare lingered at the periphery of his mind, taunting him with its horror.

She filled a kettle with water from the sink and put it on the stove. Sounds of rummaging in cabinets and containers and bags hitting the counter were the only noises. Her lack of words had him gulping down a surge of panic. As a master negotiator who used silence as a weapon, he recognized her self-same skill. He would answer her questions honestly, even if what he wanted most of all was to bury himself in her kisses and never let go.

"Are you still cold?"

He shook his head, blankly absorbed by the sights below him. Little activity marked the street at this hour, with nothing enthralling to keep him turned away. He was avoiding her and avoiding this discussion. He was a pro at keeping his thoughts to himself. If only the room didn't fill with the scent of vanilla and warm woman.

"Do you like marshmallows?"

That made him turn in disbelief. The pleasant grin didn't quite reach her eyes, but she put a brave face on whatever she was feeling. In one hand, she shook a container of cocoa powder at him. It was only when he examined the spoon in the other that he noticed she trembled.

"Marshmallows?"

"In your hot chocolate. It's soothing for both cold and grief."

He shut his eyes and shook his head. "You have no idea what you're talking about."

She regarded him closely. "Maybe not. Why don't you enlighten me?"

"I am not talking about it." He took a pace forward. If he intended to look menacing, he missed the mark. She probably saw the fear in his eyes.

The kettle whistled, and she lifted it from the stove and poured steaming water into the mugs. The aroma of comfort wafted through the room. She stirred the spoon in one, carrying it across to Rock.

"Take your coat off and stay awhile. I promise not to interrogate you."

Something in her words froze him in the act of taking on the mug. He met her eyes, the terror something he couldn't hide for a second before he forced an expressionless curtain to drop.

Acting like his behavior didn't bother her, she retrieved her mug and dropped to her sofa. "How about if I ask you yes or no questions? You can choose to answer or not. No explanations, just yes, or no. Deal?"

A shrug was the only response he gave her, but he settled into a dining chair. His eyes remained glued on her, and she gave an encouraging smile.

"Are the nightmares of something real?"

He hesitated, trying to decide if answering at all was a good idea. Still, they'd shared something amazing tonight, until his past made it ugly. She deserved to understand. Then it would all make sense to her someday. He offered a single nod.

"Did they happen to you?"

A shiver racked through him, but he nodded again.

"When you were in the military." He tilted his head to this to remind her she needed to ask simple questions. "Did they happen to you while you were in the military?"

He nodded more easily this time.

"Were you hurt?"

He looked away, and this time he spoke his response. "I was injured, but not as badly as others were."

Jenny slipped off the sofa and came to his chair, dropping to her knees at his feet. Ranger moved over readily, and she leaned into Rock as the dog did. "If you talk about it, you take away its power over you."

He snorted at the absurd idea. "It's all on me, and nothing will change that. Stop trying, Jenny. I can't talk about it. I won't." He fell silent and looked away.

"Nothing is as bad as we think it is in the cage of our own minds. Talking about it helps us break free."

The wince wasn't something he could hide, not when she pinned him in her assessing gaze. He swallowed the twin feelings of vulnerability and loneliness. He had no right to twist her life up like this. When she wrapped her arms around his legs and hugged hard, her cheek came to rest on his thigh. She let the silence fall and might have drifted off to sleep.

His hand lifted without his conscious command and ghosted over her hair. She would never know how precious this time with her was. He could never tell her, because she'd never let him go. Her arms stayed wrapped tight around his legs like her caring wrapped tight around his heart. Rock knew he should push her away, but his power to do it drained away with the last of his energy.

Jenny's even breathing produced a faint snore, a sound he found intimate and engaging. He wanted to hold on to this moment, this time when he didn't have to move forward or back but only had to keep his fingers pressed into the soft curls under his hand. Rock was afraid to sleep, afraid of what might come to visit in the middle of the dark hours, so he kept watch. He'd stay here as long as she let him, until he was forced to set her free.

Snippets of earlier came back to him. The tender pressure of her kiss as she coaxed him into another round. Her bubble of delighted laughter when he grabbed her and tickled her. Passion shared, something he hadn't hoped to experience again in this lifetime. The essence of love, something pure and right, that he never hoped to experience.

Regret chased on the heels of that thought. He would never have another chance to make amends. Penance wouldn't bring forgiveness. His soul would never be his own because of the souls of others weighing on it. This was something he had to do.

"You're thinking awfully loudly."

Despite his dark thoughts, he smiled, his hand stilling. "You should sleep."

"You should sleep too." She raised her head, pinning him with wide chocolate eyes that didn't hide her conviction. "Unless you're afraid the nightmares will come back. We can talk, if that's what you want." She took his hand in hers. "Just talk."

"Sweetheart, the nightmares always come back." The endearment slipped out naturally, as if his subconscious already recognized the important role she played in his life. She fussed with the corner of his jacket, giving it a tug.

"Why don't you take your coat off and stay awhile, soldier?" The Mae West impression wasn't great, but he enjoyed it anyway, almost as much as the sweet aroma of vanilla that always seemed to surround her.

By the time he pushed his good arm out of a sleeve, she was already on her feet, assisting the slide of material over cast. She came back and took his hand, pulling with a slight tug that had him on his feet. She walked backwards to the couch and sat, patting next to her. When he obeyed, she snuggled in tight with her arm across his chest as if she planned to protect him.

"What branch of the military were you in?"

Name, rank and serial number, ma'am. He could do this.

"Army."

He felt her slight nod. "What part?"

"Rangers."

She pushed up at that, looking between him and the dog. "Is that why you called him Ranger?"

The dog picked up his head at the name, regarding them solemnly.

"No, the shelter staff named him Ranger, because he was found near a forest ranger fire station. No one knows his story."

"Just like no one knows yours."

Her calm point made him lock eyes with her again. No guile or accusation shown there. She waited with more patience than he'd thought she'd have. He relented. He didn't think he'd have any other choice. It had become important that she understand.

"I was a hostage negotiator. Often my missions entailed defusing situations where prisoners were involved."

"Hhmmm."

The noise didn't tell him what she thought about this, but he'd be damned before he'd defend it. That was it, all he was going to say.

"So, we could say your job was to rescue people."

When she put it like that, he had to agree.

"You rescued Ranger."

He was beginning to think that had been a part of some higher power's plan.

"You rescued me."

He met her gaze. "You don't need rescuing."

She shook her head hard. "I do, and you did. You just don't realize it. It's part of who you are, and it's so deeply engrained in your make-up, you don't recognize it. People rely on you and you always step up with unselfish giving. You should give yourself credit for that."

She didn't understand, and she never would, because he would never tell her.

She didn't press him on it as he had expected. Damn the woman, she was never doing what he expected. She only smiled at him, glancing at the window.

"It's getting light outside. Another day. We never know what will happen. Today, Shelley has her surgery, and she finds out what she faces in her future. Someone will lose a job. Someone will get a new one. People are born. People die."

Her face fell into somber shadows, and he'd give anything to chase those away. She gave a funny scowl, wrinkling her nose and shaking her head. When she met his gaze head on, the tears mixed with a smile surprised him.

"I didn't tell you everything about why that day at the tree farm when we were kids was such a happy memory for me. You see, it was the last time my family was happy. Dad flew off for a business trip the next day. Mom had a routine doctor's appointment on Monday, nothing anyone was concerned about. That's when they found it. Cancer, and so widespread, there was nothing they could do. It grew so fast, she was incapacitated by spring, and by summer, she was gone."

"I'm sorry for your loss." He'd said the words enough times over the years to realize they were meaningless. Discomfort over the future and when those words would soon be uttered again made him shift in his seat.

"She's no longer in pain, and that brings me comfort. The point is, with my life falling apart, I returned to a place where things made sense. It certainly doesn't in my present situation." She shook her head, the curtain of hair hiding her face from his view. He fought the urge to push it away, to see what emotions held her in their grip now. His hand came out anyway, stroking curls behind her ear and caressing her cheek.

If only he'd met her again years ago, before significant aspects of his life took turns from which there would be no recovery. She called him unselfish, but he was going to engage in the ultimate selfish act. He knew that's what it was.

A little voice inside him murmured a single word. Coward.

Burying the roughness in his heart in a calm tone, he said, "What would it take to get your life back on track?"

She gave a watery laugh as she nuzzled closer to him. Her cheek rested on his chest, and her arms encircled him once more. When he dropped his face into her hair, he wanted to forget about the past and the future and live in the present forever.

"It would take a miracle, but I believe in them. I love to learn new things, and I don't mind hard work. I want to return to consulting, but for myself instead of inside a big company. Starting a new business is hard, though. It takes time, and it takes contacts. I'm out of both."

His lids drooped, the reactions of the night catching up with him. A germ of an idea teased the edge of his consciousness, something he could do as a final act of unselfishness. The harder he chased it, though, the faster it ran, until he gave up the fight to follow and relaxed into the embrace of her peace.

When he awoke again, he dragged himself to the surface with an effort of will. His muscles felt leaden, like he'd slept for a week deeper than the dead. The metaphor wasn't lost on him.

A sound caught his attention, a murmuring voice in a singsong tone with words too low to hear. That forced his eyes open, searching for its source. His gaze settled on a woman crouched low on the floor, eyeball to eyeball with his dog.

"Come on, Ranger, you have to eat. Look, I even added broth to your kibble. Princess ate all of hers. Why aren't you eating?"

Ranger gave a deep sigh in response. Rock moved a silently as possible to a seated position, but his rustling was enough to be sensed by the dog, who immediately lifted his head with brighter eyes. Jenn looked over her shoulder too, and she offered him a tentative smile.

"Good morning. You slept so deeply, I didn't want to wake you. The dogs had a constitutional across to the park. I thought Ranger might be hungry, because Princess certainly was, but he won't eat."

She was already showered and dressed in fresh clothes, he noted, and he pushed away the stab of disappointment that brought. Moving on. They'd had a wonderful, unexpected evening, something he could hold close and remember at the end, and that was going to be good enough for him. It had to be.

"He is a mystery. Ranger, eat."

At his single order, the dog dove into the food bowl and wolfed down kibble. Jenn shook her head.

"I used that same word, and he didn't listen. I guess he's so fixed on you that he won't eat unless you give him permission for it. That's some major command mojo you've got going on, Mr. Kermarrec." She stood, but he noticed her eyes wander down his frame, resting at the one spot that perked to attention and saluted her interest. He shifted to make the denim more comfortable.

A bright spot of color appeared on the cheek he could see. She moved to the fireplace that had been dark last night and lifted a poker to move a log. The fire burned with enthusiasm, almost as much as his body did for her.

"Where did you learn to build a fire?"

Jenn shrugged. "I watched you. I told you, I enjoy learning things. I pay attention to things around me, because I'm never sure when I'll need information or a skill. Situational awareness, I think that's what you call it in the military. In consulting, it's bread and butter to our work. I always try to absorb as much about human nature and what makes people tick as I can, plus build solid skills. Ergo, I have just added fire-starting to my list of accomplishments." Despite the upbeat words, her expression drooped.

"Well, you did a great job with the fire. I wonder what other things you could take on and be great at." He turned away, reaching for his jacket on the back of the couch. With her lack of response, he glanced over his shoulder, to find her staring at his ass with a bemused expression. He smiled at the thought that at least he wasn't the only one suffering from a lack of concentration.

"I learned about cheese. Not everything, of course, but enough to get started. And on that note, I have to go to work soon. Do you want a ride back to the cabin?"

Of course she had to leave, much as he wanted to convince her differently. A glance at the clock on the mantle confirmed the time. He may as well find breakfast and wait for his counseling appointment. Something told him he needed to find a quiet place and think, because something opened up a realm of possibilities in a way he hadn't anticipated.

"Thanks, but I have a meeting."

She cocked her head and he could see the sparkle of interest in her eyes, but she didn't press him. She lifted her big purse. From a ridiculously large dog bed on a platform by the window, Princess growled.

"Your dog is an interesting piece of work, you know."

Jenn gave a chuckle. "She is that. You'll note that there are no decorations on the bottom couple of feet of the tree. And there are no pillows left. And that cushion on the seat of the couch is chewed at the corner. Princess Sweet Pea stays busy while I'm at work."

He met her chuckle with his own. When she drew close, it seemed the most natural thing in the world to pull her in and place a kiss on the top of her head. She leaned back and looked up at him. "Have a nice day, Mr. Kermarrec."

Her smile brightened the room. She didn't ask if he was coming back or if they would see each other tonight. The acceptance of the status quo was so unlike her, he wondered if she regretted last night. He didn't have a chance to linger long on that thought, because she reached up and grabbed his beard, pulled his face down, and kissed him with enough enthusiasm to curl his toes.

Chapter 21

She fought the desire to stand at the window and examine every person on the street, but she failed. She also tried not to look at the clock, but it was impossible to avoid too. Thankfully, a steady stream of customers distracted her. Many, she suspected, came as much for news about Shelley as a selection of her shop's products.

"No, I'm sorry, no news yet." She'd repeated the words countless times today. At least getting this part over with and knowing what lay ahead would bring her boss relief. Jenn didn't want to consider the ramifications of the opposite. It hadn't taken long for her to become fond of the woman.

After the lunch time rush, she turned the be-back-in-fifteen sign on the door and was about to twist the lock when a form darkened the sidewalk. She did a double take when she looked up, and pulled the door open fast enough to cause a gust of wind.

"Hi."

Rock smiled, though she detected the uncertainty in the expression. "Hi, Jenny."

She'd never liked the nickname, except from his lips. Man-o-man, those lips. And what he'd done today made them even more accessible.

The beard was short, a finger length trim, and his hair was no longer the shaggy mane it had been this morning. Coupled with what looked like a new shirt and faded denims under the army jacket, he looked good enough to eat. And she, no surprise, was hungry.

"I brought us lunch." He lifted a heavenly smelling bag. Leaning closer, she sniffed.

"How did you know a Reuben was my favorite?"

He smiled a genuine grin this time. "I saw a wrapper from this place in your trash the night I brought your tree up. Situational awareness, remember?" He tapped his temple.

She grinned in return, glancing down at Ranger. "I'd invite you in, but health codes." She trailed off.

"I understand. Maybe we could sit in the park? It's a beautiful day."

Looking up, she realized it was sunny, the sky such a perfect color of blue that it should be a paint tone. She hoped it was portentous for the rest of the news today.

She grabbed her coat and purse and locked the door behind her. "I have to get Princess. She expects me to bring her out at lunch time. Sorry, it won't take me long." Maybe she could stretch the fifteen-minute rule just a bit today.

The dog was sitting on her window perch, barking loudly at the street below when Jenn entered. As if they could hear her, man and dog below looked up. Rock shook his head. Ranger dropped his ears back and averted his eyes.

"You have to behave today, Princess." Though why today should be any different from when Jenn intoned those same words to the heartless creature, she wasn't sure. "We're going to have lunch in the park today. You like the park."

Adding a coat and the red bejeweled leash to the dog's collar, Jenn rushed back down the stairs and burst on to the empty sidewalk. Glancing up and down, she found Rock a couple of doors down, head bent in conversation with another man. As if on cue, they both looked up at her and stopped whatever they were saying. The other man smiled at her, and she smiled back, willing Rock to grin too. He didn't. In fact, his expression bore that distant lack of emotion. When she drew close, Ranger whined and pressed against Rock, and his hand came down to stroke the dog's ears.

She stopped next to Rock, who was living up to his nickname in a major way. Princess barked in her arms, showing her teeth, and the other man chuckled. He looked between Jenn and Rock as if he expected an introduction. When none came from the slab of granite next to her, Jenn offered her hand.

"Hi, I'm Jenn Stanton, a friend of Rock's."

The other man pumped her hand while darting glances at the silent statue. "Ed delCampo, also a friend of Rock's." His gaze sharpened as he turned his attention back to Rock's expressionless face.

"So, see you at two o'clock."

Rock opened his mouth, and she suspected he was about to argue, but one stern glare from Ed made him turn away with a single dismissive nod. Ed gave her a smile and said it was nice to meet her. Before the time pleasantries were done with, Rock was striding across the street toward the park, with Jenn forced to race along to catch up.

He dropped on a bench and lifted his face to the sun. Closed eyes and an empty expression didn't change when she sat next to him, and she wondered what he was thinking. Whenever she thought they were growing closer, he drifted away from her to a place she could not reach. She put Princess down and nudged him.

"Twelve minutes and counting. My lunch, sir?"

His eyes popped open and looked at her with apparent surprise. He handed the bag over, and she peeked inside.

"I see there's enough for two. Did you intend on sharing this fine meal with me?"

He blinked at her and frowned.

"What? You brought me corned beef and I'm hungry."

She unwrapped a sandwich and bit into it with a contented sigh, watching Rock shake his head from under her lashes. At his side, Ranger tried to crawl under the bench, but Princess was there already and growled her usual warning.

"It's okay, boy. Don't let the little girl scare you."

Jenn smiled into her bite, wondering if Rock was talking to the dog or to himself. He joined her in eating, though, and soon, his gaze rested on her in speculation.

"You didn't ask."

She shrugged.

"Ask how I know Ed."

She swallowed and examined him closer. "Should I? You grew up here. I imagine you have plenty of friends, and they're happy to see you again. How was your meeting this morning?"

He took a large bite and chewed. A standard avoidance technique, she supposed, but she wasn't going to call him on it. Before he could repeat the gesture, she put a hand on his arm.

"Thank you for bringing me lunch. It was very sweet of you. I didn't expect it. Left to myself, I would have had a bowl of cereal." She wasn't going to explain that take-out was becoming a treat she could ill afford.

Instead of commenting, he glanced down at Princess, who was doing her best to beg her way into Jenn's lap for a bite of sandwich. "She's wearing her jewels today."

Jenn nodded with a snort of humor. "Yes, she is, and you'll soon see why."

She finished off the last bit of this half and closed the paper. Princess's tail stopped wagging and she jumped back to the ground, as if she knew there'd be no treat for her. As soon as she hit the pavement, she grabbed the leash in her teeth and began wrestling with it.

"You see, that's why this is our favorite leash. She can't bite through the rhinestones, and soon, she gives up. Those little teeth of hers are like a piranha's mouth."

Ranger peeked around a leg to see what was going on. Princess dropped the leash, her attention focused on a bird settling in a nearby shrub.

"I think she has the doggie version of ADHD," Jenn said.

"Ranger has PTSD, so it's possible," Rock replied, then looked away as if he wanted to take the words back.

She blinked, opening her mouth to ask how he knew. Rock gave his watch a deliberate examination. "You'll be late."

Jenn wanted to pursue the conversation, but she recognized it would be futile. Rock would talk when he wanted to, and nothing she said would change that. Putting the best face on things might be her only option.

She rose, letting Princess sniff at the end of her lead. "Thank you for the lunch, kind sir. I hope we can enjoy a nice meal like this more often. Now, to work for me, and an appointment on the horizon for you."

He grimaced, though if it was at her nonchalant tone or the message, she wasn't sure. He rose too. Ranger stayed plastered to the concrete, whining with his eyes on an approaching Princess. Jenn scooped up the dog just in time.

Rock looked at the bundle in her arms and back in her face. She wanted to reach up as she had this morning and kiss him. As if he had the same thought, he put a big hand on her Yorkie's head to remove the threat.

His lips were warm. He tasted of rye bread and dressing and all thing unctuous that had nothing to do with a sandwich. An arm wrapped around her as if he didn't want to let her go. She echoed that sentiment in quadruplets. As if he read her mind, he deepened the kiss, dancing tongue on tongue. She swore she heard jungle drums.

The jerk when he moved brought her out of the reverie. "Ouch." He shook his hand and she saw blood oozing from his palm.

Princess looked damned pleased with herself, and Jenn could only groan.

>>>>>

Ed's silence during his relentless examination of Rock's face and his hand and back again didn't shut down the questions in his eyes. He might have been biting off a grin as he leaned back in the chair, enjoying this far more than Rock had ever seen him.

"So? Want to talk about it?"

Rock looked at Ranger. The dog stared back as if he too wanted an explanation. The sight of blood on his master's hand had made the dog frantic with worry, which played out by wrapping his body as tightly between and around Rock's legs as he could. That made walking up the stairs to Jenny's apartment a challenge.

Jenny only stopped apologizing to lecture the monster in her arms. Her exasperation and embarrassment were clear in the tone she used when she locked the dog in the bathroom with an admonishment to think about how sorry she was.

"How about this, then? A little bird told me you were lip-locked with the vicious attacker's owner when you got bitten."

Rock pivoted his gaze to Ed, who was now smiling widely. If he didn't confirm or deny, maybe the counselor would drop it.

Ed shrugged. "Small town. News travels fast. It so happens my boss was on the street and saw you. She wanted to help, but your girlfriend seemed to have things well in hand, so to speak." He chuckled.

"There's nothing to know." Rock bit out the words as hard as Princess took her ounce of flesh from his hand. This was going to raise more than eyebrows at the ranch.

Ed dropped the feet of his chair back to the floor and tapped a pencil on his desk. The counselor's face was again serious and thoughtful.

"Why did you adopt Ranger?"

The dog sat up and glanced between them, as if he knew he was the subject of the discussion.

"Isn't that why the dogs are at the shelter? To be adopted?" Rock dropped a hand to rub the creature's head automatically, rasping the bandage against his fur.

"No, you deliberately misunderstand me. You're good at that, you know. When a topic isn't the direction you want to go, you deflect. I know that's part of your training. You shouldn't need that skill in civilian life."

How little Ed knew about that.

"Why did you adopt Ranger specifically, and not some other dog?"

The dog pressed against his thigh and gave a contented sigh as the petting continued. His eyes drifted down and sheer bliss marked his doggie face.

"The cage."

Ed stilled. "All shelter dogs were in cages. Why is that significant in Ranger's case?"

Rock wasn't sure why he was saying this, certainly after skirting the past in all previous conversations. "I know what it's like to be trapped in a cage."

The dog dropped a chin to his leg and stared at him with pride.

"That's where you were held?"

Rock nodded, finding it easier to say the words for reasons he couldn't understand. "For almost two months."

Ed didn't say he was proud of him for sharing or probe further. Rock bit his tongue. He wasn't sure why he'd said anything at all, but now that he had, he didn't feel like he could stop.

The vision pressed in on him without warning. The heat drying sweat before it had a chance to cool you. Stench from unwashed bodies and blood from the beatings and feces and urine from the buckets that were rarely emptied. Only when the smell grew bad enough for the guards to complain were they allowed outside for that brief task. Screams from tortures and nightmares and the reality of their condition.

Pressure built in his head until it was almost unbearable. He'd prayed for death more times than he could count, his self-preservation gone in the arid desert sun. When they'd dragged him out that final time, he hoped it was because they were ending his misery. Little did he know his hell was just beginning.

"Rock. You're safe. You're home. It's done. Rock, look at me, man."

He struggled against the hands gripping his arms, holding him upright when he only wanted to fall to the ground and weep. He was crying, its liquid the only soothing touch on his face. With a blast of noise and pain in his head and a stab of sheer madness in his brain, he screwed his eyes tight against the pressure.

"Rock, you with us, man?"

The voices weren't from the past but the present. The grips lessened, and he registered something firm and supportive at his back. Wet continued to train down on his face, and as he peeled an eye open, a pink tongue attached to a whining Ranger swiped at him again.

He blinked, trying to clear his head. These bursts from the past left him so fucking tired. He wanted to curl into a tight ball and let emptiness engulf him.

"Rock, say something."

"Something."

The raw word wasn't meant as humor. He studied Ed's face, finding relief. Ed glanced past Rock, and that's when he noticed the other man, another counselor, stood on his other side. Ranger's paws pressed against his chest. They supported him against a wall. Without their support, he'd have crumpled to the carpet.

Ranger jumped down and snuggled his way between the other man and Rock, pressing in. Ed nodded, and the other man took a step back. Embarrassment made Rock meet his gaze to apologize, but the man gave him a friendly smile.

"Humor is the last thing to go and the first thing to come back. Congrats, dude." The man slipped out before Rock could respond.

Ed kept a firm grip on his arm. "Do you think you can make it to the chair?"

Rock nodded. By the time he'd settled and Ranger's chin appeared in its usual place on his thigh, a bottle of icy water pressed into his hand. He emptied it in one pass. Another appeared to take its place.

Ed reseated himself, never breaking eye contact. When it came, the question wasn't the one Rock expected. "What made Ranger's plight unique?"

Rock didn't want to say. Something told him that the more he talked about it, the less he'd liked what he learned about himself.

'Maybe we both need rescuing.'

The words in Jenn's voice flashed in his mind.

"Cages are weird things. Bars, but we can see and hear and sense things. Openings, but too small for us to escape through. There are physical cages, and there are mental ones." Ed stopped, waiting as if he expected Rock to respond.

He'd heard that before from the Army shrink at the hospital and every counselor since then. His understanding of this never seemed to matter as much as it did now.

His voice remained raw when he spoke. "You're saying my cage is in my head and breaking free is a matter of choice."

Ed grinned and nodded like he was a star pupil. Ranger jumped up from his place on the floor and gave an excited woof of agreement. Rock stared between the two of them, knowing what the two of them didn't.

He had no choice, no without losing what little honor he had left.

Chapter 22

"Why do you hate me, Princess?"

The dog attacking the chew toy with as much energy as she had Rock's hand ignored her. Rock had been stoic about the wound, while Jenn couldn't stop apologizing. She'd even offered to show him Princess's shots record to prove she was up to date on rabies. Rock looked at her like she was crazy. Maybe she was.

Ranger had responded to the snarls directed his way by cowering in a corner. She felt so bad for the dog because he could be terrorized by something a fraction of his size. What Princess lacked in size, though, she made up for in attitude.

"You can't keep acting like this. What is wrong with you?"

The dog ceased chewing and sent her a pointed look in turn, as if to ask what was wrong with her.

Jenn wasn't sure. Rock left without saying he accepted her apologies on behalf of her dog. He didn't mention seeing her again, nor did he kiss her on his rapid retreat out her door. By the time she returned to the shop, ten minutes late, she wondered if the day could get any worse.

The ringing store phone greeted her as she unlocked the door. She scurried to answer it, a touch breathless. After her standard greeting, silence was the only response.

"Hello?" She held the phone away from her ear and checked the connection. It was still engaged. A voice began speaking, and she hurried to pull it close again.

"Is this Jennifer?"

"Yes."

"Ah, good. Jennifer, this is Shelley's sister Patti. I wonder if you could do us a favor."

"Of course, Patti. How is Shelley?"

"Well, that's just it, dear. We don't know yet. The surgery took longer than they thought, in part because things were more widespread than they thought. Tests take time, don't you know. Anyway, I was going to come into the shop and work for Shelley for the next couple of weeks, but I think she's going to need my help with other things. Would you mind taking care of the shop for a while on your own?"

Assuring the troubled woman things would be fine was one thing. The reality of what that meant when she hung up was another. She looked around the store, her eyes picking out merchandise depleted from this morning's rush. The order book came next, with its stack of holiday specials to cover Christmas and New Year's and events in between.

A single thread of trepidation wound its way into her chest and wrapped around her nerves, tugging hard. She forced herself to cut off that thought with a ruthlessness she knew some wouldn't expect of her. Failure was not in her vocabulary.

The door chimed and she turned, ready to give the customer a distracted smile, when she registered the face. Miss Emie stood inside the door flanked by Deke. The woman smiled. The man glanced around the place with marked interest, and when his eyes finally settled her, he sent her an apologetic shrug.

"Hello, Jennifer. It's so nice to see you, dear. Tell me, what have you heard about dear Shelley?"

"Nothing yet, I'm afraid. She had her surgery and her sister says she's resting comfortably. They're waiting for the results to come back from pathology."

"That sounds promising. I'm going to pop over there and say hello as soon as we're done here. Deke, say hello, and tell her what you need, and get on your way. Those cattle won't sell themselves."

Jenn didn't think it was possible for a grown man of obvious strength and character to look so chagrined at the commanding tone in the voice of the petite, gray-haired woman standing next to him.

He said, "Jenn, I am sorry. I couldn't dissuade her. She insisted on coming as soon as she heard."

Jenn stilled, unsure what they could be talking about.

Emie hummed, picking up jars of jams and reading the labels with intense interest. Deke stood where he'd landed inside the door, hands in pockets, keeping his eyes on Jenn with enough questioning focus to make her want to shift away. Whatever it was they were after, they would have to fill her in.

"Deke." The note of warning in the single word made Jenn want to grin. She might be small and she came across as sweet, but Jenn suspected Emileen Kermarrec had more steel in her spine than was used to build the Golden Gate Bridge.

"Ma," he began, only to stop when she shot him a stern look. He glanced back at Jenn, mouthed 'I'm sorry', and drifted out the door.

"I thought he'd never leave. Tell me, dear, do you have any of that wonderful brie in the tasting tray, and maybe some of those excellent soda crackers?"

Jenn doubted this was what brought Miss Emie in, but she obliged her, pulling the stool from the back of the counter for her to sit on.

Emie bit into the cheese and her humming reached a new pitch. When she finished the taste, her benevolent smile landed on Jenn once more. She reached out and closed her hands over Jenn's.

"So, tell me how it happened."

Jenn opened her mouth to reply, knowing she had to come clean about it. She was so ashamed of her dog, she didn't know where to begin. All she could do was beg Rock's mother to forgive her and promise never to let the dog close to her son again.

"Miss Emie, I don't know what to do about her. All she does is snarl and bark and chew and bite. She's been like this ever since I was forced to sell the condo, and now, no matter what I do, I can't make her happy. Nevertheless, she behaved herself at Rock's cabin, for the most part, until he had that nightmare, and then we had to spend the night in my apartment upstairs. He never said anything after Princess bit him. And now I'm afraid Shelley will fire me, and we'll be homeless again."

She fought the urge to drop her face into her hands, because her embarrassment reached dramatic proportions. She respected Miss Emie, and even if nothing happened with Rock, which she hoped it would, she would enjoy being friends with the women of that family. Not wanting to appear uncaring or useless in their eyes suddenly gained in importance.

Emie's smile faltered a bit, then faded. Her scrutiny would have been uncomfortable, but it seemed more caring that judgmental. When she finally spoke, her tone revealed her confusion as well as determination.

"Rock kissed you, in public. You didn't mention that part. The rest I wasn't aware of. You and Rock spent a night together. You're worried you'll be homeless. Dear girl, maybe you better lock that door and start at the beginning and bring out a little more of that good cheese while you're at it."

>>>>>

His usual hour lasted three today, and by the end of it, Rock felt so drained, he wasn't sure which end was up. The last person he wanted to see was his brother, lounging on the front bumper of his truck, his face turned to the last of light from sunset.

"Don't tell me they called you."

Deke looked surprised. "No one called me. I came here two hours ago at the end of your appointment, and they said you would probably be a while yet. I left you a note at the desk, and they promised to give it to you."

Rock closed his hand around the piece of paper in his pocket. He hadn't opened it, figuring it was another appointment reminder or change in his schedule. He pulled it out but didn't open it.

"What does it say?" It hurt to speak.

Deke straightened and lowered his head to look him full in the face. "That I was going to run some errands and come back for you. To call me when you finished so I could give you a ride home. That is, unless you're not going back to the cabin tonight."

Rock waved a hand, too bone weary to argue with the last of the fight kicked out of him. "I'm not coming back to the ranch."

Deke's response to this sentence was a wry smile. "So, you're staying in town." His grin grew.

It could have been anything. Maybe it was the episode from before, or the draining half-hearted explanation to his counselor. Lack of sleep from both pleasure and pain last night mixed up his mind. The constant reminder of things gone wrong pulsed in his palm. He pushed his face into Deke's and snarled, "What the fuck are you talking about?"

The smile vanished in an instant, and concern retook its place. Deke stepped off the bumper and took another step closer. "What happened to you today?"

Rock spun away. He didn't want to land a punch in his brother's face, but the likelihood of that grew with each passing second. Full explanations were impossible to provide, and the partial ones met with disbelief, conflict and lectures. He wanted none of the above.

"Rock, what's going on?"

A strong hand closed on his arm, and that flashpoint was all he needed. He twisted his body and slammed into Deke, breaking his hold and gutting him with a blow to the stomach. His brother crumpled in half, holding his waistline with both arms and breathing with difficulty. Rock was panting too, though it wasn't an injury so much as the welling pain nothing seemed to help. Ranger barked once, as if in warning.

The siren song of the obvious called to him. He had a way out, a way no one else would approve of, but that wasn't their business. The throb of growing pressure would make the end of this worth it.

Deke put a hand on the hood of the truck and raised himself from bent to half-standing. His breathing still labored but color no longer burned in his face. His eyes, the same turbulent dark blue Rock was sure reflected in his, never strayed from Rock's face.

"What was that for?" The rasp in his voice didn't hide his anger.

"Leave me alone."

"I would, except Ma won't. She's already heard, you see."

Rock shook his head in dismay. Who at the center revealed what happened this afternoon? Actions inside stayed inside and confidential, or so was the rule.

Deke made it to standing and woofed out a gasp. "If you're going to kiss a woman and you don't want anyone to know about it, don't do it on Main Street, Flynn's Crossing."

Rock deflated like a punctured balloon. So that was what Deke meant. His first thought was to warn Jenn. His second was remorse about bringing her into this. At his side, Ranger whined as if to anchor him in the moment.

"You know, it's not a bad thing to start something with a woman as nice as Jennifer."

Rock wasn't sure what he was doing with her. He turned fast enough to knock the dog off his feet and accelerated back toward the cheese shop. What he planned to do once he got there was no clearer than why he'd punched Deke in the first place.

"She's not there."

He paused, waiting to hear what else Deke planned to say.

"She and Ma left over an hour ago. I don't know where they went. Ma isn't answering her cell phone, which isn't that unusual for her."

Whatever energy he had remaining left him in a wave of collapse. He crouched low, mainly because the effort of standing didn't seem worth it anymore. He could return to the cabin, though since it was already evening and he'd never been back to dry the bedding and its interior today, it would be strikingly cold.

"It's supposed to snow tomorrow," Deke said in a conversational tone. "Come back to the ranch."

It was a tempting offer, made more so by the fleeting thought that perhaps Ma had convinced Jenny to come over for dinner. Just as quickly, he rejected the idea. He belonged in the forest, in the cabin, doing his solo penance. A good snowfall tomorrow would be a first step in the only direction he could take.

"No," he said, not looking back to see how Deke took that news.

In response, the truck's big motor fired up. He turned toward the sound, hoping his brother left him. It would give him something to be angry at that wasn't his own damned fault.

Instead, Deke sat behind the wheel, meeting his gaze with a level one of his own. Never once had he offered a recrimination or reprimand for Rock's behavior. He wished Deke would get mad and try to kick his ass. Then he'd have a reason to hate him.

As it was, the only one he could hate was himself. With a sigh echoed by the dog at his side, he trudged toward the truck.

Chapter 23

Nothing helped a woman overcome remorse and uncertainty like a sympathetic ear and good food. When the listener happened to be the mother of the man in question, things could get dicey. Luckily, that wasn't the way Emie Kermarrec was wired, a fact Jenn had come to appreciate in the last few hours.

"Start at the beginning, my dear, wherever you think that might be."

And Jenn had, with the story of the tree farm from long ago, and her mother, and then losing her job and her reasons for coming here. Emie clucked and consoled at all the right places. Then she insisted they take the conversation upstairs to Jenn's apartment when the tears began, and Jenn couldn't get them to stop.

Princess was delighted to see the older woman, and they settled at one end of the couch, the dog in her lap gazing at her with tongue-lolling adoration.

"Why can't she be that way with me?" That question was grounds for new tears streaking down Jenn's face.

"Now dear, animals take to me. I exude calm and love and forgiveness. They know that. Don't take it personally."

When Emie coaxed her to continue, Jenn glossed over the night she and Rock spent together in the cabin, but there seemed no harm in explaining last night. It was chaste and platonic for the hours they were here. The sly smile on the face across from her let her know she figured out the rest and found the idea endlessly pleasing.

That didn't make it right, not when Rock so clearly seemed sorry it had occurred. If he'd been as enamored of their intimacy as she was, why would he storm out?

"And that was when Princess bit him," Jenn finished, coming to the kiss in the park. It seemed Miss Emie had spies everywhere, because she not only knew the kisses had happened, but that up until then, they appeared to be having a wonderful time according to onlookers. Jenn wasn't sure what to make of small town living after learning everyone got in everyone else's business.

Emie picked up the dog in her lap and lifted her to eye level. "Did you bite my boy? Now why did you do that? Your human tries to take very good care of you, but that doesn't mean she shouldn't take good care of herself too. You be nice to Rock from now on, young lady, and his dog Ranger too."

Princess's ears drooped as if she understood the disappointment and didn't like the prospect of what was expected.

"So, I guess that's it," Jenn said.

"Why do you think you'll be homeless?"

Jenn shrugged and toyed with the torn corner of the chair cushion. "When Shelley gets better, she'll come back to work. She already told me the winter months are slow and she usually covers them herself with no employees. Without work, I can't afford this place, and I'll have to go back to my sister's. Eventually, I'll have to take any job to get back on my feet."

"Why can't that be here?" Emie regarded her with puzzlement.

"Miss Emie, you've been very kind to listen, but I don't think I can grow a business overnight, one that will support me and my monster. Besides, consulting is what I know. How many businesses in Flynn's Crossing need those sorts of services and can afford to pay me for them?"

A slow smile came to the woman's face. "More than you might think. Tell me, what do you want out of life?"

"Why, what everyone wants. A loving life with family and friends. Rewarding work. Security. A future." She didn't say the one other thing on her mind, namely, a man with ever-changing emotions in his eyes and a warm heart when he revealed it.

Emie stroked the longer furs on Princess's back, making the dog snore contentedly. "There's a Native American saying that the human spirit when it passes only carries with it the regret that it did not love others and life on this side of the great beyond. All other things drop away. With that in mind, doesn't it make sense to try to love yourself as well as others when you have the chance?"

Hours later, Jenn was still pondering what it meant. The woman's confidence that she could grow the life she wanted here might be wishful thinking, but what happened if she never tried? She knew what waited for her if she returned to the Bay Area, and none of it pleased her.

As she watched a steady drift of large snowflakes fall outside the shop's window the next afternoon, she remained undecided. Shelley would know nothing from the doctors for at least another day or two. She wouldn't be leaving the hospital until then. Jenn's sisters both called urging her to come back, and she explained she had a job and a commitment to keep things running for as long as it took. Emie checked in with her, and Marlee joined in the discussion, claiming she had a retail client who would like to discuss a potential consulting project.

"Jenn, there is more business here than you realize, and I can honestly say you'll be as busy as you want to be. If you want the work, that is."

"I love small businesses. When I help them, it makes me feel like I've done some good for hardworking people who deserve it. But would they even be interested in me?"

She had little she could offer in terms of references from her former employer. Marlee's assurances to the contrary, she needed to find a way to get past her blacklisting. Without that, her background was useless.

The only one Jenn wanted to hear from who maintained radio silence was Rock. His approval of her staying around had become pivotal to her decision, even if they had no future together. This was more his town than hers.

Wanting to know his opinion of her possible plan was the reason Jenn overcame her fear of slippery roads and growing snowfall and covered the miles to the tree farm at a cautious pace. On the way, she rehearsed what she planned to say with Princess as her unwilling audience. By the time she pulled into the drive and approached the chain, she had no stronger confidence in her strategy than she had the night before.

Vague lights backlit the trees, even with the thicker flakes falling. By the time she stood outside the cabin's door, it was piling up fast. She prayed he wanted to listen and invited her to stay, if for no more pedestrian a reason than the snow was getting worse by the moment.

"Now remember, behave yourself."

Princess whined at the prospect, and Jenn almost smiled when it made her think the dog was saying the effort was too much. She forgot about the dog and her speech the moment the cabin door swung open.

Haggard lines cut into Rock's face and his hair stood on end. The cabin was hot, too warm for comfortable standards based on the blast that hit her in the face. The thin shirt on the man who wasn't smiling at her fitted each muscle and tendon with more form than should be legal. Jenn tried to hold back the whine of pure appreciation. Meeting Rock's cold gaze cast thoughts of that out of her mind.

"Why are you here?"

His tone of voice bore no emotion, but Jenn sensed a protective slouch to his body, as if he expected her to lash out at him.

She smiled with a brightness she wasn't really feeling. "I come bearing groceries. Princess and I felt like an adventure, so here we are."

None of that would make common sense to anyone, she knew, but she had to try. Ranger peeked out around Rock's legs and sniffed at Jenn's purse and its resident Yorkie. For once, the little dog kept her yap shut.

Dropping to the stoop on one knee, she held out her arms to the dark tan dog, and Ranger glanced up at Rock before approaching her with as much hesitation as the man seemed to show. He came to her, though, staying as far as possible from her bag while nuzzling her shoulder.

"Yes, I brought you goodies too, big boy. Do you think your master would be interested in a juicy steak and a baked potato and a nice red wine? If not, you and I can share it." She glanced up to see if her words had any effect on Rock, but the limited light hid his expression.

"Why are you here?" His voice sounded weary and old in repetition of the question.

She stood and stepped into his personal space, forcing him to take a step back into the heat of the room. Keeping her eyes on his, she took another pace, putting her purse on the floor inside the door. When she lifted her arms around his neck, she noticed the light begin to return to his eyes as he searched her face.

"I am here because this is where I want to be. A very wise woman recited a Native American ideal to me, that we live with regret if we don't take the risks in life to love others. I choose to listen to that and act on it." She took a deep breath, willing her voice not to waver. "The question is, are you with me or not?"

His arms came around her like tight bands, trapping her against the hard muscles of his chest. He winced, but when she would have pulled back, he shook his head.

"Why are you here?" This time, she heard wonder in his voice. When his head dropped and his lips settled on hers with the slightest bit of pressure, she smiled. He lifted his head almost immediately.

"You shouldn't be here."

"I disagree. This is my choice, remember? You should allow me the right to make my own decisions about this."

He opened his mouth again as if he wanted to argue, then closed it just as fast. He dropped his arms and stepped back, turning away and running his hands through his hair. She took that as invitation enough and closed the door behind her.

"You got your cast off already."

He glanced at his arm as if just noticing. His eyes shifted to the corner, and she followed his gaze to the blue plastic frame lying discarded on the floor.

That sign, she realized, was only one of many that he'd tossed the place upside down and sideways. Furniture stood in odd places. Papers were strewn on the floor near the stove, as if he'd been feeding them inside to heat the room. That room was sweltering, now that she was fully inside, and she took off her coat and hat, draping them on a peg by the door.

"What's going on?"

He shook his head at her question. He looked at the floor, the papers, the fire, at anything but her. His fists opened and closed at his sides, like he was fighting a losing battle with himself.

"Rock, will you help me get the groceries from the car?"

She turned and lifted random papers from the table, clearing an area for the bags as she stacked the pages. She tried not to look at them, but scripts noting who spoke and who replied jumped out at her. Ranks that were no doubt military denoted individuals.

He grabbed the pages out of her hands, pulling hard enough to tear a couple of corners. She looked up at him in confusion, to find him staring at the page on top.

"I'm sorry. I'm not reading them. I need someplace to put the bags."

Whatever he was looking at brought anguish and guilt to his face. She had a suspicion trying to coax the reason from him now would be fruitless. He seemed frozen in place, unable to break whatever spell the pages held on him.

She was torn between trying to break that hold and reaching for normalcy. She wasn't sure which would be better, and in her indecision, she turned blindly and opened the outer door. The gust of dense snow blowing in cooled the room considerably, even as it drove the fire taller.

She made a trip to the car and back, and Rock still stood in the same place. By the time she got the second load, he hadn't yet moved, but now, he was crying. His grief pulsed in the atmosphere around them, and she found her eyes tearing too.

"Tell me what's wrong. Tell me. We can face this together, whatever it is."

He shook his head, slowly at first and then with marked vehemence.

"No."

"What should I do to make it better?"

He said nothing.

"Rock, I'm here because I want to be. Please don't push me away. Tell me what I should do to help."

He shifted but didn't say a word. She listened to the crackle of the fire as a river of sweat beginning at the base of her neck headed down her spine. Stepping back enough to lift the sweater over her head took only a moment, but in that space, Rock began to shake.

"I'm going to close the woodstove and cool things down in here," she said.

"No." His tone was more command than denial.

"Why?"

He turned to her, exposing a face scored with deep lines of tension. "This is how it was. This heat. It's a reminder. I can't be allowed to forget what it was like."

She went to him, wrapping her arms around his waist and locking her hands when he tried to push her away. "Tell me what it was like. When you share the nightmare with someone, it loses its power over you."

"That's not how it works." He met her eyes, his dead with grief and drained of fight. "Sharing it makes it worse."

She leaned back and kept her gaze steady, never letting him go. "Try me. I can handle it."

He examined her face like he didn't recognize her. His gaze flickered over her features, slowly at first and then more rapidly. A change came over his expression, lessening the sadness even as he raised one corner of his mouth. As if it came with reluctance on his part, the other side of his mouth lifted in a tentative smile.

"I do believe you would try."

He put out a hand that shook and touched her cheek, and she tilted into his touch. The caress whispered over her skin, cool and gentle as a light breeze. The contrast to the oven the cabin had become couldn't be more profound. "The dogs aren't comfortable in this kind of heat," she said.

As if the idea hadn't occurred to him, he lifted his head and searched the corners of the room. She could hear Princess panting her little woofs of air in the confines of her carrier. In the corner, Ranger curled as far from the stove as possible, his tongue lolling with his own means to control his discomfort.

Rock dropped his hands from her face and she released him. The slam of the stove's door echoed in the room, and immediately, the reflective heat lessened. Rock threw open the cabin door and did a double take, as if he had no clue it had been snowing outside for quite some time.

"You'd better leave. The road will become impassable for your car."

"That's okay," she said.

Confusion made his face almost comical, but remnants of pain lingered. Again, she wanted to ask him what was wrong. Patience was never her best trait, but in this case, she'd work harder at it.

"You'll get snowed in."

She shrugged. "For a night, maybe. The county will clear the roads. I checked. The snow ends overnight. I'll be fine."

He lifted his arms and stretched, pulling the cotton fabric tighter over his chest. She sucked in a breath. She might be safe from the snow, but the magnetism of the man was another story altogether.

"Are you sure?"

She nodded, fumbling with her keys.

It was like the man flipped a switch and turned into the consummate host. He hurried to the table and gathered the papers. She had no idea where he hid them, because by the time she had the groceries stored out of dog reach, the room bore none of the signs of turmoil from before.

He said, "So how do you like your steak?"

She played with a curl of hair, twirling it around her finger. "That's not exactly what I'm hungry for right now."

He looked up in surprise. She could see him trying to process what she said. When she drew closer and placed a single kiss on the fabric over his heart, he dropped the bag of potatoes on the counter and raised his hands to her shoulders.

"It's not too late to go home, Jenny."

Oh yes it was. It had been, the moment she'd first met those blue-green-gray eyes. Nothing had been the same since. She shook her head.

When he looked like he planned to protest again, she put a finger over his lips and smiled. She stepped back and lifted her hands to the hem of her shirt, lifting it like a slow striptease. His eyes followed her movements, and his hands flexed at his sides. Her turtleneck hit the floor. She crooked a finger in his direction, grinning openly, and his mouth lifted into a reluctant smile.

"You'll get cold," he said, advancing as slowly as her retreat.

"You'll keep me warm."

His hands ripped the t-shirt off in a move so fast, it blurred in her vision. The next moment, his clever fingers had her bra off and flung into a corner. She dimly heard Ranger give a happy woof and Princess's answering complaint of a growl. That all disappeared the second his lips came down on hers.

Gone was the gentle persuasion he'd used last time. His tongue demanded entry and his teeth nipped at her lips. The whirlwind of energy ripped through her as he pushed her fast, harder, further than she thought she could go, and with each pulse of it, her demands rose too. The inferno inside them ignited into a passion so intense, she swore it melted the snow outside with its ferocity. She screamed, acutely aware he yelled her name too. When they'd climbed peaks higher than any mountain on the planet, neither one of them had the strength left to move.

Sweat cooled on her skin, and she burrowed closer to the man who was her source of heat. Heat, fire, sun, Rock was all of those and more. She had the unreal feeling that, like that winter day by the lake long ago, nothing would be the same after this night.

Chapter 24

Ravenous didn't even begin to describe how he felt as first light grew. The strange reflection of it, like the sun rose in the north instead of its usual place, disoriented him for a moment. A murmur of female singsong came to him like a morning bird call, and he smiled. A high yapping followed by a whine came next.

He didn't want to move. His best hope, the one he wanted to act on, was that Jenny would come back to bed, and they'd make love for another leisurely few hours. It was early yet. They still had time.

But how much time? That was his decision to make, and while he would have embraced its rapid approach with a welcoming sigh a few weeks ago, now he was less sure. Things had changed for him, and it all came about as a result of big brown eyes, a determination that never quit, and lips made for kisses.

The sound of the front door opening roused him from that more difficult path. A delighted gasp came next, followed by "Princess!" The exasperation in Jenny's tone was another reason to smile. The question of who was in charge in that relationship had him chuckling. Jenny liked to think she could fix anything and direct people to the best solution, but the dog proved she didn't have the same control over other creatures.

A cold wet nose burrowed under the covers and nuzzled Rock's armpit with a pitiful whine. He ran a hand over the dog's big head. "Good morning to you too. Go on, chase after your nemesis. It's okay." Ranger gave a single happy woof and headed out the door too.

Jenny appeared in his line of sight, tousled and tangled and looking utterly too good to wait. He grabbed her around the waist and pulled her down on the bed, rolling her under him with the urge to tickle her into submission.

"Stop, wait. We'll get to that. Think you can keep the motor running while I chase down the dogs? While Ranger won't go far, I don't think Princess has the sense of a pea when it comes to the forest."

"You have a point." He made a point to dig his in too, only satisfied when she moaned and gave him a hard kiss. She used that to leverage herself up. He lifted to an elbow to watch her.

"My, Ms. Stanton, what would your clients say if they knew you were going commando? And braless too?"

Jenny gave him a grin more enticing than anything he could remember seeing in years. "I'm not going to get all dressed up to corral dogs, then come back and have you take everything off me again. I like to be efficient."

The door swung closed on her calls for the dogs to come. He hoped they obeyed. Like he'd obey anything she asked, anything, except revealing the past. She'd said nothing more about the papers she saw, but he knew it would only be a matter of time. She wasn't going to let him off the hook that easily. Once she knew, she'd understand why what they had, precious as it was, could only be a short-term thing. The promises made decades ago didn't count in times like this.

It was silly, really. They'd been children and had no idea what they promised. And yet, he remembered that afternoon as clearly as the day it happened. Now they both needed rescuing, and he was afraid it was him more than her. She would never understand there was nothing she could do to save him now.

His thoughts froze on Ranger's sudden deep cascade of barks, a tone and intensity Rock had never heard before. Rock reached for his jeans, trying to interpret the frantic nature of the noise. He was pulling up the zipper when an ear-piercing scream that could only come from Jenny echoed in the forest.

His reaction times, while slowed by lack of use, were still faster than the untrained. He didn't need to think. He yanked open a drawer in the cabinet by the door and was outside before two ticks passed on the clock. Scanning right and left, he noted pawprints and boot tracks heading toward the lake. He picked up his pace at the fast stream of hysterical words he couldn't make out, though the voice was the same one who cried out his name in passion over and over in the past few hours.

The clearing wasn't far, and Jenny stood at the edge of it, her hand wrapped in Ranger's collar as he strained forward at her side. Her sobs now came to him clearly, and dread, a too-familiar feeling, took up residence in his stomach.

"Princess. What can I do? Ranger, stop pulling. Get away. Go. Get."

She waved an arm, and Rock moved to the side to see past her. Princess in her ridiculous red and green plaid coat was easy to spot about twenty feet in front of Jenny, and the risk to the dog was now also clear. Three coyotes, noses low and tails in ground-sweeping curls, surrounded the little dog. To her credit, Princess growled and curled her lip, like associating with low life such as them was out of the question.

He could shoot them in rapid succession, but Princess wouldn't have that kind of time. It would only take a quick snap of teeth to bite the little dog in two. His gaze zipped to Jenny's face, noting the desperate tears mixed with anger and worry. She lifted her free arm and waved at the animals again, but they weren't paying attention to her.

Rock took a cautious step to the left and searched the ground for a branch long enough to poke at an animal and keep it back. He stood a chance of rescuing Princess if he could drive them to the side. He'd probably get bitten by the little monster as thanks for his actions, but he'd worry about that later.

"Ranger, no!" He lifted his gaze in time to see the big dog break free of Jenny's restraining hand and take a massive leap toward the wild animals, giving a ferocious bark. She lunged after him on instinct, then seemed to realize that would throw her into the fray too.

He didn't want to watch, knowing three against one were terrible odds when hungry pack animals were in play. They were no different from brutal humans in that regard. He lifted his arm, ready to take the merciful move if necessary, because he couldn't stand to see any creature suffer. Jenny wouldn't understand, which only underscored the difference between them as a yawning chasm.

Ranger's paws landed in the soft snow without a slip, and in a blink, he stood over Princess, ears laid back and teeth gnashing at the coyotes. They chortled and hissed in response, one taking a step closer. Ranger advanced on him in turn with a threatening growl, and between his legs and keeping pace, Princess made her own menacing noise. Big dog and little one stood aligned as one, ready to take on the pack. Rock's heart was already hurting for the loss of a creature who was proving his magnificence when he could no longer thank him for the act.

He'd never know what he would have done, or even if he could have done it. He'd done too much killing in his life to measure, and he'd like to think most of it was for a good and righteous cause. One more death on his conscience would be the last straw. He wished it could be different.

The move was so fast, he wasn't sure he saw it clearly at first. Ranger stopped growling and twisted low, and when he faced forward again, he held Princess's coat in his mouth, the dog dangling and yapping and baring her teeth at the coyotes. The pack exchanged glances, but Ranger had his own plan. With another leap that had to cover three times' the dog's length, the brown blur rose in the air and sailed over the back of the smallest attacker. He landed neatly on his feet in front of Jenny. He deposited Princess, who'd gone quiet as if in surprise, and turned to resume his menacing protection.

Rock didn't think. He lifted his arm to the sky and curled his finger like a gentle caress. The early morning exploded with the single gunshot, scattering the marauders into the forest. As it reverberated off the trees and hillsides, Jenny turned with her mouth open in a perfect circle of shock. He didn't lower his arm, meeting her expression of horror with a stoic one of his own. Before he gave in to the urge to explain, he turned and retraced his steps to the cabin, sure the questions would come soon enough.

Jenn shivered, unable to move, with Ranger panting at her side and Princess still growling at her feet. The big dog glanced at her with a pause, then followed in his master's wake at a fast trot. She scooped up Princess, too confused to do more than head for the safety of the cabin.

The door stood open when she reached it. Her brain wasn't processing at its usual warp speed as she tried to reason out what she'd seen. Rock had a gun, a big-assed gun, and he kept it loaded. The reasons why he'd need a gun living in the rural wilderness weren't lost on her, but somehow, she had a feeling protection from wildlife wasn't the only reason.

He stood at the woodstove, watching newly-kindled flames lick at the logs inside. The gun was still in his hand, cradled inside his elbow as his arms crossed on his chest. His bare chest, she noted, as it had been in the forest. His feet were bare too, and it didn't take a genius to realize he'd probably yanked on the jeans and grabbed the gun when she screamed.

The look on his face in that clearing, desolate and frozen, stuck in her mind. She knew he must have fired the gun before. He'd seen action in the Army. The killing he must have done was not something she wanted to contemplate.

"I'll check the road. The county should have been through by now. I can push you out if you get stuck in the driveway." He kept his gaze on the fire.

Her head pounded with a dull pain. She had a long list of questions she wanted to ask, but she was afraid to hear the answers. His words registered, but she struggled with the message. If he thought she would run so easily, he'd learned nothing about her. If he wanted her to leave, she wasn't ready, not by an effing city mile.

Princess squirmed in her arms, and with a reluctant reminder to behave, she put her down on the floor. The dog scampered off for a far corner. Jenn went to Ranger, laying in his dog bed and panting with what might have been a doggie smile of pride on his furry face. She dropped to a knee and wrapped her arms around him, since she doubted Rock would accept her thanks as readily.

"You are a good boy, Ranger. Impetuous, and nuts for taking them on, but Princess and I are in your debt. I'm going to buy you the biggest steak I can find."

She rose from the floor, eyeing the man by the stove.

"You have a gun."

He scowled.

"Is it for protection?"

The hesitation before his nod wasn't lost on her.

"Would you have killed those coyotes?"

His direct gaze, unflinching and unblinking, gave her the answer.

"I don't like guns."

He kept staring without comment.

He shifted his body again, from side to side as if her steady consideration was uncomfortable to him. His chest heaved, and he looked down at the gun in apparent contemplation.

"I think you should go," he said.

From the dog bed, Ranger gave a disconcerting whine. The dog looked between the two of them as if he understood the conversation and didn't agree with the idea.

If Rock didn't want her here, she couldn't come up with an argument to stay. He'd come running and saved her yet again, and she doubted he'd listen to her thanks.

"Thank you for coming to Princess's rescue."

Rock inclined his head, looking at his dog instead of her.

Jenn gave up trying. This was all too impossible. One minute it felt like they were drawing closer in ways that were more than just sex, and the next, he pushed her away. The pounding in her head now rivaled the shot's noise in the woods. It didn't matter what she felt for him, not if he didn't return those feelings. In her brand of logic, if he cared about her, he wouldn't push her away.

"Princess, come. It's time to leave." She snapped her fingers a couple of times. The dog didn't appear, not an unusual occurrence, and she sincerely hoped the Yorkie wasn't eating a hole in something important. Those papers Rock whisked away to hide came to mind.

Ranger gave another whine. Rock shook his head and sighed. Dog and man regarded each other steadily.

The click of nails announced Princess's return from whatever she'd been up to. Jenn was about to grab her and the rest of her clothes and pray the road had been plowed when she focused on what the dog dragged across the room. It was Princess's favorite squeaky rhinoceros. The plush toy thing was almost as big as she was, and she yanked and growled at it as if lecturing it on coming along. She'd have to hope that kept the dog occupied while she found her underwear.

Jenn searched the floor, seeing the pieces she was missing under the small dining table. Talk about a walk of shame. She'd never done one before. She shoved the panties and bra in her big purse, turning to grab her little dog and race out the door.

Rock stood in her way, but he wasn't looking at her. His expression of disbelief had her following the direction of his gaze to the big dog bed. Ranger watched too, as Princess wiggled her butt and backed up, dragging her toy behind her. When she got to the dog bed, she dropped the toy and looked at the bigger animal, wagging for all she was worth.

"Ruff," the little dog said, and she followed it up with a nose push to the purple rhino in Ranger's direction. The dog's ears perked up and he stretched out his head and sniffed. Princess advanced too, and Jenn readied herself to grab the little monster by her Christmas-themed coat. It would be just like the ungrateful creature to bite her rescuer now that the fun was over.

"Princess, come." Jenn was already moving when Rock put out an arm that stopped her in her tracks, even though they were feet apart.

"Ruff," Princess said again, and leaned forward too. Her nose touched Ranger's and the big dog didn't move. Princess drew closer, and both dogs sniffed wildly. The tail that had been wagging got into a serious blurred rhythm, and as if he understood, Ranger's longer one brushed the bed, picking up speed.

Princess went back and gave the toy a shove with another happy bark. Then she marched up to Ranger, sniffed his nose again, and curled up against his side. Big dog and little one put their heads down and stared at the humans as if they wanted to deliver a message.

"I'll be damned," Rock said, shaking his head. When he turned his face up to hers, the half-smile gave it a rueful expression. Jenn's heart beat a little harder at the boyish charm, and she pulled in a deep breath.

"If they can do it," she said, "how about if we give it a try?"

Rock tilted his head and the smile faded. A wary expression came after it. Underneath, though, she saw the hurt and pain. He expected her to bolt, not because he wanted her to go, but because he thought she would run.

She dropped the purse and her coat. In a movement she doubted he expected, she lifted off the sweater and tossed it into a corner. Slipping off her boots took a little more effort, but she kept an unwavering gaze on the man who was again doing his best impression of a rooted tree. By the time her jeans headed in the same direction as the sweater, he was shaking his head.

"Are you sure?" Stress was easy to read in the strangled tone of his voice.

She glanced at the gun, now dangling at his side in a grip that didn't look like it had lessened. If he noticed her moment of hesitation, he didn't show it. She nodded, meeting his eyes with a defiant lift of her chin.

"I guess if Princess can thank her rescuer, I should thank mine," she said. Her eyes flicked once to the gun hanging in his hand, then returned to his face.

Rock stared at her for a few moments, and she couldn't read what he was thinking. He was good at that, hiding his feelings and his meanings behind a blank façade. As if her constant regard was what he was looking for, he walked over to the dresser and pulled open a drawer, and the gun disappeared.

Chapter 25

Jenn busied herself sorting through the mess that was Shelley's organization system to find the phone numbers she needed. Her fingers itched to set things straight, enter the contact information into the computer, and see which of these companies had online ordering available. It would make Shelley's life so much easier if she had the ability to order even when she couldn't reach anyone by phone. Only the memory of her promise not to change anything while her boss was gone stopped her. It didn't stop the itching, though.

Shelley was itching too, though, specifically going crazy about being in the hospital, even though she insisted she felt fine. Privately, her sister said it was worry over the result that had her fussing so much. Shelley was calling at least three times a day.

Near closing time, the bell on the door tinkled. She recognized the answering rise in her heart rate. Each time, she secretly hoped it was Rock, coming to explain. Each time, she was disappointed.

The doorway filled with a laughing set of Marlee and Marguerite, arms laden with packages. Both women were still laughing as they buzzed up to Jenn. Packages landed on the counter with a thud that made the display of cheese knives jump.

"Oh, but we have had a wonderful day of shopping. And we saved our favorite stop for last." Marguerite's accent made the words sound more joyous than the holiday season.

Marlee, loaded down with fewer packages than her sister-in-law, made a face. "My feet hurt. My back aches. And I'm not even done yet."

"Relax. You have that handsome husband to rub your tired muscles and massage your feet. If that's what you want him to rub, that is." The Frenchwoman gave an exaggerated wink in Jenn's direction. Cheeks heating, Jenn looked away and busied herself straightening papers on the counter.

"Sorry, Jenn. Marguerite can be a little risqué at times. No, you shush."

The women bickered in a good-natured fashion that spoke of fondness. Envy shot through Jenn like a lightning bolt, surprising her with its ferocity. That emotion wasn't a stranger, but it had been a long time since a bite of tears followed it.

"Jenn, is something wrong?" Shadows of the two women approaching made Jenn blink rapidly.

"It's Rock, isn't it? What did he do? Believe us when we say we know how headstrong and stubborn the Kermarrec men can be. We'll give you the down and dirty on how to work around them."

If they attempted to console her, Jenn knew she'd spill it all. Pasting on a bright smile she was sure fooled no one, she turned to them and asked, "What can I get for you today? I have a new brie I think you'll love."

Marlee and Marguerite exchanged a measured glance as they nibbled samples. Marguerite stepped forward and put a hand on Jenn's shoulder. "What time will you be closing the shop today?"

She didn't have to look at the clock to know it would only be half an hour away.

Marlee made a point of examining the sign on the back wall, and said, "We'll get rid of these packages and come back for you. It looks like you need a glass of wine and a heart-to-heart with people in the know. That's our version of tea and sympathy, in case there's any question in your mind."

Her smile was kind and understanding, which made Jenn's ready denial seem bad mannered. Refusing their warmhearted offer would be rude.

"We will not take no for an answer, you understand. *Non*, you are coming out with us and you will unburden yourself of whatever transgressions little brother has carried out. Oh, and I will take a very large piece of that brie. It is delightful."

They sailed out the door like forces of nature. Declining would be impossible, she guessed. It would be up to her to keep her thoughts and activities of the last few days to herself. The time passed too quickly for her to come up with alternatives, though, and before she knew it, they were back.

"That new restaurant up the street will be perfect. They have private booths in their bar area. I love their tea, and they carry Marguerite's wine." Marlee linked arms with Jenn on one side.

"And their appetizers are quite lovely as well. The pimento almonds pair exceptionally well with my Syrah. When I was pregnant, that is what I craved. Deke had to buy them in five pound bags." Marguerite grabbed her other arm like she expected Jenn to run in the opposite direction. It was an amazingly astute observation.

"I should check on Princess," Jenn protested.

"Your dog? When did you check last? Two hours ago? And how much trouble could she get into in that time? We will not be all evening."

Jenn wanted to protest but stopped before she said more. Since the incident with the coyotes, Princess had been on her best behavior. It might be too early to celebrate this as a change in character, but she would enjoy it while it lasted.

By the time they were settled in deeply cushioned benches with wood walls rising around them, Jenn fought the urge to squirm. Marlee concentrated a speculative gaze on her, and Marguerite, once she'd ordered for all of them without consultation, leaned back and folded her hands like an expectant interrogator.

She could do this. She'd made her living getting others to talk, forgetting their inhibitions and their nerves. Life stories, corporate problems, and opposing philosophies were her bailiwick. Jennifer Stanton prided herself on deflecting a discussion heading her way and getting rocks to talk. Too bad the one Rock she wanted to have a conversation with seemed to cut her off at every turn.

"So spill, sister. What did Rock do?"

"Marlee, I believe there is a gentler way of probing for the answers." Marguerite shifted her attention to Jenn. "Kermarrec men are too good-looking for the peace of mind of any red-blooded woman within twenty miles, and they know it. They are more stubborn than any creature on the planet, once they get an idea in their heads. And their loyalty is only exceeded by their firm belief that they should champion anyone they trust before themselves. Have I missed anything, sister?"

"No, sister, you have not. And now, let's hear what our new sister has to say."

They both stared at her, even as the table filled with almonds and olives and cheese Jenn recognized from the shop. Wine was poured into her glass without consultation. Marlee dunked a teabag into a pot but didn't look away. Marguerite was already nibbling on almonds when Jenn stole a peek at her, but her gaze too was planted squarely on Jenn's face.

She struggled to come up with anything innocuous to say. Turning the conversation around on these women seemed an impossible feat. Talking about her future in Flynn's Crossing might help, particularly since she wanted Marlee's advice.

But when she opened her mouth, she couldn't control what came out. "He saved my dog. I mean, Ranger saved Princess, but Rock saved Ranger, and then he shot a gun into the air and they all scattered. And then he was so nice to me, I mean, before, and when I got upset but told him I wasn't going anywhere, he seemed happy about it. That is, until he told me to get out."

Both women blinked when she drew a breath. This time they didn't even bother to hide their unmistakable pointed curiosity. Marlee got her wits together first. "We know he helped you when you fell at the tree farm. And he returned your dog's leash. But you're going to have to start in the middle and fill us in on the rest."

Jenn opened her mouth to apologize, ready to protest that it was nothing, but the firmness in Marlee's expression and the equally scary determined set to Marguerite's mouth told her she wasn't getting away with that. With a resigned sigh, she began at the beginning. Not three weeks ago or even the past year, but decades ago.

"When I was young, my family came to the tree farm to cut the annual tree. The last time we did it, I met Rock. He'd broken his arm, the same one he hurt when he fell because of me, so he couldn't carry trees like his brothers were. He was nice to me, and we took a walk to the pond. Do you know the pond?"

Both women shook their heads.

"We took a blood bond oath and promised to always come to each other's rescue. Except, I seem to be the one who needs rescuing more than Rock does."

"I wouldn't be too sure about that." Marlee shot a meaningful look at Marguerite.

"He has a gun and I think he keeps it loaded."

Marlee sucked in air at that. "That's not good."

"There's more. Every time I think we're drawing closer, and we're happy and joking around, he suddenly gets this pensive look and withdraws. When I ask him about it, he shakes his head, gets mad, and tries to send me away."

"Rock, joking around?" Marguerite sounded nonplussed by the idea. "But I agree with Marlee. A gun is not good. And this sadness you mentioned, it is also unfortunate. But tell us, is the sex good?"

Jenn opened her mouth, about to respond to the casual question, when its subject hit her. Marguerite gave her a sly smile, and Marlee shook her head, but she too grinned.

"You will have to forgive her. She is woman with sex on the brain. Not that it's that unusual, given the men we're talking about. Ignore her. Back to your story. Tell us about the dogs."

So she did, beginning with Princess biting Ranger and the big dog scared of the little one. When she related the part about the coyotes, Marguerite muttered something in French under her breath and Marlee let go a single curse. By the time she got to the part where Rock told her to leave, they both looked puzzled.

"Now you understand why I feel like I'm the one needing rescuing." Jenn nodded at the others, expecting their logical assent.

"Why did you throw icy water on him?" Marlee steepled her fingers under her chin.

Jenn shifted, feeling like she might be giving away something so personal, even these two relatives shouldn't know about it. But Rock needed something, someone on his side, and it didn't look like he wanted that person to be her.

"He was having a nightmare and thrashing around. I couldn't wake him up, so I filled a pan with water and I threw it on him. It would have been better to think that through since we were both then soaked, and the furniture was too, and it was really cold. We went to my apartment to warm up and dry off."

Marguerite raised questioning eyebrows, but before she could ask, Jenn jumped in. "It was strictly platonic." No need to go into what happened all the other times since.

By the look on the other women's faces, she doubted they had any illusions about how far things had gone, but thankfully, they didn't ask for details.

"You saved him," Marlee commented. "Plus you drove him to the hospital when he fell. I think those count as rescues." She bit her lip as if deciding whether to say more. "Would it be okay with you if I told my husband about this?"

"And Deke too?" Marguerite added.

"I don't know. I'm not sure, I mean – " Jenn stopped, realizing she was stammering. It stung her to think she was the cause of more problems for him, and she had a sneaky suspicion he would see this as her spilling his secrets.

But she hadn't shared the deepest ones. Had he told her more already than anyone else? She wasn't sure, and she didn't want to explain that part, feeling like it would be the ultimate invasion of Rock's privacy.

Marguerite placed a comforting hand on her arm and patted. "You see, his brothers are very worried about him. No one knows what happened to Rock overseas, because he is unwilling to talk about it. He returned with post-traumatic stress, and according to the boys, he is not the same man they knew growing up. He rarely talks. Joking? Out of the question. Miss Emie tries her dear self to pieces, wanting to get him to tell her what is wrong, but he hangs his head and turns to leave as quickly as possible. I doubt even his counselor at the center knows much. Ah, but keeping a secret is also a Kermarrec trait, as we can also attest to. Sometimes, though, the best way of learning a secret is sharing one of your own. Do you agree?"

This was the first Jenn had heard of Rock seeking professional help. "He's seeing someone? But that must be good, right? He sought help."

Marlee leaned in again. "Not exactly. Jake and Deke made him go. Someone from the family dragged him there for the first couple of months. Then he started going himself, at least, until he broke his arm. That old truck of his is a stick shift, so he's pretty much stuck until it heals."

"His cast is off." And what a difference that made, she thought, but she kept the words to herself. It was impossible not to remember his tender lovemaking or the fiery parts. She let her eyes drift closed as her heartrate picked up.

"And yes, we have confirmation. The sex is good."

Jenn's eyes popped open at Marguerite's purr of satisfaction.

"Give the poor woman a break. She might not be willing to share and share alike, not like you do, anyway."

Marguerite shrugged at Marlee's protest, but she gave Jenn a wink. "I cannot help it. I am French, after all."

Over their shared laughter, Jenn heard the ringing of a phone. Marlee reached into her pocket, her expression softening.

"Ah yes, that would be Jake calling her. She gets that same tender look every time."

"Except when I'm pissed with him," Marlee retorted. Her fingers were busy over the cell's screen.

"Yes, that is a Kermarrec trait as well. They are loving, except when they are bossy."

"Amen to that, sister. And they are committed to causes they believe in." Marlee nodded to Marguerite.

"That is also too true. And finally, as we could both tell you, they fight for what they want."

Both women stared at Jenn as if expecting her to say something profound. She couldn't. With a sinking feeling, she realized that loving feeling she felt probably wasn't shared by Rock. He didn't want to fight for her. If he did, he wouldn't be so set on sending her away.

Chapter 26

It solved nothing. It solved nothing. It solved nothing.

The words were a mantra playing over and over in Rock's mind with each downward path of the ax and the crack biting into wood. He'd split enough to last much longer than he would need it, but it was easier to keep working than deal with his troubled thoughts. The ache in his arm remained a reminder of how things had to be.

Jenny had been grateful, only he knew deep down, it was more than that. She thought he was sleeping when she watched him, a nostalgic lonely expression on her lovely face and tears at the corners of her eyes. When he opened his to meet her gaze, she gave a laugh that sounded forced and rolled on top of him.

Grateful didn't begin to describe how he felt about her. She was a goddess inside and out, despite her meddling ways and long list of things he should do and her insistence that he needed to find balance in his life. He saw her glance more than once at the drawer where he stored the gun. He couldn't promise her he'd get rid of it, even as he saw the yearning request in her eyes, just as he couldn't promise her a future.

The cold didn't feel as biting as his bitter reflections. He'd shed the jacket long ago, which Ranger now used as a convenient blanket perch. Occasionally the dog lifted his head and stared intently at the road, and Rock would hear a car pass. The dog drooped when it drove by.

As tightly as Rock and Jenny had been wound around each other, he feared Ranger and Princess had become inseparable. Both dogs moaned and whined as Jenn packed her things and Rock shoved his hands deeper into his pockets.

He needed them there, because otherwise, he'd grab her and beg her not to go. He couldn't travel down that road. Both dogs hung their heads in apparent depression when Jenn and Rock said goodbye. He and Ranger stood at the bottom of the drive as the hybrid disappeared around the turn in the freshly plowed road. It was a hell of a time for the county to become efficient.

Ranger lifted his head again and gave a warning bark. Rock paused and heard it too, and it only took a moment for he and the dog to sag. The vehicle climbing the driveway had the distinct whine of a powerful gas engine and thick tires. When Jake's patrol SUV pulled even with the woodpile, Rock went back to chopping.

His brother stepped down and adjusted his gear belt. His face turned to the pile of split timber, then to Rock. His sunglasses hid his eyes, but Rock thought he detected a shadow of a grin around his mouth.

"You got the cast off."

In response, Rock took another swing with the ax.

"Will you need therapy for the arm?"

He hoped the crack of the wood rending in two answered that question.

"It's only been three weeks."

Rock picked up another length of wood and balanced it on the chopping stump. He could hear the lecture coming already. Three weeks wasn't long enough for the arm to heal. But he was tired of the chafe of the cast and he'd rid himself of it on his own.

It had been an excellent idea, because it freed his arm to hold Jenny closer than he'd been able to before. Making love with her writhing below him was an experience he wished he could enjoy many times. But time was drawing short. He put more force that needed into the next down stroke, and logs shot off into the woods.

Jake avoided commenting as his eyes followed the trails of the logs. He walked over to Ranger and crouched down, and the dog sat up without his usual timid worry, enjoying the loving he was getting. "I heard this one's a hero," Jake said.

Rock's surprise brought just enough hesitation to his stroke to bury the ax in the stump, wedged in tightly enough to be unwilling to let go.

"Where are you storing it?"

Jake still stroked the blissed-out mutt, but his tone held a note of warning that he didn't need to raise his head to transmit. Rock wasn't going to say. Admitting what he hid would be considered a ticking bomb by his brother.

A deep sigh marked Jake's disappointment, and he pulled off the glasses and rose. The grim line of his mouth and crossed arms told Rock he wasn't going to escape providing an explanation. If he said nothing at all, Deke would appear next, and he'd be harder to turn away.

"Well?"

Rock released the ax handle with deliberate care and lifted his shirt to wipe at the sweat on his face. The sting of cold penetrated his body, but he ignored it. He'd become skilled at ignoring the physical discomforts of his life. The mental ones were another matter. He doubted he'd ever come to terms with those.

"I took the cast off because it got in the way of things I have to do."

Jake quirked up a corner of his mouth as if he appreciated the response. Then he waited. He was good at the silent treatment, but Rock had him beat by a south county mile. Too bad his brother knew that.

The deputy didn't wait for a comment, pacing toward the cabin like he planned to toss the place. Rock didn't want that.

He had too many things hidden that he hoped no one would find until it didn't matter anymore.

"I keep the gun for protection, like from the coyotes the other night. There was a big cat sighted at the junction last week. And you know how the bears get."

Jake stopped and turned. "A mountain lion? Did a warning go out?"

Rock shrugged, pleased he'd sidelined his brother's intended investigation. He knew it was only for a moment. Using the break to his advantage, he began his own offensive.

"Who told you about Ranger's daring deed?"

Jake performed a sideways glance that Rock had seen often growing up, until his brother grew older and realized it was a significant tell that he knew something he shouldn't. Rock wanted to swear, because it also probably meant he knew more than he should now, and that was not good.

"Marlee and Marguerite took Jenn out the other night. They want to get to know her better, particularly since you're interested in her." He crossed his arms once more.

"Jenny is very nice, but I'm not interested in a relationship."

"Bullshit."

The word had no less wealth of meaning, said in a conversational tone.

"If she's said differently, she's deluding herself." Or he was trying to fool himself. Rock had a sick feeling it was the latter.

"Yeah, go ahead and tell yourself that. What are your intentions?"

A gruff laugh with no humor burst out of Rock before he could stop it. "I'm a man, big brother, not a boy, and the days of me sharing my deepest feelings with you are long gone."

The silence his words brought fell in the clearing like the aftermath of a toppled tree. Jake said nothing, and the teasing quirk disappeared. Grim lines returned, and he stood as still as Rock did. When they were growing up, the boys shared their thoughts and feelings and dreams for the future. While they teased Rock about being the baby, the three brothers had been inseparable.

Deke and Jake would not understand many of the things he'd had to do in the name of duty, and he couldn't explain what he had to do in the name of love.

Love. The thought behind the word brought a crash against his brain, harder than a kick to the head and three times as deadly. Jenny. He didn't need to draw on his memory to feel the tingling of his fingertips, the glide of her skin, or the warmth of being buried deep inside her. He would protect her from himself, because that's what he had to do.

"There was a time when it wasn't like this." Jake's tone held sadness. He sighed and blew out the air in a hiss that had Ranger perking his ears. The dog extended his head and sniffed wildly, and Jake looked down at him with a cheerless smile. "I wish you'd talk to us, tell us what happened to change you like this. Damn it, Rock, we're worried about you."

He didn't want them to worry, which was why he'd planned it out with such care and precision. He couldn't reassure his brother any more than he could share his deepest remorse with the woman he loved. He had a mission, and he intended to complete it.

Chapter 27

She was happy to see the older woman, and glad the news was as good as it was. Shelley informed Jenn her condition was not life-threatening and treatable with a course of care lasting over the next few months. Between treatments, she planned to return to work, and she saw no problem keeping her former schedule. Privately, her sister said she wasn't as sure, but Shelley remained determined.

When Shelley dismissed her for the day, Jenn didn't feel a sense of relief. She'd worked every day since her boss's hospitalization, except for the snow day. The clock was ticking, counting down. Soon, she'd have no job, and then she'd be in a pinch. Besides the money, she'd miss the distraction from the constant ache in her heart.

Marlee had been encouraging when Jenn proposed that she start up a business consulting practice in the area, focused on the back office management needs of the retail shops and small companies in the area. "But what you must know, Jenn, is that it takes time to build a client base. I have some ideas, but you'll need to get to know the people and build your resume on projects with other owners they trust. It will probably be slow at first."

Time was something Jenn didn't have. Already, she felt a stress headache coming on with the thought of her lack of savings and the reduced hours Shelley had discussed. She had to get her ideas out there and prove herself, and she needed to start with someone who might buy in because they knew her already.

She drove out to Rock's cabin with mixed feelings. Trepidation at her reception sat on one side of the scale.

Excitement in seeing Rock again weighed down the other. Balance between the two wasn't something she could maintain, not even for a minute.

"I don't know what to do, Princess."

The dog yipped from her front seat perch in the carrier.

Pulling into the driveway, she was surprised to see the chain missing from its usual stretch between the posts. That made her slow down, unwilling to confront the man if he already had company. Telling herself it was ridiculous to feel like she was invading as an unwelcomed visitor, she put her foot down a little harder, making the hybrid's engine whine into gas mode and lurch forward.

That drew the attention of the three people standing in front of the cabin. Rock towered over his mother and the bent form of Uncle Rowan. His head came up and he met her eyes, but at this distance, she couldn't tell if he was happy or disappointed to see her. Miss Emie shaded her eyes and a grin came to her face. Uncle Rowan waved a dismissive hand in Rock's direction, like he was angered by the direction of whatever they'd been saying, and he paced to the old ranch truck and got in the passenger seat. She could hear the slam of the creaking door even before she opened hers.

"Why Jennifer, what a lovely thing to see you here. Isn't it lovely, Rock?"

His mother might have dug an elbow into her son's side, but Jenn wasn't sure. She was too mesmerized by the transformation in front of her.

Rock had shaved. The facial hair was gone, and without it, he looked younger. She hadn't realized how much older it had made him appear until now. The pale vulnerability of bare cheeks and chin matched a forlorn slump to his shoulders. He glanced away, his attention on Ranger, who bounded over to her car with a happy sounding woof.

"Ranger, my hero." Jenn bent to greet the dog with genuine joy, but he only paused for a moment. In the next, he was in the driver's seat, and Princess barked an excited happy yap. Ranger whined and lowered his nose to her carrier, and Jenn watched in amazement with the two dogs licked through the mesh.

"I'll get him," Rock said, but he didn't move.

"Don't worry. They'll be fine." She crossed her fingers as she opened the carrier. Princess leaped out, barking with renewed excitement. Ranger gave his own low woofs, his nose at little dog level and his hindquarters up in the air, tail wagging madly. The two dogs sniffed and barked, and when Princess took off, Ranger ran hot on her heels. They disappeared inside the cabin, muting their joyous noise.

"Looks like at least those two know how to get along," Miss Emie said. Stony-faced Rock had no reaction to her intentional poke and meaningful look. Her interest swung to Jenn. "And what brings you out here on such a fine day?"

"I have a proposition to discuss with Rock."

Another poke. "A proposition, son, did you hear that?"

Rock said nothing, watching her with that expressionless look she hated.

"You'll join us for Christmas, Jennifer."

The command wasn't hidden behind the smile of the older woman.

"I, ah, can't." Not without Rock's permission. "I have plans." A little white lie.

"Ah, plans. She has plans, did you hear that?"

This time, her dig of elbow brought a roll to Rock's eyes. Despite the reaction, Jenn smiled inside. It was fun to see a man as formidable as the one in front of her brought down to size by a woman he could probably bench press with ease.

"Will you visit your sisters?"

Caught off guard, Jenn said, "Oh no. One is on a cruise, and the other will be spending the holiday with her husband's family."

Emie's face fell into a puzzled frown. "But then what are your plans, dear?"

Jenn shifted from foot to foot, conscious that Rock's gaze now seemed pinned on her. She shrugged, because any excuse she could come up with this quickly was bound to fail under the eagle-eyed scrutiny of Miss Emie.

"I thought so. Now, you join us. Bring this big lug with you. I swear he is as difficult now as he was a-borning. Did I tell you I was in labor with him for a day and a half? Didn't want to come out yet, nope, he did not. Stubborn then like he is now. Oh, the years in between were the same too. Always wants to do things his own way."

Rock sighed loudly, frustration washing over his features. When he couldn't hide behind the beard, it was a bit easier to see his expressions.

"Give me a kiss, son, and then go see your lady friend."

Rock bent and pecked his mother on the cheek, and she wrapped arms around him and pulled him in for a hug. Jenn watched him hug her back, a rock-hard gesture that spoke to the depth of his love for his mother. His eyes fell closed and his expression turned vulnerable again. Jenn felt tears well in response. By the time they parted, his face wore that blank look again.

"Give me a hug too, dear. Now remember, Christmas out at the ranch. Rock will give you the details. You two can drive together. He can even pick you up." Emie took her hug and made her way across the yard to the pick-up, climbing behind the wheel. "Now Rock, remember, you need to move a little faster, or someone's going to mistake you for your nickname and pass you by." Her pointed determined look extended to Jenn.

The older woman had the engine fired up and the truck in gear within seconds. They both watched her head down the driveway. When her tires hit the main road, they squealed from a rapid acceleration. Rock wore a fond smile on his face when she turned back to him, but Jenn didn't miss the longing in his eyes. Longing for what wasn't clear, but she swore she was going to find out.

"Jake hates it when she does that."

She wasn't sure what to comment on first, how different he looked shaved, or that she missed him. Standing feet away from him now, she realized she'd really, really missed him. It had only been three days.

Still watching the place where his mother drove away, Rock said, "You can go now. You don't have to attend the holiday shindig. I'll tell Ma something."

Her heart squeezed like a hand clutched around it. The distance in his tone exceeded boredom, but not by much.

He set his eyes on hers, close enough now for her to marvel at the shift of colors. The bare face made him seem more open. More available, but not welcoming, at least not to her. If she told him why she was here, he would help her. She had no doubt about that. The rest she'd have to leave up to chance.

Instead of responding to his dismissal, she said, "Rock, I need your help."

He stilled, his face a frozen mask of indifference. When the frown came, her ability to appreciate it fully accented its darkness. Scary stuff, his frowns, but not enough to chase her off. Nothing would be scary enough for that.

"I don't have anything to offer you."

She stepped closer, forcing the intimacy she was sure he tried to fight. "I want to start a business consulting practice in Flynn's Crossing, and I need a few projects with clients that locals trust to establish my credentials here. Otherwise, I'll have to return to the Bay Area and take whatever job I can find. I don't want to do that."

Nothing she said was a falsehood, making it easier to stand up to his intense scrutiny. The hint of a possible dimple on his cheek had been hidden by the beard, and she bet if she could make him smile, it would appear as a crazy attractive divot. She wanted to make him loosen up to see if she was right. She'd settled for him relaxing the stance that screamed military even though he wasn't saluting.

"I don't need anything." He turned and headed for the cabin, his pace a rapid march.

"What about the goat business? I've been doing more research. It's a great way to make a living for someone who doesn't want interaction with other people."

She bit her tongue, willing him not to hear the last part of that. He halted his retreat and turned back to her.

"I don't need to manage goats to make a living. Talk to Uncle Rowan. He's intrigued by the idea."

He spun away again, and she ran to catch up to him. When she put a hand on his arm to stop him, he looked down at it like she'd bitten into his flesh.

Oh yes, she'd enjoy taking a few love bites out of him. Up close, his cheeks appeared soft, like the skin had hidden for so long, it aged slower than the rest of him. His woodsy masculine scent lingered in the air around him, a tempting cloud luring her in. She didn't fake the sway closer, drawn as she was to him in every way she could imagine.

If only he'd take her into his confidence and tell her what was wrong. It was easy to see how post-traumatic stress could explain his mercurial mood swings and nightmares. What third party resources couldn't tell her, though, was what caused his.

Words swirled around in her brain from years ago and their recent conversations, forcing her to focus on things other than wanting to jump his bones. He rescued her, and she rescued him. That's what the universe intended them to do, and she wasn't going to fight the universe.

"I think having you as one of my first local clients will go a long way toward convincing others to hire me."

He shook his head. "They don't know me, so why do you think that would help?"

It was her turn to deny the words. "Of course they know you. You received a Purple Heart and a Bronze Star and so many commendations, you probably need a filing cabinet to manage the paperwork. What happened to the medals?"

Helplessness washed over his features, and he cringed as if the idea brought him heartfelt anguish. Without responding, he turned back to the cabin and strode so fast, she had to run to stay on his heels.

"Okay, forget that. All I'm saying is that people recognize you as a hero, and if you hire me, it will mean something to them. You'll help me establish my credentials. Do you trust me, Rock?"

He was inside with his hand on the cabin door, staring at something out of her view. When she drew even with him, she followed his gaze to the dog bed. Ranger stretched out to as full a length as he could against the cushion's surrounding bolster. Mimicking his pose, Princess pressed against his belly. Both dogs snored contentedly with matching rhythms.

"They're friends now." She couldn't keep the marvel of this out of her voice. It was like the incident with the coyotes had brought Princess a change of heart, and now, Ranger trusted her. If only Rock would agree to copy that.

"It isn't a question of trust," he said in a quiet voice. Melancholy made the words sound so forlorn, she stepped closer, intent on offering him comfort.

He swiveled away, throwing out a hand to block her when she would have followed. "I can't help you," he repeated.

"Go back to San Francisco. I'm sure you'll be able to negotiate a return to your old job without any problem."

"I don't want to."

Jitters threatened her resolve not to beg, but she had a sneaky feeling she would, if she had to.

He put his hands on the table and leaned down, his eyes closed. "Tell me why you can't. There's almost always room for negotiation if you're willing to be flexible on the terms. Give a little and often you can gain a lot. Draw a line in the sand, and you lose."

"Is that what happened to you?"

He reared back and stared blue fire at her, fierce and feral. "Who told you that?"

She stepped closer, betting he would tell her if she bared all too. "No one. I'm guessing, based on the way you're acting. You were a negotiator. You lost something important to you. You're letting it destroy you."

"You don't understand." Sorrow colored his words, even as his face stayed furious. Ranger raised his head and whined, in tune with Rock's feelings.

"Maybe I don't, and since you refuse to explain it to me, I won't be able to learn about it."

"Give me one good reason why you can't search for a new job in the Bay Area. Just one. There are dozens of firms who would be happy to have you, I'm sure."

She inhaled deeply, willing herself to tell the story calmly. "My company won't give me a reference, which is as bad as saying I did something wrong. Not that I did, I mean. But they aren't being helpful when a potential employer calls for references. Believe me when I say I don't have any options left. They fired me, they won't give me a good recommendation, and effectively, I'm blacklisted from working as a consultant in any major firm."

Jenn wasn't aware her voice dropped to a whisper until she got to the end of her recitation and gasped out a sob. Rock watched her with sharp interest. She could almost hear gears grinding as he processed what she said. A narrowing of his eyes told her he'd reached the part where he registered the implications of being blacklisted. Frustration came next.

His voice was gentler when he said, "So, no going back."

She shook her head, not trusting her voice.

A grim line pulled his mouth tight and he looked at the dogs. Ranger had dropped his head down, but his eyes stayed on his human. He looked like he'd spring into action if Rock required him. Meanwhile, Princess still snored from the safety of her cuddle.

"Does the other company, the opposing side, know who told them about the discrepancies?"

She shook her head again. "No. My firm denied there were issues. If they told the other side, they'd have to admit what I said was right. They can't admit to their dishonesty."

"It goes beyond dishonesty. Their business ethics are worth shit." He paced, running a hand over hair a good inch shorter than it had been three days ago. "You are better off not working there. You understand that, don't you?"

He pinned her with a sincere gaze, and she knew he was now on her side. If only he'd admit they needed to work together too, she'd feel like they stood a chance.

"Yes, I know. That doesn't put kibble in the bowl, though." She tried a smile, wondering if her tension showed in her face.

One corner of his mouth lifted in a grin. Yes, there was that dimple. It shown like a beacon of hope in his face, or at least, she hoped so.

"What if I help you develop a strategy to return to work? Not here, but back in San Francisco. Something you can use to negotiate a return to work, not with your old firm, but a new one."

"I don't have a lot of time." Another truth, since Shelley wouldn't need her long once she returned to work.

"Neither do I," he replied.

She felt the frown crease her face, and her mouth opened to ask what he meant by that. As if he anticipated what she would ask, he said, "I'll be leaving soon."

"Leaving? Does your mother know?"

He grimaced. "No, and please don't mention it to her. It would ruin her holidays. I'll tell her afterwards."

So, no hope for the two of them, either, unless wherever he went next would be a place where they could try a long-distance relationship. By the expression on his face, she suspected he dismissed that as a possibility outright.

She tried not to let that disappointment show on her face. He watched her, hiding whatever he was thinking and feeling behind a blank expression. She wished she knew what he was thinking, because she had a feeling she wouldn't like any of it, and that was the sole reason he hid it from her.

He waited, wondering if the inevitable question would come. Where was he going? Could they stay in touch? How long would he be gone?

Not far. No. Forever. The words he couldn't say sang through his head, taunting him and shaking his resolve. He loved Jenny, and he ached to tell her. A promise was a promise, though, even one he only made to himself.

She surprised him when she asked none of those things. A shy smile came to her face. "I like the no-beard Rock."

He glanced toward the door. "Ma's work. It is impossible to say no to her. Ask any of her sons. Ma's word is gospel." Which is why he could never tell anyone what he intended. Ma would find a way to talk him out of it, and his grief would never end. A pang he recognized as guilt was only assuaged by the knowledge of what he planned to leave behind.

An explanation. A letter might be deemed highly inadequate, but it was all he could give them. That, and analyses and reports supporting his contention. He didn't deserve to live on after the others died. The curse of their memories haunted him every night and every day.

Another Christmas none of them would ever see. The change of seasons his buddies from the Midwest so loved to enjoy. The powerful feeling of success for the medical personnel when they saved another life. Simple things, like a favorite food or a beloved pet. Families left to mourn and grieve.

Another twinge of guilt washed over him. None of his family would understand. He wished it was different. He and Jenny were more alike than she would ever know. They both operated from a set of moral values and ethics many would consider obsolete. Too bad he couldn't explain it to her. She, at least, would have an inkling of what he felt.

"So, can I stay?"

He blinked at the question.

"You wanted me to leave. You told me to forget about Christmas. But you said you'd help me devise a re-entry strategy." She had a peculiar look in her eyes, like she hid something from him. He suspected he knew what it was. She hoped that working together, she would be able to break down his defenses and change the future. Too bad that was impossible.

"We only have a little time together, Jenny."

She nodded, but uncertainty clouded her eyes. "How long until you leave?"

He wrestled with that question every day. The snows promised to fall in depth over the holidays. Temperatures were dropping. Things would align into the perfect conditions within a couple of weeks.

"Soon."

She nodded again, lowering her head. Her hair fell to cover her face, obscuring how she took that news. A hitch in her breathing and a lift of her shoulders told him she might be sobbing, but when she raised her head, she wore a teary smile.

"Well, we'd better get to work then, I guess."

He wanted it to be so much more, but that wasn't going to be something he could negotiate.

Chapter 28

Neither of them said it. Neither of them asked anything. Jenny brought over a suitcase and a bag of dogfood. She draped herself around the little cabin. For as long as they had, they had each other. That didn't mean he couldn't save her one more time when he was gone.

"That will be your best solution. Your advantage is in knowing you saved that other company. If you tell them you are their anonymous informant, they might be willing to clear your name."

"I can't do that. Rock, they won't see me and if they did, they wouldn't believe me. My old firm made it clear to everyone that I was let go because they said I was the one lying about the analysis. Let's not discuss it anymore. Let's enjoy the time we have without thinking about the future."

He grew frustrated when she resisted. Even as he laid out the risks and she agreed the possible reward outweighed them, she fought him. He understood. She didn't want to go back at all.

He didn't want to leave either.

Rock struggled with keeping quiet. It wasn't about what he would do, but how he felt. The three simple words were on the tip of his tongue so many times, he bled with biting them off without revealing them.

I love you.

Yes, there had been other women he'd cared for deeply. A doctor's face rose the most clearly from the massacre. When he returned to consciousness two years ago, her sightless eyes stared back at him. Blood stained the floor around her, pools of it from the many dead. His buddies. The platoon protecting the makeshift hospital. Everyone but him, dead. For what purpose? The iron stink of too much blood stung his every breath even now.

"What are you thinking about?"

Jenny nestled closer to him, warm despite her naked skin. She traced a hand up his chest, then down, down, until he grabbed her fingers. Play time was over. He had something serious to discuss with her.

"I have something I need to say."

Her eyes grew large at his words. He saw the hope there, and he hated to quash it. They'd had days and nights of utter bliss. Christmas was now a single day away.

"I'm not going to like it, am I?"

Her perception, as usual, was too on target for him to argue. He nodded, and he saw her light dim. She put on a brave front, smiling like it was nothing and shifting away. She pulled on a sweater, and moved away from him, pushing her shoulders back and avoiding his gaze.

He couldn't say it. He wanted to, but the words didn't come.

"Well, I have something to tell you too. I have a meeting with the CEO of the company I helped save from that bad deal, two days after New Year's, bright and early. I'll go to my sister's the day after your family's Christmas dinner. I need to prepare my presentation."

"I think they'll see you as a hero."

Jenny snorted and shook her head. "It's a nice idea, seeing as the CEO seems to value honesty and integrity based on his public persona. We both know, though, that corporate pressure and politics being what it is, this could backfire. But I agree, this is the right thing to do, maybe the only thing I can do."

"I'm glad you were able to get in to see them so quickly."

She looked at him with expectant curiosity. "Well? Now it's your turn. What did you want to tell me?"

This was going to be hard. He'd told no one about what happened. Not the umpteen shrinks and counselors who'd grilled him, each in their own styles. Not his brothers, who took a rip-off-the-bandage approach to these kinds of things. Not Ma, who was wise enough to recognize the pain in his eyes and leave things be until he was ready. He'd never be ready to explain completely, but he could give Jenny a summary.

"You've asked me why I'm so messed up."

She began to protest, and he put two fingers over her mouth. Those lips were red and swollen with their hours of kissing. His body had never been so sated, and her presence in his life was bringing him peace inside too. The course of action, when it played out, would turn out as it was supposed to.

"I am messed up. I have post traumatic shock from what happened. People died, everyone but me. I was supposed to save them, and I couldn't. The brass saw things differently, which explains medals and commendations I can never accept as mine. I have them hidden away. Others judge me differently, but I know what I did."

Jenn leaned into him, putting her hand over his heart.

"I know the heart that beats in here," she tapped his chest, "and it is a good heart. You're a good man, Frederic Kermarrec, and I think the military is right about you."

He stopped her tapping fingers with a clutched fist. "Hear me out, okay? I'll gloss over specifics that don't matter. It was the desert. Midsummer is a brutally hot time of year in that part of the world. I was assigned to protect an underground hospital, not with a gun, but with my words. I was their negotiator with the outside world. I bent the rules and broke down barriers and got the other side to give them allowances, all in the name of saving lives."

"You are a hero."

When he could respond, the booming pain in his voice brought a whine from Ranger, curled in his bed with Princess by his side. "No. My band of brothers and sisters protecting the hospital above ground were in constant danger. They were injured, threatened, and bribed to reveal the location. Their presence alone was enough for the other side to know there was a facility in the vicinity, but none of us would give it up. They couldn't because they didn't know where the entrance was. Only I knew, a standard protocol of protection to minimize their risk."

His throat grew parched with the memory. The arguments between the soldiers grew heated at times. His special status as a Ranger and his assignment as a negotiator was respected, but some regarded him with suspicion. They might have suspected he had a personal interest in the safety of the hospital team.

"I was involved with one of the doctors." The telling grew even more painful with that admission. Jenny seemed to sense it, and she laid her head down on his chest and matched her breathing with his. She didn't ask, only waited.

Ranger sensed his agony, laying down against his flank. With Jenny's hair under one hand and stroking the dog's thick coat with the other, he let his gaze drift to the woodstove and its dancing flames.

"She was an amazing surgeon. So many people, rebels and children alike, owed their survival to her skills. She had hope, such profound hope, that her countrymen would see reason and the war would end, and she could go back to being what she'd trained for, a pediatric surgeon."

"What was her name?"

"Ilya. She dreamed of working for a worldwide organization that performed transformational surgeries on children who might otherwise live their lives with crippling disfigurements which meant they were outcasts in their cultures. Instead, she sewed up fighters and removed bullets from kids and when nothing could be done, she held hands and prayed with the dying."

"She sounds like an amazing person. Were you in love with her?"

"No." He knew that now. For a long time, he thought he had been, until Jenny came back into his life. Now he knew the depths of love in its best and worst.

He felt the heat of parched desert air and his own screams in his words. "I couldn't save her or the others when it counted. I couldn't negotiate a way out of the final battle, the one that killed those who were left. The soldiers. The doctors and nurses and patients. Everyone died but me."

"But you escaped. You survived. That's the legacy of that battle. You live on to tell their story."

"No, they let me live because I gave them what they wanted, the location of the hospital and my troops. I must have."

She stared at him without speaking, a thoughtful expression on her face. "What if it wasn't you? What if someone else knew? What do the reports say?"

He shook his head. She didn't understand, and he wasn't going to enlighten her. He couldn't read the reports, not without wanting to put his gun to his head and pull the trigger. He had to be the only one who knew.

"They're inconclusive," he said.

"But you're still a hero. Rock, didn't the delay save people? Did some of the patients and your unit survive?"

A few had, slipping away under the cover of barrages of gunfire or dense too-quiet darkness. Some had made it out alive. That was the only page in one thick folder he was able to read without dense anguish overwhelming him.

He shrugged and looked away, unwilling to respond to her questions. She gave him a way to explain it, though.

"That's what I'm going to do. I'm going to live out the legacy of that battle. I'm going to honor the ones we lost."

She drew back and gazed at him with admiration on her face, a caring he didn't deserve. "So you'll be telling their story? Is that where you're going?"

He nodded, since it was, in a manner of truth.

"But that's wonderful. You'll be amazing at this, I know it." The smile she gave him was a blessing he didn't deserve. Then her face grew solemn. "And when you're done? Where will you go?"

He heard what she didn't ask. "I'm not planning to come back here."

She looked away, biting her lip in that way she had when she craved to ask a question but knew she wouldn't get an answer. It had become an unspoken rule between them. Neither of them asked anything they suspected would produce an answer the other didn't want to hear.

Truth. They told the truth, or they said nothing.

Princess wandered over, yawning widely, and poked her nose into Ranger's face. The big dog gave her a lecturing swat, and she accepted it. These two had also become too close for words to explain. Little dog crawled into Rock's lap and settled herself on Ranger's head, and big dog crossed his eyes and tried to look up at her. Both of them sighed and rested their eyes on Rock as if waiting for a continuation of the story.

He felt the uptick in her heartbeats as if they pulsed in his own chest. Jenny grew too quiet, and the weight of her sadness dragged him further into the abyss. He wanted to make only happy memories with her, something for her to take out occasionally and enjoy as a pleasant reminiscence. He smiled, trying to make light of it.

"Promise me you'll get help. You can feel better about the outcome, Rock. I know you can feel better about yourself. I feel it."

He chuckled without humor at her calm assurance. She was so sure things could be better for him. Things would get better for her too, once he was out of the picture. She would move on, successful in her quest to clear her name.

"Well, I feel something else, and you can do something about it." He took her hand and drew it down to his lap, wrapping her fingers around the hard press against the blanket. She giggled, and it sounded a little watery, but she seemed game when her fingers closed, and she began stroking.

"Want to go to bed?" The suggestive glint in her eyes was unmistakable when she lifted her face to his. In response, he lowered his head and kissed her with every emotion in him.

She carried him to a different place, a place where things were peaceful and calm even as their joint fire burned so brightly. By the time she rose over him, he was straining to hold on. He wanted to hear her cry out in passion and watch her face transform with ecstasy. It was never enough. Saying goodbye to her might be the hardest thing he'd ever have to do.

"Come with me." Her voice was rough with passion as her hands clung to his shoulders with a fierceness past anything from before.

"You first."

She shook her head, leaning down and giving him a kiss that seared his thoughts. In a second, he was seated to the hilt and nothing ever in his life had felt so exquisite.

Breaking the kiss, she gave him a breathless command he could do nothing but obey. "Together."

He couldn't stop his body from responding, and she egged him on with each matching move. Their eyes held, even as he fought off the impending wave ready to crash over him. Jenny's soul shown in her wide gaze.

"I love you, Rock."

His heart might have stopped. He wanted to say it, but if he did, her pain would only be a thousand times worse.

When they hurtled over the edge, oblivion didn't claim him as he hoped. All he could see was the matching emotions of joy and sorrow in the eyes of the woman he loved and know that the devastation at his silence was something he felt powerless to fix.

Chapter 29

Jenn stretched her toes, not that they hadn't stretched plenty over that night. Curled too. She wanted to purr with contentment, but that nagging idea that something wasn't right kept her from enjoying it fully.

She was sure she could convince Rock to stay in touch. Once he'd had time to tell his story to the world, he'd be ready to pick things up again. The trip would be difficult but cathartic, and perhaps bring him the calm he needed. She was sure he returned her love. She saw it in his eyes, even if it was coupled with a sadness without bounds.

Princess gave a yip for acknowledgement, and Jenn opened her eyes to find both dogs sitting up and staring at her from a spot next to the bed. She glanced over at Rock, sprawled on his back with an arm thrown over his face. The other was wrapped firmly around her. When she moved, he tightened it immediately.

"The dogs need to go out."

He came awake instantly and lowered his arm. The unguarded yearning in his face did weird things to her heart, like make it want to leap out of her chest without a leash. She gave him a quick kiss which he instantly deepened and pushed him off with a laugh.

"I'll take care of them. Then we can go back to bed for a while."

He rubbed a hand over his face, and with the motion, he replaced the yearning with a neutral smile. "What time is it?"

A glance at her cell gave her the answer.

"We need to get moving. I have something I'd like us to do before we leave for the ranch."

By the time she was back in with the dogs, he'd banked the fire. He pulled her in close, keeping an arm wrapped around her as she tilted into his strength.

He was such an amazing man. He didn't realize it, she suspected, but his strength was probably what saved him when everyone else died.

"Take a walk with me?"

She nodded, and they dressed in silence. Cups of coffee in hand, they walked outside, and he stopped in surprise, the same kind she'd felt moments before.

"It's snowing."

She nodded. "I wonder how much is predicted."

He tilted his face into the falling flakes and a few caught on his long lashes. He closed his eyes, a mixed expression of joy and sorrow on it that made her feel nervous. Blinking off the snow, his intense gaze fell on her.

"You might need to leave earlier than you expected."

"Oh no, I couldn't do that. I mean, your mother's expecting us. I don't want to disappoint her."

He looked up at the white sky again. Underfoot, he kicked at what had accumulated and frowned. "If it looks like this is going to keep up, you might not be able to get out tomorrow. Then you'll miss your meeting."

As if he didn't expect her respond, he took her hand and pulled. Ranger bounded past, with Princess in her plaid coat leaping to keep up. A little dog bark was all it took for the larger beast to slow into a walk, and she could jump from paw-step to paw-step in his wake with happy abandon, based on the speed of her wagging tail.

Jenn didn't want to ask where they were going, preferring to enjoy the silence unique to a snowfall. She'd experienced too few of those over the years, and this one was special with the man by her side. He walked ahead of her, breaking a trail in the few inches hiding the packed earth. At times, he kicked snow to the side, letting her see a root or vine so she wouldn't trip.

When he stopped, she peeked around him and drew in a delighted gasp. The pond rimmed with white held a magical quality.

"Our lake," she said.

"It's a pond." Still, he chuckled indulgently and tucked her into his side. She'd happily stay like this forever if he let her.

She didn't want to go away, even for a day. An hour would be too long when she didn't know his plans. He wouldn't tell her when he was leaving, keeping his answers frustratingly vague.

Rock kissed the top of her head, and she tilted back to look him in the eyes. His shimmered as if he held back tears. His arms tightened briefly before they let her go, traveling down her arms to grasp her hands in his.

"I have something to say to you."

This was it. She'd finally hear the words.

"I release you from our oath, our blood bond." His probing gaze stayed on her face with the words.

A shock rang through her, a bolt as deep and alarming as when he'd fired that gun into the air. "Wait, what do you mean?" She couldn't keep the stammer out of her voice.

He lifted her hands and kissed her fingers one by one, his gaze never breaking from hers. "I release you from our blood bond. You no longer need to feel like you must rescue me."

That also meant he didn't feel committed to rescuing her.

"I don't understand." Frigid numbness began to penetrate every cell in her body.

"You don't need to worry about me, Jenny. I mean it. No oath."

'Blood bond. You and me. We'll always rescue each other.'

The old words rang in her head like a chiming bell.

"These past few days have been a wonder for me. Your presence this past month, a miracle. I'll carry the vision of you with me for the rest of my life."

His words were pretty, but the dejected emptiness in his eyes spoke louder.

"Why are you doing this? Why now?" She heard the panic in her tone, but she couldn't hide it.

"You'll be better off if you travel home with a clean slate. I hope you remember me with fondness, or better yet, don't think of me at all. Please understand that you have been the best thing to ever happen to me." He stopped short, as if he wanted to say more but decided against it.

"You're sending me away again."

He tilted his head and closed his eyes. He nodded.

"And you aren't going to tell me why."

Instead, he looked skyward. "The snow's getting heavier."

"But I can stay. We'll have Christmas here. I'll drive out a bit and find cell service, and I'll call your mother, and then I'll delay my appointment. I'm sure everyone will understand."

He was already shaking his head. The sadness in his face made her wish she could turn back the clock and freeze it instead of her heart.

"You need to go. You'll never feel settled until you close the loop, Jenny. Explain everything and then, no matter what, you'll find your answers and your future."

The words he didn't say, a future without him, weren't something she could ignore.

"I want to go wherever you go," she said, leaning into his body. His arms came around her slowly, as if he fought the urge and lost.

His voice broke with raw emotion as he whispered, "No, you don't."

>>>>>

Ma wasn't pleased with him. Her sharp gaze saw too much when he explained Jenny's sudden departure for parts west as the need to get out before the snow became too thick. She couldn't dispute it, though, since six inches were predicted to add to the half a foot already on the ground. Jenny's little hybrid would never have made it down the hills.

He thought about calling her, wondering if she made the drive okay. At the ranch, he pulled out his cell phone and triggered the phone app, finding that she'd entered her number in his contacts list when he hadn't been looking. He pondered the significance of that for a moment, then put the phone away. Creating an expectation when there could be none wouldn't be fair to her.

Later, when he'd played with the babies and had a good-natured argument with his brothers over college football teams, he thought about how normal it all felt. Normal was anything but for him. Then he pulled out his phone and swiped to the photo gallery, stopping at the pictures he'd taken when Jenny wasn't aware.

Most were of her sleeping. In a couple, she was reading something with serious concentration puckering her forehead. In one, she looked right at the camera with a laughing face.

She'd caught him then, and she pulled out hers and demanded to take some in turn.

He hoped she deleted them, and soon. He didn't want her focused on the past, and that was all he could ever be. His finger hovered over the delete button too, but he couldn't bring himself to do it.

"What's going on?"

Deke's deep voice didn't hold anything other than curiosity, but Rock knew his brother would only be pushed off for so long.

"What do you mean?"

With a hand that waved at Ranger romping nearby with one of the ranch dogs. "You, coming alone. I understand the story about Jenn not being able to drive in the deeper snow, but you both could have gone back to her apartment in town. It's a lower elevation, and she could have traveled back from there."

Rock shrugged, realizing that was an angle he hadn't prepared himself for. He usually planned for every possible line of debate or questioning. Not this one.

"She wanted to go. It was time. She's going back to her life, the life she's meant for. End of story."

Deke didn't look like he was buying it. "You know, Ma's not going to let you off the hook so easily. Just wait until dessert's done."

Rock met his brother's warning grin with a reluctant one of his own. "Maybe I'll skip dessert."

Except he didn't want to. He'd welcome Ma's interrogation, because he'd been worked over by the best and never said a word. He'd never been sure how the enemy had discovered the hospital's location. He had been positive he hadn't given it up, not even when he was out of his mind with pain and their threats, until the reality of being the only one who knew wasn't something he could ignore.

Deke watched him, waiting with a level of patient calmness Rock had envied when they were kids. Jake was the planner of their trio, figuring angles to reach the best possible outcomes. Rock tended to act first and apologize later, his fast temper and impetuous nature getting him in trouble more times than he could count. When the time came to pick a career track in the Army, Rock decided to work against type, channeling his older brothers' temperaments to build his negotiations persona.

"Are you going to tell me what's going on, or do we need to beat it out of you?"

Under other circumstances, that would have raised a smile in him, but not today.

"Everything I said was true. Jenny's interview is important. She could get her career back, and that's important to her. I couldn't stand in the way of her future."

"I get all of that. What I don't understand is your behavior today. You seemed, I don't know, forced, like you're intentionally acting like your world is rosy and bright."

"Maybe it is," Rock said, turning to the wrestling dogs. He wasn't sure why he'd saved Ranger from kennel hell, only to abandon him again when the time came for him to leave. He'd had to add a few steps to his master plan to make sure the dog was taken care of.

"I used to be able to read you like a large print book," Deke muttered, shaking his head. "Now, I don't what's truth and what's bullshit coming out of your mouth."

"Everything I say is true," Rock replied. Being pushed to be on the offensive was not a position he liked. Besides, it was what he didn't say that would bring hardship and pain to the family. He didn't want that to be their last memory of him.

"What's going on?" The question fired from Jake as he joined them made Rock roll his eyes and Deke utter a single curse.

"I don't know. That's what I'm trying to learn from our baby brother here."

The two looked at him with matching lop-sided grins, probably expecting him to rise to the taunt. He'd been on the receiving end of worse, and he lived to tell about it. Stoicism had nothing on a blank stare and expressionless face, he'd come to learn, and that's what he deployed now.

"He's not going to tell us," Jake said in a conversational tone. "But what until Ma gets him in her clutches. He'll be begging for mercy."

He'd begged, mercy not for himself, but for the others. Their captors had laughed, saving their best tortures for him. The only reason he survived was because they needed him. Once that need no longer existed, they didn't even have the decency to finish him off.

The flash of pain came without warning. One minute, he was looking at his brothers' smiling faces in the snowy countryside, and the next, he was creeping along the bomb-blasted inner wall of the town, alone, hoping for the best and fearing the worst. The entrance was hidden down an alley, under a pile of rubble that appeared immovable and solid to a casual glance. A small cave opened in the back, just wide enough for him to crawl through. He wasn't sure how they lowered patients down the tunnel. He had to crawl on all fours with his belly sweeping the floor.

Ilya pushed hair from her forehead, leaving behind a streak of blood. Conditions could not be called sanitary, but it was the only hope these people had. She lifted her face and caught him staring, and she regarded him without a smile and got back to work. She had no hope for their future, while he had assured her he'd get her out. He'd return to the U.S. with her by his side. She called it his romantic notions. She never responded to his declarations of love.

Then in another flash, he was parched and tired and hurting. A hot wind blew on him, making his thirst worse.

Cracked lips and swollen eyes made communicating difficult. He thought he was the only one being held hostage. It wasn't until later that he found his military brothers in the same stinking black hole. Then they were begging, and it wasn't from the captors, but from him.

'Tell them. Please, Kerm, tell them. I'm dying here. I'm gonna bleed out and die in this miserable hell, all because you won't tell them. What does it matter if it's now or later? They're gonna find it anyway, you know that. They said they'll let us go once they know.'

A couple of the men were stoic, watching him with dagger looks. They said nothing, leaving it to those who had it in them to plead to do their dirty work. Everyone assumed the ones who were missing were already dead. How they got ambushed was unclear. Captors and captives were now pinned down under a steady barrage of indiscriminate artillery fire and despite Rock's reports to the friendlies, sometimes it took one of their own along with their rivals.

When they dragged him out that final time, their glee bordered on psychotic. They cackled and grinned and kicked him, not hard enough to do harm but like they would a ball in a casual game. Throwing him down to face the reality of what had happened with curses he had no trouble understanding, they laughed even harder at his screams of grief.

This time, though, it wasn't Ilya's blank-eyed stare facing him. The blood-matted hair was silky brown, the creamy skin was pale, and the vacant dead eyes were a chocolate he knew would soon fade to a milky white. Soon, no trace of vanilla would linger in the air over the tortured stench.

"No!" The scream ripped out of him, because she didn't deserve to die. Jenny needed to live, to have a life full of love and happiness, and someday, when she was old and gray and musing about life's strangeness, she might remember a boy with a cast walking with a girl in an elf's hat along a pond's edge and stealing her first kiss. She might close her hands together and recall how they held hands all the way back to a cabin in the woods.

"Rock. Rock! Man, what's the matter? You're here. You're safe. Get Ma."

He heard the frantic words, felt the bands of arms pinning him to something so cold and wet, he couldn't comprehend what it was doing in the desert. Blood gone cold was slippery and sticky. This was refreshing, but it didn't ease his pain and burden.

Then a whine and something warm. More whining, and a boney shove to the side of his head.

"Off. I said get off him, Ranger. Grab his collar. Rock, where are you?"

The stabs of pain in his head faded slowly. Deep-toned yips accompanied the whines, held at a distance. He registered the activities around him. Turning his head to the side, snow buried one eye. With the other, he saw Uncle Rowan holding a straining Ranger, who noted his stare with a happier bark and sat down.

Deke pressed a knee to his chest and pinned his arms to his sides. The fear on his face was as real as it got. Rock couldn't think of a single time when he'd looked any worse.

"Let him up, Deke."

Ma's voice lost its hippie lilt. A five-star's bellow to the troops wouldn't have held more command.

"Ma, I'm not sure – " Hesitation colored Deke's tone.

"Get off me," Rock said, unsure his voice carried far. He went completely still, which drew his brother's attention. In a firmer voice bleeding roughness, he tried again. "I said, get off me."

"I think we should call an ambulance," Jake said.

"Let's get him inside. Rock, can you walk? Boys, help him up and carry him if you have to. He can't lie in the snow like that. He'll catch his death."

The bubble of laughter was completely inappropriate. It came out of nowhere, and once he started, he couldn't stop. Not when he looked at the horror in Jake's expression, or heard the cursing coming from his uncle. Ranger jumped on him with evident joy, which made him laugh harder.

Catch his death. If only he could. He'd make it happen anyway, and the snow was just what he needed. Relief that it had all been a nightmare washed over him. Jenny was safe and sound, alive and heading on to her life without him, to a place where he couldn't drag her into his abyss.

It wasn't until later, when his brothers were mollified with a story about PTSD bringing on these episodes, that the significance of Jenny in his nightmare made an impact. She would be disappointed if she ever learned she hadn't saved him. Nothing could.

"Here, this will warm you up. Just like you like it."

Ma put a mug in front of him. Rock glanced down at it, about to tell her he didn't need it, when she wrapped her hands around his, and then around the ceramic. It was a mug she'd made during her pottery stage. That had come after the painting and before the quilting. The mug wasn't perfect, but it was made with love.

"Is it helping?"

He looked at her lined face. Most times, her eyes sparkled with youthful mirth and her smile lit up a room bright enough to blind a man's vision, but not now. Somberness aged her to her real years, and he regretted being the cause.

"I don't know. I'll tell you when I drink some." He blew on the hot chocolate, dislodging marshmallows and sending up steam.

"Does being with Jennifer help?"

He snapped his attention to her, but there was no teasing crinkle to her eyes and the set of her lips told him he'd better come up with an answer. He always wanted to tell her the truth. He nodded once. Ma looked satisfied with that.

"You know that you can always come to us, to your family, for anything you need. Any help at all. We'll all come running for you. You know that, don't you, son?"

He felt all of five years old, like that time he'd put his pet mouse in the barn because he didn't want his dad to find it in his room. The barn cat got the mouse and displayed it with pride, leaving it on the front doormat as an offering to Ma. He'd been devastated. Ma had understood.

But she wouldn't understand this.

Chapter 30

Jenn paced the traditionally furnished dining room, complete with glass-doored breakfront exhibiting her sister's wedding china. Minus its usual hubbub of activity, the house felt cold and too silent. She'd become used to the noise of two children and their friends' invasions, busy parents, and full lives. Today, it was just Princess and her.

The dog had become uncharacteristically sweet and quiet. She cuddled. She tore up nothing. She was on her best behavior. Jenn suspected Princess Sweet Pea had a major crush on one Ranger dog and hoped with all her doggy heart that her good behavior would mean their return to Flynn's Crossing.

"You and me both, sister."

The dog yipped her agreement and wagged her tail. The expectant tilt of her head came right before she ran to the front door, then back, yipping again.

"And no, we can't go back now. We might not be able to go back ever."

Princess sat and threw her a disgusted look.

Jenn sighed. Much as she would love to go back, to crawl into the safety and assurances of Rock's embrace with an unwavering belief that they could work it out, she knew he wouldn't welcome it. When he pushed her into the car and slammed shut the door, it sounded as final as it got. He didn't lift a hand to wave as she drove away. It was only because she had to concentrate in the unfamiliar snowy conditions that she didn't give in to the tears.

Her phone rang, and her heart jumped in anticipation. He found her number under the contact she'd added. She even put herself in his favorites folder, so her face and name appeared in an otherwise empty list when he opened the phone app. He'd had second thoughts. He wanted her to come home.

Home, funny how it hadn't taken her long to find that in Flynn's Crossing when she hadn't felt it anywhere else in ages.

The second cadence of ringing whipped her into action. She grabbed the phone and swiped the screen alive. The photo of her sister's face filled the screen. Dejected, she pressed the green button and waited for Kate to speak.

"Hello? Jennifer, are you there? I'm so glad you came to your senses and decided to come back to the city for the holiday, and I'm sorry I'm not there to share it with you. Will you be able to manage on your own? Do you want me to come home?"

Jenn closed her eyes and waiting for a couple of beats, because the first words that jumped to mind were a fast retort that she could damn well take care of herself. An instant later, remorse washed over her. Her sister was only worried and trying to make things easier.

"I'm fine, Kate. I don't mind being on my own, you know. I've lived alone for a long time." And even a house full of people would be lonely without the person she loved. That knowledge came to her on the long drive back, made longer by bad weather and short-tempered drivers. She'd fallen into bed in the same clothes she'd worn at the cabin, hoping for the oblivion of sleep, but she either thought about Rock, or she dreamed of him. Neither option made for a restful night.

"I can be on the road in a few minutes and there in a few hours. Really, I don't mind."

Focusing on the desperate tone in her sister's voice, Jenn smiled. "Are the in-laws such terrors this year?"

Kate made a disgusted hiss. "Pre-teen crazies, hubby having a midlife crisis, in-laws determined to plan a two-week family vacation to a place we have no interest in going to. You name it, it's happening. Please, please tell me you need me there."

Jenn chuckled. "I'm sorry, Kate. I can't rescue you by saying I need back-up. And I'd never make it to LA and back in time for my meeting tomorrow."

"What kind of meeting? Who plans a meeting for the holiday week?"

"Oh, just something exploratory. It's with a company who was part of a consulting project I worked on."

"Why that's wonderful, Jenn. You see? Your career will be back on track in no time."

The pang of guilt wasn't new. She'd never told her family the full story of why she'd been let go. In their understanding, her company had down-sized and she'd been a casualty. She couldn't tell Kate why meeting with the opposing side was so important to her now. The only person who knew the full truth was Rock.

Screaming in the background brought a resigned sigh from Kate. "Were we monsters as pre-teens? I swear, these two are out of control, and I'd like to blame hormones."

They wished each other a Merry Christmas and signed off, with Kate shouting her good luck about the meeting over kids yelling for her to referee. When the call disconnected, the silence in the big house was even more pronounced.

The forest should have been silent, but it creaked and rustled and breathed, day and night. The cabin nestled in the woods had its own set of sounds, like the crackling of wood burning and the squeaks of structure expanding and contracting in its warmth. And the man, despite his intended silences, had his own rhythms too. Most of all, she missed the man who made it all come alive for her.

Jenn couldn't block Rock from her mind, so she gave up trying. She picked at her memories, flipping through them like pages in a photo album. She had a bad feeling about leaving Rock alone, and she couldn't put her finger on what it was. Hours later, her eyelids finally drooped, and she wrapped a blanket around herself on the couch. Squinting at the lights on the Christmas tree, she drifted off.

In her dreams, Rock smiled. He laughed, a full-bellied sound that she'd never heard in real life. They made love, and as he loomed over her, linked in the most intimate way possible, he repeated the words she'd wanted to hear.

'I love you, Jenny. I love you. I love you.'

When she blinked herself awake, she wasn't surprised to find her cheeks damp with tears. The words she craved to hear weren't to be. She had to come to terms with that. Rock said he had no future. The thought made her uneasy, and she thought about trying to call him, even though she knew it wouldn't connect at the cabin.

Her eyes strayed to the clock as she stretched, and she bolted upright. Her meeting was in an hour and a half, and the drive alone might take an hour, depending on traffic. She transitioned to lightning speed to get ready, going over the points she wanted to make as the shower spray beat on her head. Taping her list of bullets to the mirror, she prepped hair and make-up while drinking a power shake. By the time she was behind the wheel, her nerves made the vanilla mix dance in her stomach.

The receptionist didn't hesitate to ring her through to the CEO. The man who appeared in the doorway and beckoned her back behind the inner door wasn't a stranger to her. He'd been on the other side of the table at countless meetings, but she'd been on the perimeter then. He evidently recognized her, though, because his greeting was warm. Idle chat about the holiday filled the time for a short walk to his corner office.

"I don't want to waste your time, Ms. Stanton. I understand you have a strategy that you believe will help our company, now that the merger is off the table. I've had others say the same thing, and what they suggested was ludicrous. What makes you think your idea will be different?"

Jenn didn't flinch. This was a make or break moment, and she focused her energy on bringing her best to the game.

An hour later, the CEO leaned forward with a reluctant grin. "I have to say, I admire your tenacity and your insights. I wasn't aware that you left our friends across the great divide, though I hold you in higher esteem for it."

Jenn pressed her hands to her thighs under the table and licked her lips. She hoped he was truly impressed with her ideas, because now she had to explain that departure, and when she did, he might not be so interested in her anymore.

"In the interest of full disclosure, I have to tell you something about that. I didn't leave by choice. I was let go."

He frowned, retreating into the chair. All good nature had fled his expression as he examined her over steepled fingers. "I see."

"Do you remember the anonymous tip you received about fraudulent information in the financial analysis?"

A perplexed look came to his face, and his eyes darted up to meet hers. "How do you know about that?"

She took a deep breath. "I was the one who made the call."

He settled forward with a speculative narrowing to his eyes and lifted a finger to tap his chin. "What did you say on the call?"

Jenn didn't hesitate to repeat her words, almost verbatim. She'd had plenty of time to think about it over the last year, and she remembered it too vividly to forget.

"When your team made those areas of the analysis points of focus, they could trace the work back to me. I was the only one with access to some of the key documents with the missing information too. I didn't try to hide it. I didn't agree with their tactic of withholding the data."

He watched her for a long time, long enough for her to wonder if he thought he a traitor too. Those were the words her boss had thrown at her when he'd raged about her reveal, right before he told her she was fired.

"I have to tell you, Ms. Stanton, that at first, I thought your message was a sham. Something thrown at us to test our seriousness about the deal, perhaps. It wasn't until my guys dug in and found the discrepancies that I believed it. Frankly, I'm glad you came forward, because I owe you major thanks. We would have been screwed over if the deal went through. So, thank you."

He rose and extended his hand, and with a sinking heart, she did the same. His dismissal came too easily. If the company applied her ideas, she wished them the best. They deserved it.

Still, as she prepared herself for his swift rejection, she knew she'd done the right thing, then and now. Telling him she was their anonymous tipster meant she wouldn't carry the burden of that secret any longer.

"And now, since you're no longer under their thumb, I assume you have the time to take on projects of your own?" He cocked an eyebrow at her.

"Yes, yes I do."

"I'd like you to come back next week and present your ideas to my full senior team. We've been looking for ways to capitalize on exactly the business sectors you brought up. Opportunities have gone missing for long enough. I want you to help us get there, Ms. Stanton."

She felt the air press in close before it expanded with a rush. "I'd be delighted. And please, it's Jennifer."

She only avoided a happy dance in his office because it would be undignified. As it was, she waited until she was in her car and stuck in traffic to give a two-handed fist pump and a whoop of exhilaration. As the adrenaline spike wore off, though, she turned somber.

If she worked for them, she wouldn't be able to return to the foothills. The man she loved was there, and she doubted he'd be willing to move here. By the time she reached her sister's house an hour later, her melancholy over the choice had reached epic proportions.

"Princess, I think I got the job and lost the guy."

In response, the little dog whined and lay down, her chin resting on her paws. Her whining didn't cease, as if she too mourned the alternative.

As Jenn hung up her coat, she realized the victory of vindication felt small compared to what it meant she would lose in her future. The man who had encouraged her to take a courageous step forward might not listen to her message for days if he didn't leave the cabin, but she needed to tell him.

Rock's phone rang, and she waited, hoping he'd set up a personal voicemail response so she could hear his voice. When the phone clicked on, momentary surprise had her speechless.

"Jenny?"

"Rock? In person? Where are you? No, that doesn't matter. You were right. You were so right. I gave the CEO my ideas, and then I told him I was the tipster, and he thanked me. You rescued me again."

He didn't respond immediately. In the space of his hesitation, she wondered if even this joy wasn't something he felt he could share. He deserved it, just like he deserved to have a full and happy life. If that wasn't with her, she'd have to accept it. But he wasn't going to blow off her appreciation. He'd lit a fire under her, in a way only he could do.

"I'm glad it worked out for you, Jenny. Really glad. I assumed it would, since you negotiated from a place of honor and ethics. If it hadn't, it wouldn't have been the kind of company to deserve you."

Tears crept to her eyes, missing him more than ever. "The only person I thought of celebrate this with was you, Rock. Just you."

His silence communicated how far she'd overstepped on that score. She might be ready to jump into arms with gladness, but he didn't sound like he was willing to catch her.

"You deserve to celebrate with someone who can enjoy the victory. Someone else, Jenny. Please, delete my phone number. Remember me as a passing phase, a short vacation from the real world. Believe me, it's better for you that way."

Fierce protectiveness surged through her. "I will not delete your number, and you are not a passing phase. I don't see any reason why I can't run a consulting practice from Flynn's Crossing. It's too late to hit the road today, but I can be back before lunch tomorrow. And when I get back, we'll have a real celebration."

"I won't be here when you get back."

Choices always loomed on the horizon. Forget the job and get the guy loomed larger than anything right now.

"But I can travel with you. Where you go, I want to be. I love you, Rock."

"No."

His single word froze her in place, the glass of water she was about to fill poised under the refrigerator dispenser. "Why?"

"I don't want you going where I'm going. You deserve a long, happy life."

"But – "

"No."

Something in his tone raised the hairs on her skin, prickling over her like cheap wool. She couldn't draw in enough air to argue, and the sensation of being punched in the belly with a fist of enormous proportions made her double over. He didn't want her. She loved him, and he didn't want her.

"Goodbye, Jenny. Have an amazing, joy-filled life. You deserve it."

Deafening silence told her the line had gone dead. Any equally loud ringing took up residence in her ears. She didn't register the crash of the glass falling from her hand, or the bite of broken pieces digging into her knees as she slipped to the floor. When Princess licked her face and yowled in protest, she wound her fingers through the dog's silky coat and held on for dear life. Rock had hung up on her without giving her time to change his mind, and she had a bad feeling the result would be permanent.

Chapter 31

He tried not to imagine what her face looked like as her happy words tripped over themselves. The huge eyes, infectious grin, and delighted musical range of her voice danced in his consciousness anyway. It would be better if she forgot him, better if she never knew.

His aimless wanderings brought him home in the waning daylight. Ranger had loved the drive for supplies. The large bag of dogfood in the back guaranteed the dog wouldn't starve. He'd hate being locked up in the cabin and he'd make a mess and raise a ruckus, but no one lived close enough to hear. Rock had made plans for that too. Deke would take care of him.

"So, buddy, this will be it. End of the line. You forget me too, okay? Have a good life. I know they'll take good care of you."

If a dog could frown, he bet this would be the expression. Ranger's ears pinched up high and lines he didn't usually have appeared around his eyes. He whined, unwilling to get out of the truck when Rock parked it in front of the cabin.

What would Uncle Rowan do with the place now? At least there would be time for his family to figure that out before the next holiday season. Someone would step in.

The interior looked as it did when he left this morning. He'd needed a couple of things for his final mission, but he'd prepared the rest not long after Jenny's departure. Files stacked in the plastic tote in chronological order told the story of what had happened in that desert hell. He hadn't read all the reports, because he didn't have to hear what others thought they knew about it. He'd been there. You couldn't argue with death when it stared back at you with the empty eyes of people you cared about. He could recite their names like a litany of prayers, but that would never bring them back.

He owed it to them to follow. He'd failed them, all of them. It had been his responsibility to keep the hospital safe. He'd failed. They'd all died, probably because under the haze of torture, he'd said too much and revealed their location. Because of him, his unit perished, and the courageous medical staff and their patients had been slain.

He deserved to die too.

Ranger whined, unwilling to leave his side, even to take care of business. Rock gave up trying to convince him to wander, sitting himself on the stump next to the firepit and staring at its emptiness. It was like looking in to the yawning cold emptiness of his soul. The dog finally took a few paces away but returned in less than a couple of minutes. He pushed against Rock's legs and whined.

"It's okay. We'll go inside now. You'll get cold sitting in this snow. I hope the warmth from the stove lasts long enough tomorrow." He didn't want the animal to suffer.

He couldn't bring himself to lie down on the bed. The sheets smelled of Jenny and vanilla, bringing an ache to his heart that even peace with his decision could not lessen. Thoughts of her kept him from sleeping, a kind of blessing by itself. Tonight, he didn't want his last night filled with nightmares. He'd be in them in hell soon enough.

Guilt made it harder to sleep too. He couldn't let her think he didn't care, not when she'd been brave enough to bare her feelings and he chickened out. The letter he buried in her ridiculously large bag would reveal the full truth. He'd ended it with a string of emotion that proved impossible to hide.

'I love you, Jenny. I love you. I love you.'

He'd written that the place he was traveling to was cold, the forever kind of cold he never wished for her. Not hell, perhaps, but purgatory for sure. Souls burdened his, and there was no way to release them as he'd coached her to do. By her voice, he hoped she'd found her load lifted by telling the full truth.

"It was probably a mistake, laying that on her, but she deserved to know I returned her love a thousand times more."

The dog didn't seem to agree, based on his heavy sigh.

He must have dozed off, because he was having the most amazing dream. He and Jenny ran hand in hand through a field of tall grasses, the kind blanketing the spring meadows before the rains ended. She laughed, teasing him to catch her if he could. No matter how hard he ran, she remained just out of reach. Then she stopped, and he did too. She lifted her hands to him, and he took them. When they touched, though, she disappeared, and the meadow was barren and cold with snow.

He woke with a start, feeling the chill penetrate his bones. The fire had long since faded, allowing the frozen world outside to penetrate the old building's walls. Stacking wood and adding kindling, he had it burning brightly in short order. The view made him think fleetingly of the brimstones of hell.

He drifted off again, and this time, he and Jenn splashed in water. It was the pond, he realized, though not the one they knew. This one had a waterfall and a stream running warm and clear. He dunked her, and he dove away to avoid her reciprocation. But she didn't come back up, and his worry made him sink and open his eyes, searching for her. He saw her suspended in the clear filtered light, her eyes open and on him, her lips trying to tell him something. He swam closer, wanting to urge them up to lifesaving oxygen, but she fought him off. She floated deeper, deeper, deep enough to make the water almost black. He reached for her, but she vanished.

This time, Ranger's whine brought him back to the room. "The shrinks would have a field day with that one, wouldn't they, boy?" The dog licked his face, and he took that for agreement.

Outside, the faint dim light of a new day outlined the trees. By the look of it, the sun would shine today. He'd hoped for clouds, more fitting with his chore, but the universe would disappoint him once more.

He opened the outer door and urged Ranger to run. He filled two buckets with water and set them on the floor by the dog's usual drinking bowl. He filled another with kibble and left the bag on the floor too, where a strong paw could tear its paper if needed. He didn't think it would take Deke that long to check.

When the dog came in and fell on his food, Rock kneeled next to him and wrapped an arm around him. "Goodbye, buddy. I don't think they allow us to visit the Rainbow Bridge where I'm heading on the other side, but if I can, I'll come see you there too."

He lined things up on the table, straightening the boxes of folders even if they didn't need it. He put his wallet next to his military identification. He kissed the pictures of Ma and his brothers.

And finally, he pulled up the photos of Jenny. His hand hesitated over the delete button, but he couldn't do it. His plan included leaving the phone behind, but he wanted this visual reminder of her with him until the end.

When he walked into the day's fresh sunlight, he took a last look around the clearing. His eyes lingered on the path to the pond. Memories, so many of them good, flooded over him. His eyes teared and he fought the urge to wish things had turned out differently. It would serve nothing. He was a soldier. He'd failed in his duty and his assignment, which was why he had to complete his final mission.

Her eyes were so swollen from crying that she could barely see her reflection in the mirror. At some point during the night, she'd roused herself enough to change out of the suit with its marks of blood from glass cuts. The old sweats usually comforted her, but not tonight. Jenn felt sick to her stomach with grief and longing and no amount of reasoning could make her understand why things had to be like this. She didn't have to choose one or the other. She could work from Flynn's Crossing as easily as here. If only Rock would listen to her with an open mind.

Worst of all, she'd forgotten to plug in her cell phone in her turmoil last night, and now when she needed to see his picture the most, it was dead. She couldn't remember if she'd put her charging cord in her purse or left it at the cabin. It would be a great excuse to go back.

She dumped the contents of her big bag on the floor, not caring when it scattered. Lipsticks she hadn't once used in Flynn's Crossing rolled behind the toilet. Her notebook, offering someplace to capture ideas not matter where she was, fell to the side, and more paper landed next to it. She didn't remember having so much junk in here. Princess's leash tangled with the white charger, partially submerged under the pages. It wasn't until she got the plug in the wall and reached for the other end that she registered the envelope with a slash of writing on its face.

Her heart kicked in her chest. She hadn't seen a lot of it, but there had been enough to recognize Rock's bold scrawl of her name. He'd left her a letter. She dropped the phone without plugging it in and grabbed for the cream colored paper, turning it over a few times and marveling that it was there.

He'd written her something, and it was inside this envelope. Once she opened it, she'd know what he'd really been thinking. The possibilities of that were endless. So were the risks. But he wouldn't have bothered if he didn't have something he wanted her to know. She ripped at the flap and tore out the pages.

His handwriting was neat and the strokes sure and strong, like the man himself. It looked like he'd written this and never hesitated in his thoughts, blasting through instead with a repeat of the story he'd told her about what happened to him. Except now, there was more.

He wrote what it was like to see his friends dead, the people he sought to save by not speaking despite the pain and torture he'd been through. The other soldiers. People at the hospital. Ilya. Regret came through in every word.

'Their eyes stared back at me with accusation. They blamed me. I was the only one who knew, and I protected that information to the best of my ability to the very end. At least, I thought I did. But otherwise, how did the enemy know? I must have told them.'

She wanted to reassure him that it couldn't have been his fault the truth was tortured out of him, but there was no way she knew that, and neither did he. The fact that he was released, only to live the horror again and again in the tribunal reviews that followed and, in his nightmares, made his pain more obvious. Jenn wept over his descriptions. In his estimation, he'd gone from being a man with purpose and honor to someone who did not deserve to live.

'Now you know the whole truth. I caused good people to die, as readily as if I'd pulled the trigger and put the bullets in their foreheads myself. For that reason, I am going to take my eternal punishment now, rather than dragging down everyone around me. I can see the pain in my family's eyes when they watch me with such caution, just as I could see the worry in your beautiful face, even when you smiled at me.'

"Princess, come!" Jenn crawled across the tile floor, uncaring when something dug into a cut on her knee. Grabbing anything she could reach, she shoved it back into the bag, winding the leash around her hand. She'd use it to hogtie the dog if necessary. She had to find him.

The Yorkie raced into the room and sat, her tongue hanging out and her eyes wide. For once, she did as she was told, and Jenn sent a quiet prayer up to the doggie gods to thank them. She had her phone in her hand, the first thought in her head that she needed to call Rock's family and alert them. The dead phone mocked her, with an angry yell, she plugged it in and waited impatiently for it to boot up.

"Come on, come on, come on." Where was her car charger? Glovebox? Console? Hell. Her usual organizational skills failed her when she needed them most.

"Hello, this is Deke."

"Oh thank god. Deke, you have to find him."

"I'm sorry I missed your call. Please leave your name and number and I'll – "

She screamed in frustration, tapping the counter in the hope that the rest of his message was short. Finally, the voicemail signal beeped.

"Deke, it's Jenn. Please go to the cabin and find Rock. Please. It's urgent. I think something's wrong."

She wanted to race out the door, but she had to make sure someone there was doing something. She scrolled down until she found Marlee's number and clicked to dial. On the third ring, the call was answered.

"Jenn, a belated Merry Christmas. We're so sorry you – "

"We don't have time for that, Marlee. It's Rock. He left me a letter in my purse. Someone needs to go check on him."

"Stay by the phone."

She clicked off while Jenn was trying to tell her she was on her way too. Her thumb hovered over the next number on her list, the one belonging to Miss Emie, when the phone jumped with a ring in her hand.

"Yes?"

"Jenn, it's Jake. Tell me why you think something's wrong. Tell me what Rock said."

She heard the wail of sirens in the background, and static noise that might be radio communications. She read the salient parts of Rock's letter to Jake, and he cursed on the other end.

"Okay, got it. I'm on my way. Marlee's tracking down Deke. We're all going over there. Someone will call you when we know something." He hung up on that assurance.

Her fingers gripped the pages so tightly, something tore. She smoothed them immediately, unwilling to let go of this little bit of a man she'd come to love and trust and respect above all else. Her eyes glazed down to the rest of it, below the part she had now recited aloud with fear making her voice waver.

'I know you are a strong, smart and capable woman. Your life will fall back into place. You don't need me to tell you that. You will be able to carry on, getting over this bump in life's road and making a rich future for yourself. But I couldn't say goodbye without telling you this.

'I love you, Jenny. I love you. I love you.'

She yanked at her bag and the cell. The phone's cord came out of the bottom and it again went dead. Dead as Rock would be, if they didn't find him in time.

Her mind flashed with sudden clarity to the gun. He hadn't bothered to hide it. She'd checked the dresser drawer when he was otherwise occupied. Its dull shine looked deadly even in repose.

She looked at the phone and back at her dog. Princess gave a furious series of barks and ran toward the front door, and Jenn followed. She could search for the charger while she drove. She had to get there. She had to find him. Rock needed her rescue.

Chapter 32

The bright beauty of the day was a disappointment. It would have been more appropriate to have leaden clouds hanging overhead, ready to pitch their fury of snowfall at any moment. Ice hadn't yet formed on the lake, despite its elevation. Somewhere down below, past the pines and granite, his family worked at the ranch. Even further away, Jenn began the next wonderful stage of her life, a life where he hoped she forgot about him. He took a deep breath of the icy mountain air and looked down at the lake.

Rock knew it would be hard to do this. No creature welcomes its own demise, sentient humans most of all. Nightmares' pains and physical torture were nothing compared with the idea of putting the barrel in his mouth, aiming up, and pulling the trigger. He'd turn his back before doing the deed, and his body would fall into the water below and sink in his heavy boots and clothing. It might come up at some point, when bloating made it buoyant, but no one would pass this way until spring, and by then, he'd be a pile of bones feeding wildlife or sunk to the silty bottom.

Ma would never understand this, so he hoped that reading the folders and their stark reports made her realize why his honor demanded it. Deke would sit in silence and shake his head, unwilling to believe this of his brother and wanting to fight it, even though he'd see the reason for it. Jake would snarl and rage and curse him. The thought of his usually controlled brother losing it that way brought the only relief to his tension. He'd like to see that.

His mind wandered through the faces he'd known and the places he'd been. A nearby rock proved a suitable resting place as he said his silent apologies and farewells. The sun rose higher in the sky, warming his face. He tilted into it, wishing its warmth could penetrate his soul.

When he couldn't avoid it any longer, his mind drifted to Jenny. He didn't need a photo to see her face. Didn't need to think hard at all to hear her coaxing voice. The soothing smoothness of her skin made his fingertips burn with the desire to feel her again. Against him. Over him. Surrounding him.

But that would solve nothing. She'd understand someday why this had to be.

He pulled out the phone, ready to toss it as far into the center of the lake as he could, when he noticed the message icon. He didn't want to listen to it, afraid of what he'd hear, but he needed to make sure it wasn't Deke saying he couldn't take care of Ranger. His last call had been to his brother, asking him to check on Ranger since Rock had been stuck out of town. Once Deke saw the table, he'd read between the lines.

But that call went to voicemail, and Rock wasn't sure where Deke might be. It could take too long for someone to get to the dog, and he didn't need that on his conscience too. Reluctantly, he triggered voicemail, expecting to hear Deke's reply. What came instead had him shocked into stillness.

'If you do this, Rock Kermarrec, I will track you down and I will kill you myself.'

The fury in Jenn's voice made him sit up straighter. She hadn't listened to him, of course, and for some reason, that made him profoundly happy.

'You don't get to make all of the choices here, goddamnit. I love you and you love me and we have a blood bond. You can't break an oath like that, even if you think you released me. You rescue me, and I rescue you. That's how it's done.'

Her voice cracked. He could tell she was crying. In the background, a horn blared, and she cursed the driver. She was breathless a moment later when the message continued.

'Whatever you're doing, wherever you are, stop. Right now, stop. We'll figure it out together, if only you'll come home. There must be another explanation, and we'll find it. What happened was not your fault. Please Rock, I'm begging you. I love you. You love me. Nothing else matters. The world is filled with possibilities. We will figure this out.'

A shiver ran through him. Didn't she realize there could be no other explanation? He was the only one who knew where the entrance was. None of the others could have revealed it.

The final words of his captors raced through his brain. Their glee in the telling was even more vicious when surrounded by the carnage he couldn't look away from.

'You have been useful to us, but it was too late. Too late, for you, for your friends. I suppose we should say thank you for an amusing pastime. But you see, we already knew it all.'

In his ear, Jenny's voice in her message played like a soothing melody, drowning out the filth of years ago.

'Rock, you're the one who told me the truth, once revealed, lifts the weight off your shoulders. It did for me, and I wouldn't have had the courage to do what I did without you. You said you didn't read the reports, but they gave you medals. You're a hero, Rock. Don't fail me now. Blood bond. You and me. We'll always rescue each other.'

A sob marred her strong words, then another. On an abrupt gasp, the message ended. His vision blurred with tears.

He didn't deserve her. Releasing her from their bond was the right thing to do. The right thing trumped any hope or dream he might have. She probably didn't think it now, but she'd be free to live and love and grow in joy. That capacity for happiness was something he'd always remember about her, no matter what.

He stepped to the edge of the lake and hurled the phone as far as he could throw it, watching the resulting splash with pangs of sorrow and guilt. If he played her words again, who knows what he would do. The deadly metal in his hand burned colder than the air around him. Jenny's face swam in his vision, blocking his view. He'd done the right thing, forcing her to go.

Rock turned his back on the lake, not wanting the distraction of its beauty. Calling to mind Jenny's laughter and determination wasn't hard to do. She was the most amazing woman he'd ever known. Her love knew no boundaries, and he was grateful for that.

Finally, he lifted the gun like an old friend one last time.

Trucks and cars and two sheriff SUVs filled the clearing when she slid to a stop. She didn't bother to grab anything other than Princess. She tripped when she saw Rock's truck parked beside the cabin, its doors open. When someone with CSI emblazoned on their back stood from leaning into the interior, she inhaled sharply and raced for the cabin door. It opened in front of her and Ranger burst out with Miss Emie on his heels.

"Oh thank god you're here. Do you know where he could be?"

At least he wasn't in the truck. Twin emotions of relief and worry bombarded through her again, making clear thought impossible and grief overwhelming.

Dogs barked and yipped and she put the Yorkie down, uncaring when the leash trailed out of her fingers. The older woman seemed to have shrunk as she grabbed Jenn in a tight hug, one she could only cling to and pray for a good outcome.

"I don't know, Miss Emie, I just don't know."

Jake was beside her next, giving her that intense stare she recognized now as a Kermarrec trait.

"Have you heard from him? We've been trying to call you."

She waved her hands. "I was speeding and I had to use both hands in the traffic and the phone fell on the floor and pulled off the charger and it's dead and why aren't you out there looking for him?"

The grim line of his mouth didn't change.

"You know this is big territory, and Rock knows it like the back of his hand. Many roads still haven't been cleared from the snowfall, so we can consider that a blessing. Unless he hiked someplace, in which case, who the hell knows where he is?"

Deke came next, shaking a sheaf of papers in his hand. "Have you read this?"

She shook her head. "He had some of it out one night, and I tried to read it, but he grabbed it and hid it before I could. Some kind of incident report, about the killings, I'll bet."

Deke nodded with a brisk snap and a grimace twisted his mouth in a face the color of old ash. "Did you know he won medals for his bravery? I haven't had time to figure it all out yet, and it looks like the last report in this file is dated six months ago. The Army was still studying what happened back then. There's probably more, but I can't find it."

"If he'd had more for us to see, it would have been there on that table. He left it all for us to find." Miss Emie's body shook but she lifted her chin, and Jenn hugged her closer, not sure who supported who at this point.

"How long ago did he leave?" Jenn tried to put as much force into her voice as possible, but she figured her tears and exhaustion showed too.

"He left me a message this morning, asking me to pick up Ranger and take him to the ranch since he'd be detained out of town. I thought he might be with you when I first heard it. I intended to come by once I'd been out to check on a herd, and that's when Marlee called and I listened to your message," Deke said.

Something squawked through Jake's radio and he stepped away, speaking in a low tone. Jenn wanted to scream at him to speak up, that they all needed to learn what he did, but she didn't want to make a bad situation worse. They were hurting as much as she was.

Deke followed Jake, and Miss Emie gave her a squeeze. "Come inside. You're shaking. You must be beside yourself."

Jenn couldn't move, her eyes pinned on the worried glances shared by the two men. "He told me he loved me, Miss Emie. In the letter. He never told me face to face, but he wrote it. I told him I loved him, and I thought he loved me, and it didn't make any difference. He sent me away."

The older woman sighed, and Jenn pulled away to look at her with fresh concern. The possibility of losing a son would wear on anyone, and Miss Emie didn't look like she was weathering it well.

"That's what these stupid men do, I'm afraid. Why, the boys' father told me to go back to the flower children, said he couldn't imagine a hippie girl wanting to live a country life of hard work and adult seriousness. It took me a while to figure out that he didn't think his life was good enough for me. Called me the light he never thought he'd find in his life, when he finally got around to it. I know the boys never could figure out what kept us together, but I know. That man loved me enough to want to let me go."

Jenn felt hot tears on her cheeks, watching the little rivers follow the tracks of deep creases on the face in front of hers. They both held on tighter when Deke and Jake paced back.

"So far, no luck on the APB. We can't file a missing persons because it's too soon, but when we do, that will plug us into the federal system as well. Meanwhile, every possible patrol unit is out looking."

"Unless he's out of sight already," Miss Emie said. Her sons nodded with grim faces and matching cold gray eyes so like Rock's, Jenn hiccupped a fresh sob.

Barking erupted as the dogs romped a distance away. Jenn was about to call them back, because they were at the edge of the clearing. It didn't take much to imagine what hid in the winter woods. Ranger's deeper noise accelerated, and he raced into the forest, with Princess bounding after him as fast her shorter legs could manage.

"Princess, come. Ranger, come." Jenn let go of Miss Emie and ran after them. If she lost Princess and Ranger now too – she bit off the thought because it was too awful to contemplate.

Ranger's barks turned to high yips, and she ran faster, aware that the men were now running too. She followed the dog tracks through the trees, tripping but not falling, and realized she ran in a circle when she ended up on the driveway leading in. She pulled up short, thinking she must be hallucinating, because she couldn't see straight.

Ranger had his paws on the shoulders of someone who looked like a mountain man. A furry hat covered his dark blond hair. In a big hand, Princess's red and green plaid looked like a toy. He had her raised to eye level, and she was licking him happily. Then he looked up and his smile grew wider.

Jenn had never seen a better sight.

"You came back." She wasn't sure her breathless voice carried over the distance between them.

He nodded once, his expression growing wary. Jenn dimly noted bodies pushing by her, Rock pushing Ranger off, setting Princess down and putting his hands up. Deke hit him first, a fist on the chin that sent him careening off a tree and into the snow. Jake jumped on him next and pinned him to the ground, his hands reaching behind him where handcuffs hung on his belt.

"Where's the fucking gun?"

"In the lake," Rock said, trying to buck his brother off.

She wasn't sure what she saw next, because snow flew in the massive pile-up of bodies on the ground. The three threw punches, and by the grunts, some of them connected. She should do something to make them stop, but Jenn didn't know how to respond, her brain still stuck on the miracle that Rock was here.

They had a chance.

"Stop, now."

The voice wasn't raised but the authority in it made them all freeze in their grappling on the ground.

"Stand up," Miss Emie said. The way she said it made Jenn straighten taller too.

The three men stood up. Jake's uniform jacket missed a button and a knee was torn on his regulation pants. Deke's knuckles bled, and a black eye already bloomed. Rock's nose had a trail of red under it, and his lip was split. And he still looked like the best damned sight she'd ever seen.

"Come here, Frederic."

Rock stepped forward without hesitation until he stood in front of her. Miss Emie lifted a hand and put it to his ear, and she tweaked it. By the grimace on Rock's face, Jenn bet his mother hadn't gone easy on him.

Then the older woman wrapped her arms around him and pulled him in close. He leaned over her and drew her in, chin on head, and his mother's shoulders heaved with loud sobs.

They stood like that for long enough for Jenn to think she should fade back. This was family business now. She didn't belong here. Later, when things calmed down, maybe she and Rock could talk.

But that would be the easy way out, and if there was one thing she learned from all of this, life fully lived wasn't going to be easy. She wasn't sure where she ever got the belief that it should be.

As if he could read her thoughts, Rock lifted his head and pinned her in a blue gaze so bright, she thought it rivaled the clear sky above. His expression told her nothing, though.

"Rock, I, we, I – "

That was as far as he allowed her to get, because the next thing she knew, strong arms enclosed her and pulled her in so tight, she couldn't breathe. It didn't matter. Air was highly overrated. His mouth closed over hers and while the kiss tasted of blood and the hand he wrapped on her neck chilled her with bare cold, she didn't care. She never thought she'd have the chance to hold him in her arms again, and now that she did, she didn't plan on letting go.

It might be snowing. It might be summer. She had no idea how long they stood there. His heart beat fast under her trapped hand and the world around them was a blur. When he lifted his head, she felt dizzy.

"I love you, Jennifer Stanton. I love you. I love you."

His voice broke as if his emotion matched hers. She felt the wetness on his cheeks as he pressed his face into her forehead, and she drew back, intending to wipe away the warmth of what must be a fresh trail of blood. When she pulled away to look at him, though, she saw the tears on his face, even as joy lit his features.

"You rescued me."

She opened her mouth to ask how or why, then closed it. It didn't matter. They had a blood bond, an oath that would carry them through the rest of their lives, and that was enough for her.

"I love you, Rock Kermarrec. And don't you ever scare the hell out of me like that again. I'll follow you to the other side and make you pay for it."

She felt the rumble before the sound, and when it came, it was a glorious thing. Rock laid his head back and his laughter boomed off the trees around them. Dogs barked in accompaniment. Jenn couldn't help it. The chuckle started in her toes and rose up, and soon, they were holding each other up with happy tears falling.

"You know, when you kissed me by the pond all those years ago, I knew you were going to be trouble." Rock chuckled again.

"I kissed you? You kissed me back."

"Whatever. I love you, Jenny, and I probably always have. Rescue me again. Kiss me."

"Only if you rescue me back," she murmured into a forever kind of embrace.

Epilogue

This date would be more fitting than any other he could think of. The perfect sun rose in a perfect sky with wandering fluffy clouds. Late season rain kept the grass green. The ranch never looked prettier, but nothing compared to the beauty of the woman by his side.

"I have to take care of something, okay?"

Rock dropped his head down and met Jenny's lips, still the sweetest taste he could imagine. She stood by him, through trouble and joy. There had been plenty of the former, with enough of the latter mixed in to balance things out.

He was so proud of her. Jenn's local consulting practice grew steadily. That Bay Area company wanted her full time, but she declined. She didn't want them to move to the city, she said. His city girl had turned into a country lass with a serious attitude. Just look at those boots covered in dust and the jeans that fit her curves and straw stuck to her back from their romp a few minutes ago. She'd wanted to show him their newest goats, and he wanted to show her something else altogether.

It still gave him a twinge to think back to the desert, to the pain, to the empty eyes, but he rarely dreamed of it any longer. He'd doubled down on the counseling, taking the sessions seriously instead of trying to hide. The truth was hard, but it would be harder to disappoint the woman he loved more than anything. And anything was what he'd do for her.

His feet made little sound on the old wood floors of the bunkhouse. It took no time to pull his surprise together. It hadn't been easy, he thought, slipping off the denim. He chuckled as he picked straw out of his hair and gave it a brushing. The length wasn't what it should be for this show, but he didn't think anyone would care. Jenn liked it longer, and so did he. It wasn't to hide behind, but it fit him and their lifestyle.

What there were going to do with twenty goats for grazing duty and the five Jenn now milked with a zeal he didn't think would be possible was still a mission awaiting full execution. She traveled for work sometimes, and he went along when he could. They poured over information about goat husbandry, something Uncle Rowan jumped into with excitement too. She'd figured out how to make cheese and had enlisted Ma in her endeavor. So far, the results tasted good.

He straightened a crease and rubbed a spot. It was good as it was going to get. Bright sparkly things had a way of making a woman smile, he'd learned, and while the engagement ring he'd wasted no time sliding on her finger was one thing, he thought this might please her even more.

He turned and paced out the door, his shoes squeaking a little with unforgiving leather. Patent was never meant to bend. He smiled at the thought, remembering how his buddies always hated this parade.

The others floated through his mind too. He chose to remember their good works, their sacrifices for their patients, and their unwavering commitment good in the face of danger. He'd committed himself to that too, and this was the final public step he had to take in that direction. The rest, the private battles that he knew he'd occasionally face, were ones he knew he could win.

Even the Army had agreed in a long overdue report. A man in Rock's unit followed him to the hospital's hidden entrance one night. He'd been the one to give it away. Rock could understand. Fear and pain could make people want to do desperate things.

The tables were set up under the big oak tree. Twenty yards away, the American flag flew proudly with the ranch's smaller insignia flapping underneath. It was a good day to be alive, Memorial Day. He'd never felt prouder.

Vindicated. Loved. Free.

People fell silent as he marched across the dirt. He kept his body rigid as he'd trained to do, his dress uniform crackling with starch with each swing of his arms. Something glinted in the sun on his chest, a few somethings, and he allowed himself a smile of pride.

"Oh my," Ma said. She lifted her arms up, then let them fall as if she wasn't sure she could hug him. He wrapped his arms around her and she fluttered before her hands came up and pressed over his heart. "I'm proud of you, son."

He moved on to Deke, he gave his outfit a once-over glance before slapping a hand against his arm. He did the same back. Then Deke snapped a passable salute, the pride on his face making Rock's heart swell.

Jake huffed and slapped his own belly, clad in a white t-shirt tucked in to his jeans. "Hell, if I'd known we were playing dress up today, I would have worn something a little more appropriate." But his grin shared his respect too.

Finally, he stood in front of the only woman he dressed to impress. Her mouth was open in a round of surprise and tears coursed down her cheeks. In another step, the finger wearing his ring glinted in the sunlight and reflected near the medals on his chest, the ones he'd sworn once upon a time to never wear. He deserved them, just as he deserved the woman in front of him. And together, they deserved a long future full of happiness.

"Ma'am, this soldier would be honored if you would be so kind as to rescue him. I love you, Jennifer Stanton."

She drew in a long breath and blew it out, and he bit back the grin. He was hers, and she was his.

"Well solider, you're lucky that I'm a sucker for a man in uniform. Those medals suit you, Kermarrec, just like you suit me. Rescue me forever, Rock."

She reached up for him as he broke his stance of attention. Right before their lips collided, he allowed the widest grin of all to cover his face. Mission. Finally. Accomplished.

THE END

About the Author

I love to hear from readers, so feel free to contact me through my website, www.yvonnekohano.com, or directly on Facebook as Yvonne Kohano, on Twitter @yvonnekohano, and at yvonne@yvonnekohano.com. Please leave an honest review of this novel at your favorite book discovery site of choice.

A HOLT Medallion Award of Merit recipient in Romantic Suspense, Yvonne enjoys channeling her characters' voices and passions as they overcome real world problems and discover love. Her Flynn's Crossing contemporary romantic suspense series is set in a fictional northern California foothills town not unlike the one where she used to live. Of course, the beauty and wonders of the Sierra Nevada Mountains and the surrounding counties play costarring roles in her work.

The first six books in the Flynn's Crossing series follow the developing love interests of the girl tribe, a group of successful women who work through real world conflicts and challenges to find acceptance and love - with some suspenseful happenings thrown in! In the next six books, single guys in the wolf pack find their true loves, but not without their own issues to conquer. Periodically, Yvonne will be adding seasonal novellas to the series, featuring the first-person voice of a character from one of her previous books experiencing an event that we can all relate to.

www.ingramcontent.com/pod-product-compliance
Lightning Source LLC
Chambersburg PA
CBHW021204250626
47155CB00008B/2663